SAFE HOUSE

BOOK NO. 5 – FOLEY & ROSE SERIES

GARY S. GREGOR

LARGE PRINT EDITION

ACKNOWLEDGMENTS

A number of people play a role in getting an author's story from an initial idea to a published book. For some of them, that role is small, for others it is significant. All who contribute in some way, regardless the level of input, are important to me, and although it might be cliché, it is true that this book would never have seen the light of day without each of them.

If I must nominate just a few, I would start with my former colleagues in the Northern Territory Police Force. You wonderful folk are the inspiration for my characters and, while those characters are fictional, I occasionally draw on the personality traits of some of those I have met in the job. If you recognise yourself in any of them, please remember that you are there because you inspire me.

My beautiful wife, Lesley, who tolerates my long hours in front of the computer without complaint, I love you and I thank you, although I still insist my love of writing is not an obsession.

Last, but by no means least, I thank all at Next Chapter Publishing. The Next Chapter team took a punt on an unknown, and that's rare in this business. I hope I can justify your gamble. I know I'll never stop trying to honor that leap of faith; thank you.

This book is respectfully dedicated to the memory of police officers everywhere who have paid the ultimate sacrifice in the service of their communities.

PROLOGUE

SIX MONTHS AGO

They came for Jackson Traynor at three o'clock in the morning, the time it was believed most people reached the deepest phase of the sleep cycle. There were two of them. The raid was well planned and, up to the point of entry into Traynor's home, it was well executed. From that point onwards, however, it all went to shit.

Jackson Traynor, more commonly known as 'Jack' to his friends and colleagues, was not at home; that was the first set-back for the intruders. He should have been home, all the research leading up to the raid suggested he would be, but sometimes plans have a way of going awry.

Jack did not sleep well. Having lived with chronic insomnia for many years, he was well acquainted with a pattern of poor sleeping. The night

1

they came to his home in the pre-dawn hours was just another example of the hundreds of sleep deprived nights he had endured over more years than he cared to remember.

Jackson went for a run, something he did often when he couldn't sleep. Before he left, he leaned over the sleeping body of April, his wife of fourteen years, and kissed her lightly on her forehead. Careful not to wake her, he climbed out of bed, dressed quickly in the dark, and crept silently from their bedroom. He moved quietly along the hallway and paused outside the door to his twelve-year-old daughter's room. The door was slightly ajar; Jessica liked it that way when she slept. He pushed it open, just enough to get his head around the opening, and listened for a few seconds to the soft sleeping sounds coming from Jessica's bed. Satisfied she too was sound asleep, he gently pulled the door back and continued along the hallway. In the small laundry attached to the kitchen of his home, he slipped into his sneakers and left by the back door, locking it behind him.

He found them when he got home, following an hour's hard run around the perimeter of the suburban football ground at the end of his street.

He knew someone had been there as soon as he reached the back door. It was wide open. Jack never left it open. He distinctly remembered locking it when he left. In light of recent events relating to his most recent career, he was way too security conscious when it came to leaving the house late at night with his wife and daughter home alone.

He had a gun, one of two he possessed, buried under a pile of rarely used hand-towels in a laundry cupboard high on the wall above the washing machine. His wife knew it was there and, while not happy about guns in the house at any time, she accepted they were a necessary part of her husband's profession. His daughter, however, did not know. As far as Jack was aware, Jessica never went to that particular cupboard. There was nothing inside she would conceivably need and, besides, she couldn't reach it even if she wanted to. It seemed, at least to Jack, it was a safe place to keep it. His second gun, a Glock 9mm, he kept locked in the drawer of his bedside table, just in case he reasoned to his wife.

His heart racing, he opened the cupboard, reached in, fossicked under the hand-towels, and found the gun, a Smith and Wesson, 38 calibre revolver with four-inch barrel. He fumbled deeper in the cupboard, and found a box of ammunition, flipped open the revolver cylinder, and began loading six rounds.

It took time, too much time. In his haste, two rounds of ammunition slipped from his fingers, bounced noisily off the washing machine, and rolled onto the floor. Conscious his clumsiness may well have alerted any intruder, he quickly loaded two replacement rounds, clicked the cylinder closed, and stepped silently into the kitchen.

Jessica's bedroom was the first room on the left, off the short hallway running through the centre of the house. The light was on and spilled from the room casting a dull glow over the portion of the hall immediately in front of the door. Further along the hall, on the same side, light also spilled from the master bedroom. At that hour of the night, these two peculiarities were so far removed from the norm that Jack almost called out but held himself in check. The gut feeling was stronger now. Something was wrong, terribly wrong.

With his back to the wall and his heart pounding a staccato rhythm in his chest, he edged stealthily along the hallway, his eyes darting ahead and behind. He held the revolver in a two-handed grip, his finger outside the trigger guard, and the barrel tracking the movement of his eyes.

Jessica's door was open. Bracing himself, Jack crouched low, and sprung into the room, sweeping the area with his eyes and the gun. Jessica was not in the room. Her bed was unmade, and her fluffy, pink slippers on the floor at the end of the bed immediately rang alarm bells in Jack's mind. Jessica loved her slippers. She almost never left her bedroom without them on her feet; it was one of the little, endearing, childhood idiosyncrasies Jack loved so much in his only child.

Maybe she woke early, and climbed into bed with her mother, Jack wondered. She did that sometimes, especially when he was working the ridiculously long hours his job demanded. Accordingly, Jessica not being in her room would not normally be the cause for concern, but this was different, and Jack didn't know why.

Jackson Traynor was a suspicious man. He had to be; his job demanded it. His mind replayed his movements from when he arrived home from his run. Finding the back door open was wildly at odds with the security precautions he was always re-enforcing in his family and, when taken in conjunction with Jessica's vacant bedroom, the light burning within, and Jessica's abandoned slippers, his instincts would not accept that what he was seeing was as benign as it might otherwise appear.

He stepped back out into the hall and moved towards the main bedroom. Outside the door, he paused and listened. He heard no sound from within. The whole house was silent. He glanced at his watch; the digital display read 3.55 a.m.

Slowly, carefully, and totally unprepared for what awaited him, he peeked around the door jamb, and glanced into the room.

April and Jessica Traynor were laying on the bed, on top of the covers, both naked, and both covered with blood, lots of blood.

Subsequent investigations would reveal both April and young Jessica were savagely raped, and then stabbed to death in what was forensically described as a frenzied, unrelenting attack. They died as a result of massive blood loss from multiple stab wounds to their respective faces, chests, and genitals.

Their assailant, or assailants, left the house as silently as they came, and Jackson Traynor's life would never be the same again.

1

Detective Inspector Russell Foley fumbled in his pocket for his mobile phone, flipped it open, and looked at the caller ID. His superior, Superintendent Cameron 'Yap Yap' Barker's name appeared in the display.

"Cam, please tell me this call is not work related," Foley answered.

"Hi, Russell. I wish it was the case. Where are you?"

"I'm in the shopping centre carpark. I've got my arms full of groceries, and I'm about to go home. Why, what have you got?"

"It's complicated," Barker said. "Can you come in?"

"It's my day off," Foley answered, sounding miffed. "But, what else am I gonna do? I live alone, television is crap, and I mowed the lawns this morning."

"You don't have any lawns, Russell. You live in a unit supplied by the department. How soon can you get here?"

"I need to drop my groceries off and change my clothes. Thirty minutes, okay?"

"Twenty would be better."

"I'll do my best."

"Oh, before you hang up, Russell, is Sam Rose working today, or is he under a woman, somewhere?"

Foley laughed. "Sam's a one-woman-man these days, Cam."

"Sarah Collins?" Barker asked.

"Yeah. They're good together. I don't think I've seen Sam this happy since he transferred down here from Darwin."

"Is he working today?"

"No. I've got him on the same duty roster as myself. We're having lunch together later. Why?"

"I'd like you both on this job. Can you bring him in with you?"

"Yeah, I can do that. I'll pick him up on my way in. This sounds serious."

"It could be," Barker said. "By the way, you will both need to pack a bag."

"Pack a bag? How long for?"

"I don't know...a few days, at least."

———

Russell Foley knocked on his partner's door and waited. When no answer came, he knocked again, louder this time, and stepped back from the door. Finally, the door swung open.

Detective Sergeant Sam Rose stood there, naked save for a towel around his waist. Water dripped from his wet, ruffled hair. With a small hand-towel, he dabbed at water droplets running down his bare chest.

"It's fortunate for you it's me, and not a couple of the lovely Seventh Day Adventist ladies knocking at your door," Foley remarked.

"I was in the shower."

"I can see that."

"It's not lunch time already, is it?" Sam asked.

"No," Foley said. "You need to get dressed and pack a bag."

"Pack a bag? Where are we having lunch, Queensland?"

"We're not having lunch. We're going to work. Pack enough clothes for three or four days."

"It's my day off," Sam complained.

"I know, it's my day off too."

"Where are we going?" Sam asked again.

"I don't know." Foley shrugged. "Wherever it is, I'm going with you. Yap Yap wants to see us both, ASAP."

Sam stepped back from the door, ushered Foley inside, and closed the door behind him.

"What's the job?" he asked, rubbing the hand-towel through his hair.

"I don't know that either. Yap will fill us in when we get there."

"Bloody hell!" Sam cursed. "I can't remember the last time I enjoyed an uninterrupted day off."

"You can always quit and sell cars for a living."

"Do car salesmen get days off?"

Foley shook his head. "Get dressed, Sam. Standing here grizzling about the job is not going to make it any easier. This is what we do. You love it, I love it, everybody's happy, get fuckin' dressed."

"Bloody hell!" Sam mumbled again. He turned away and strode reluctantly along the hallway to his room.

2

Superintendent Cameron Yap Yap Barker ushered Foley and Rose into his office and indicated they should sit. He picked up a file which lay open on his desk.

"Thanks for coming in on your day off." He looked first at Foley, and then at Sam. "We've had a job dropped in our lap, which I think you two are best suited for."

"Sounds interesting," Foley said.

"It is...kind of," Barker said, tentatively. "First, I have to give you the back-story. It might make things a bit clearer."

"Okay." Foley nodded.

Barker referred to the file in his hands. "Does the name Jackson Traynor mean anything to either of you?" He looked up from the file, expectantly.

"No, I don't think so," Foley answered.

Sam shrugged. "No, not to me either."

"How about the name, Miguel Alvarez?"

"I don't think so," Foley said.

Sam Rose shrugged again.

"Joaquin 'El Chapo' Guzman?" Barker asked.

"What is this, boss? Twenty questions?"

"Bear with me, please."

"Guzman," Rose said. "Isn't he the South American drug king-pin?"

"Mexican." Barker looked back at the file. "Guzman was extradited to the US a couple of years ago on international drug smuggling charges and is currently languishing in a maximum-security prison in the States. He was the head of the Sinaloa cartel, arguably the most powerful illegal drug trafficking organisation on the planet. Miguel Alvarez, his trusted lieutenant, is now believed to be the head-man in the cartel and personally oversees the 'dark-network' spanning the Asia-Pacific region, including Australia."

"The 'dark-network?'" Foley queried.

"These days, very little of the illicit drugs coming into Australia come directly from Mexico. Rather, they are smuggled through a network of countries in the Pacific, countries like Vanuatu, Fiji, and New Caledonia."

"Isn't this El Chapo Guzman character the dude

who escaped custody a couple of times back in Mexico?" Sam asked.

"Yeah, that's the prick. The Mexican authorities captured him some years ago, locked his arse up, and he managed to dig an elaborate tunnel and escape. He was recaptured a couple of years ago and extradited to the States. That's when Miguel Alvarez stepped up to the plate and filled the void left by Guzman. It's no coincidence that Alvarez's rise to leadership of the cartel coincided with a sudden spike in illicit drug importation into Australia.

"A few years ago, Alvarez formed a somewhat uneasy alliance with Salim Ghandour, the head of a Middle-Eastern crime family, operating out of Sydney.

"At that time, the Ghandour family were the prime movers in the nation-wide distribution of illegal drugs imported into Australia. Alvarez wanted control of the lucrative Sydney drug market and Ghandour was not about to simply hand it over. When he subsequently lost a couple of senior associates to drive-by shootings, including his eldest son, and survived an attempt on his own life, all believed ordered by Alvarez, he decided it might be healthier to form a partnership with the Mexican."

"Where does Jackson Traynor fit in all this?" Foley asked.

"Traynor is a Detective Sergeant with the Australian Federal Police, based in Canberra. He was attached to the Australian Criminal Intelligence Commission as part of a Task Force raised to investigate international crime syndicates smuggling drugs into Australia. He spent almost two years working deep undercover as a member of Ghandour's crime gang.

"Traynor worked his way up through the ranks of the organisation, to where he was a significant player in the Sydney drug underworld. He was the man trusted with the distribution of tonnes of illegal drugs smuggled into the country via the dark-network on behalf of the Alvarez cartel."

"Two years!" Foley said. "Must have picked up some pretty good intelligence over that time."

"What he didn't learn wasn't worth knowing," Barker explained. "He knew it all, identities of the major players, both here in Australia, and in Mexico. Names, dates, places, dollar values; he had enough intel to blow the whole organisation apart, including the Pacific connection.

"I am informed by our Federal police colleagues that Traynor was pivotal in the interception, and seizure, of over three-hundred-and-fifty million dollars of cocaine and amphetamines, smuggled into Australia through the dark-network by associates of Alvarez's cartel, and bound for Salim Ghandour's distribution network.

"The information, supplied by Traynor, resulted in the arrest of all of the key players, both in this country and a couple of Pacific countries. Simultaneous raids on a number of residences, warehouses, shipping containers, aircraft hangars, and sea freighters, in three states, blew the syndicate wide open. The Feds seized six million dollars in cash, not to mention several luxury homes, yachts, and cars."

"I'm guessing Traynor would be keeping a low profile these days," Foley supposed.

"And looking over his shoulder a lot," Sam added.

Barker placed the file back on his desk. "Traynor is due to testify against the Ghandour family and its connection with Alvarez's Sinaloa cartel in a couple of weeks. Needless to say, his testimony will result in a lot of people going to prison for a very long time, including Salim Ghandour, his only surviving son, Hakim, and a number of high-profile cartel associates here in Australia. Word on the street is Miguel Alvarez and Salim Ghandour are not happy campers. Our Federal counterparts believe there are two contracts out on Traynor's life, one ordered by Alvarez, and one by Ghandour. They believe Alvarez sent two professional hit-men over here to take him out."

"All the way from Mexico?" Sam asked, incredulously.

"All the way. They went to his home in the early hours of the morning, but he wasn't home...he was out running."

"Running, in the middle of the night?" Sam asked.

"Traynor is an insomniac," Barker explained. "Has been for years, apparently. He often went running when he couldn't sleep."

"So, they missed him?" Foley guessed.

"Yes...and...no. They missed Traynor, but his wife and twelve-year-old daughter were at home asleep when the baddies came. They brutally raped both, and then stabbed them to death. Traynor found them when he got back from his run."

"Shit!" Foley exclaimed.

"Shit, indeed." Barker nodded.

"How do the Feds know it was the Mexicans, and not Ghandour's crew, who killed his family?" Sam asked.

"Traynor is certain he knows who it was." Barker referred again to the file on his desk. "He says Alvarez has one particular dude he uses when he needs someone taken care of. Bloke by the name of Rodolfo Herrera, a Mexican of Spanish descent. Those who move inside the international drug trade refer to him as 'The Wolf.'"

"What about the second bloke?" Foley asked.

"Mostly, Herrera prefers to work alone. Intel suggests he is a clinical, methodical killer. He gets the job done, quickly and cleanly, and gets out just as quickly and cleanly. It seems this might be the first time he has used an accomplice, a bloke by the name of Ignacio Vargas. Vargas is a particularly nasty piece of work from a small village south of Mexico City. According to Traynor, he likes to use a knife, and almost always includes a sexual component when he kills, and doesn't much care if the victim is male or female."

"Charming," Sam commented.

"How did these two toe-rags get into Australia?" Foley asked.

"False passports," Barker answered with a shrug of his shoulders. "That's not difficult given the circles in which they move. Besides, they're both clean-skins; not so much as a parking ticket between them back in their home country."

"I find that hard to believe," Sam commented.

"It's common knowledge that the Mexican authorities don't have the best track record in regards to corruption. You want a clean record, greasing the right palm will get it for you. The international drug cartels talk about millions like we talk about weekend milk money. Our Australian authorities didn't even know they were in the country until after they arrived."

"Where are they now?" Foley asked.

Barker shrugged. "It seems they disappeared within an hour or so of arriving. The Feds have no idea where they went."

"Where is this Jackson Traynor dude now?" Foley asked.

Barker sat back in his chair, paused, and exhaled loudly. "That's where you and Sam enter the picture."

"Why do I suddenly regret asking?" Foley said.

"Traynor, his wife, and his daughter, were lodged in a safe-house in Sydney following the drug busts. Somehow, the location was compromised, resulting in the murder of his family. Subsequently, the Feds moved him interstate."

"He's here, in the Territory, isn't he?" Sam guessed.

"Been here since just after his wife and daughter were killed," Barker confirmed.

"Where?" Foley asked.

"Ti Tree. Two hundred k's up the track."

"Why Ti Tree?" Sam questioned.

"It's a quiet, nondescript town, close enough to send assistance from here reasonably quickly, if required."

"Assistance?"

Barker leaned back in his seat, sighed heavily and eyed Sam and Foley.

"There's more isn't there?" Foley asked.

"Apparently, the Feds feel the safe-house at Ti Tree may have also been compromised." Barker sat forward and leaned his elbows on his desk. "They want Traynor taken into protective custody."

"By us?"

"Yes. Traynor has a protection detail in place. A team of four working in twelve-hour shifts, two chaps sitting on him twenty-four-seven. But the Feds have requested a local escort."

"Why the escort?" Sam asked. "Why don't they bring him down here themselves?"

"Apparently, there is credible intel indicating the two hit-men, Herrera and Vargas, are still in the country. Traynor knows a lot about Herrera and in-sists he has never failed to complete an assignment. He will not quit until he has completed what he set out to do."

"Kill Traynor?" Sam asked.

"Exactly. It is believed Herrera knows where Traynor is hiding out and is on his way to the Terri-tory to finish the job, if he's not here already." Barker paused before continuing. "This is our turf. The powers that be, upstairs, want a local compo-nent in the escort team. That would be you and Russell."

"How did these roosters find out Traynor was in Ti Tree?" Foley asked.

"The Feds aren't saying. But, rumour has it the cartel has a man inside the International Crime Task Force. If Traynor is killed, Salim Ghandour and his cohorts in the Australian arm of the Mexican cartel are going to walk."

"How long is he going to be in our care?" Sam asked.

Barker shrugged. "I can't tell you that yet. He will be flown to a secure, secret location as soon as a suitable military aircraft can be dispatched to pick him up."

"Military aircraft! Sounds like the Feds might be a tad worried," Sam posed.

Barker leaned back in his chair and eyed both Foley and Rose. "Let me be perfectly clear about this job. I am informed that these two are not to be taken lightly. They are professionals. They have killed before, many times, and will not hesitate to kill again should anyone get in their way. Chances are they are not here yet, and you will not meet them. But, remember this—if you do run into them, they will kill you in the blink of an eye, and then this Vargas character will fuck your corpse."

"What, no dinner and flowers first?" Sam commented.

Barker fixed Sam with an icy stare. "I'm serious,

Sergeant Rose. If you think you've seen the worst of life's scum since you've been in the job, you're not even close when you consider these two arseholes. I hope you don't run into them, because if you do, this may well be the last time I see either of you alive." He picked up a page from his desk and handed it to Foley. "This is the location of the safe-house in Ti Tree. There's a vehicle fuelled up and ready to go in the carpark out the back."

"What about the Ghandour contract?" Sam asked.

Barker shrugged. "Intel has gone quiet on that. The word is Ghandour uses an interstate based two-man team when he wants someone hit. Maybe he cancelled the contract when he found out Alvarez had sent two men out here."

"Or, we've got four hit-men looking for Traynor," Foley suggested. "Sounds like a job for the Task Force."

Barker nodded. "Normally, it would be a job for Task Force. But we want to keep this low-key. If Herrera and Vargas are here already, we don't want to scare them off with an overt show of force. The Feds would like to bag both of them, if possible."

"Why the overnight bags?" Foley asked.

"Originally, the plan was to escort Traynor back here, where we could keep him in protective custody until the military aircraft arrived."

"But?" Foley questioned.

"If the two hit-men are aware of the safe-house in Ti Tree, it's reasonable to assume they are aware of the plan to bring Traynor back here. They can't afford to let that happen. Accordingly, I have changed the plan. You are not to bring Traynor back here until you hear from me, personally."

"Where *are* we taking him?" Foley asked.

Barker shrugged. "I am liaising with a bloke I have known for several years. He owns a couple of cattle stations here in the Territory, including Aningie Station, northwest of Ti Tree. He runs both from a station further north, up past Tennant Creek, and has a sole caretaker in the homestead at Aningie. It's isolated, forty kilometres west of the Stuart Highway. You are to escort Traynor, and his security team, to Aningie Station, and contact me when you get there. There is no mobile phone reception out there, but I am told the caretaker has a satellite phone."

"How long will we be there?" Foley asked.

"It might take a while to organise a military flight to pick up Traynor. Apparently, most of the military aircraft based here in the Territory are involved in war games with the United States, operating out of the Tindal Air Force base, south of Katherine. Could be later today or even tomorrow.

As soon as I know a chopper has been despatched I will contact you on the satellite phone."

"Who knows about this Aningie place?" Sam asked.

"So far, just the three of us in this room, the station owner, and his caretaker. When I speak to Traynor's boss in Canberra, I will inform him. If there is a leak in the system, the fewer people who know where to find Traynor, the better."

3

Based in Alice Springs, the second largest city in Australia's Northern Territory, Detective Inspector Russell Foley and Detective Sergeant Sam Rose were senior members of the Major Crime section of the Northern Territory Police Force. Both were career police officers, having joined the force as members of the same recruit training squad, Foley at age twenty-three, and Rose at age twenty-two. Now, twenty years later, they had been partners for a long time, were best friends and a very good investigative team, respected by their police colleagues and the hierarchy alike.

Rose and Foley, however, had not always been best friends. Several years earlier, when both were members of what was then known as the Criminal Investigation Branch based at Police Headquarters in Darwin, the capital city of the Northern Territory, there occurred an acrimonious split in their friendship.

Sam Rose was a confirmed bachelor, and an unashamed ladies' man. While he had a reputation among his male colleagues of being a skirt-chaser, it was a reputation undeserved. He was a red-blooded, Australian male, and in the opinion of most women who knew him, he was the complete package: tall, confident, intelligent, nice looking, had a likeable sense of humour, still had all his hair, was employed, and most importantly, he was single and available.

Despite the perceived lothario reputation among his male colleagues, Sam was faithful to the woman he happened to be with at the time and remained so until that particular relationship had run its course. Sam's one big mistake, one he regretted immediately it was over, and still regretted on the rare occasions he reflected upon it, was the time he slept with Jennifer Foley, estranged wife of Russell Foley. It only happened once, and he was so drunk at the time he had no recollection of whether the liaison was enjoyable or otherwise. What he did know was he was overcome with regret the following morning, and the fact that Russell and Jennifer had been apart for some time had no bearing on the severity of the guilt he felt.

From Jennifer Foley's point of view, Sam was just another conquest in her scheme to hurt her husband, as often as she could and as painfully as she could. In this case, Sam Rose was the facilitator. For Jennifer, seducing Sam was not about romance, it was about spite. What better way was there to hurt her husband than to screw his best friend? Subsequently, she couldn't wait to broadcast the dalliance to Russell, and indeed the whole CIB squad room. She proceeded to do so, in full voice, and in graphic detail.

The incident precipitated a physical altercation between the two detectives which ultimately led to the fracture of the friendship they had enjoyed for many years. Sam Rose subsequently resigned from the police force, and Russell Foley was promoted to Officer in Charge of the Criminal Investigation Branch.

The acrimonious split lasted for twelve months, and ended when both men, Foley in his role as a homicide investigator and Rose as a private investigator, were involved in the investigation of a series of brutal murders. The killings, committed against select members of the judiciary and the police force, were the work of a psychopathic killer responsible for killing his wife and two young children.

Subsequently, Sam was invited to return to the police force, and Foley was transferred to Officer in

Charge, Major Crime Southern Command in Alice Springs.

Russell Foley never re-married. Jennifer Foley took their two children and fled to Queensland where she diligently continued to make his life more difficult by constantly demanding he send her more money, over and above the amount ordered by the Family Court at their divorce settlement hearing. It was for the children, she insisted. Foley suspected the money found its way into her pocket rather than to the benefit of his kids, but he sent it anyway.

He dated occasionally, but the whole falling in love, marital bliss thing was tainted now following his experiences with Jennifer. Besides, he loved his job, always had, and his commitment to it was always going to make it difficult to maintain a happy, contented marriage. Best not to commit to anything resembling a long-term relationship, he reasoned.

Unlike his friend, Sam Rose, Foley was an average looking man, rather than conspicuously good-looking. In truth, 'average' best described all aspects of his physical appearance: average height, average weight. He was clean-shaven and, like Sam, he had all his hair, although it was starting to thin a little on top. Around the outer edges of his eyes, crow's-feet creases threatened to deepen over the next few years, a result of over twenty years under the blazing

Territory sun, he reasoned. Or, perhaps it was nothing more than the natural aging process. It mattered little either way to Foley, he was not one who suffered from vanity.

Where Foley differed from many of his police colleagues was in his approach to his job. The vast majority of the police force membership were a hard-working, diligent team of men and women who went about the often-difficult job of policing in a professional, dedicated manner. If that approach was to be considered the average for the force, Foley constantly strived to be better than average. The general opinion among his colleagues was that he was a 'cop's cop.' He was aware of the analogy of course; hard not to be given the gossip mill in the police force was healthier than the local Country Women's Association. Although he found it flattering, he considered it of little consequence to him in his overall application to the job.

For the most part, Foley was a 'by-the-book' cop. There were occasions when he found it acceptable, if not necessary, to bend the rules in his endeavour to achieve the best outcome; most cops were guilty of procedural manipulation at one time or another. For Foley, however, such occasions were rare, although more frequent when working with Sam Rose. Rose's approach notwithstanding, Foley never once felt guilty of compromising his principles. The end-game, after all, was all about getting a conviction and taking the baddies off the street. The best way to do that, he considered, was to present the best possible case to the prosecutors. If that meant bending the rules occasionally, without actually breaking them, he was okay with that.

4

———

Foley drove while Sam perused the file on Jackson Traynor. They travelled in an un-marked police sedan, heading north along the Stuart Highway, the main highway running from south to north through the centre of the continent.

"Interesting reading?" Foley asked, after they had been on the road for just over an hour.

"Yes, very interesting."

"Tell me more."

"Well," Sam began, "this Jackson Traynor character has led an adventurous life."

"As an undercover agent for the Federal Police?"

"Even before he joined the Feds."

"Tell me about him."

"He was in the military. Served with the SAS Commandos in Afghanistan. It says here he was awarded the Medal for Gallantry for his actions at the battle of Shah Wali Kot, in June 2010. He was part of Second Squadron Commandos deployed by chopper around Tizark, on a kill-or-capture mission hunting the Taliban and their leaders."

"The Medal for Gallantry," Foley commented. "I'm guessing he might have got a couple of the bastards."

"Remind me not to piss him off," Sam said.

"In that case, you better let me do all the talking; you've got priors for pissing people off."

"I'll be on my best behaviour. This dude killed people for a living."

"Just like the two Mexican pricks, and maybe a couple of Australian contractors looking to put *his* lights out," Foley observed.

"That would be a contest worth watching."

"Yeah, from afar." Foley slowed the vehicle and flicked the left-hand indicator on.

Sam dropped the file on the dashboard and looked ahead. "Are we there already?"

"No," Foley answered. "I need a leak, and a coffee." He turned off the highway.

One hundred and thirty-five kilometres north of Alice Springs, behind a stand of trees in the heart of Anmatjere aboriginal country, Aileron Roadhouse was set back close to three hundred metres off the Stuart Highway. The rest-stop would be easily missed by the traveller if not for the Anmatjere Man, a giant, steel sculpture of an aboriginal hunter standing 17 metres tall and weighing 8 tonnes, erected in 2005 on a hill behind the roadhouse. A lone sentinel overlooking Aileron and the surrounding area, Anmatjere Man was joined three years later by similar sculptures of a woman and child. The Anmatjere Man had a family.

"What the hell is that?" Sam asked.

"That's the Anmatjere Man," Foley answered.

"The Anma...what?"

"Anmatjere Man. He was on his own for a few years; then he met the lovely Anmatjere Woman. Now they're a happy family."

Sam stared in amazement at the giant sculptures. "I never knew they were here," he said finally.

"They were right there when we came up this way on the 'bones in the well' case. But we didn't stop here."

"Why here, in the middle of nowhere?" Sam wondered aloud.

"This land is Anmatjere country," Foley explained. "The Anmatjere people are the traditional owners. The sculptures invite people to stop, take photos, and spend money in the roadhouse. It's all about marketing."

"Well, it's working. I'm hungry, and we never did get to have lunch."

Foley parked in a designated area, got out of the vehicle, and stretched. He leaned down and spoke through the open door. "I'm gonna take a leak. You wanna order me a steak sandwich and a coffee to go?"

"It's your turn to buy lunch," Sam reminded him.

"My turn?"

"Yes, your turn! I paid for lunch last week."

"That's not how I remember it. Tell them to hold the beetroot." Foley closed the door and started walking towards the roadhouse toilet block. Behind him, Sam got out of the vehicle, muttering just loud enough to be heard.

"Bloody steak sandwich...hold the fuckin' beetroot...rip-off, roadhouse prices...I'll have to get a second job."

Foley smiled to himself and continued walking.

———

A long, sweeping, right-hand bend from the south welcomes travellers into the small township of Ti Tree, two hundred kilometres north of Alice Springs. With the population in the surrounding district hovering around one thousand, approximately two hundred people call the town home.

Originally named Tea Tree and established in

GARY S. GREGOR

1888 as an overland telegraph reserve connecting Adelaide in South Australia with Darwin in the far north of the continent, the reason for the name change to Ti Tree had been lost in the annals of time.

At the northern end of the sweeping bend, a service road branches off the Stuart Highway to the right, directing visitors to the Ti Tree Roadhouse, a typical road-side rest-stop supplying fuel, dine-in and take-away food, a licensed bar, and restroom facilities.

Foley slowed and pulled into a vehicle parking area between the highway and the roadhouse. A hundred metres past the roadhouse, a blue and white checked sign on top of a tall pole indicated the town police station.

"Do we make ourselves known to the local lads?" Sam asked.

"Our instructions are to go directly to the safe-house, liaise with the Feds, and pick up Traynor," Foley said.

"Hmm," Sam murmured.

"Hmm? What's that supposed to mean?"

Sam turned in his seat and looked at Foley. "Come on, Russ. You're a smart guy. This sounds like a straightforward escort job. Sending two senior Major Crime investigators on a candy-run like this doesn't make any sense."

"Protecting a key witness from two, maybe four, hit-men doesn't sound like a 'candy-run' to me. Do you have a theory, or are you still cranky because you had to pay for lunch?"

"I have a theory, and lunch is still repeating on me."

"Would you care to share your theory?"

"Maybe the Mexicans are back home, drinking Tequila and snacking on Nachos."

"You're could be right. But I don't think you are. There is still the Salim Ghandour contract." Foley indicated the file on the dash. "If this was a candy run, it would be the General Duties blokes doing the job. I don't think this is as straightforward as you suggest it might be. If the two Mexican hit-men know Traynor is here, they may be on their way here. They may be here already. In which case, this would definitely be a job for two highly experienced, intrepid crime fighters, such as us."

"Intrepid crime fighters?"

"Just trying to lighten the moment." Foley smiled.

"Holy Mexican murderers, Batman!" Sam cried. "Fire up the Batmobile!" He indicated the road ahead.

5

Mitchell Simms and Trevor Lowe slept soundly in the small accommodation unit they shared, behind the Ti Tree Roadhouse. A window-mounted air conditioner rattled softly, labouring against the still, humid air.

Simms and Lowe were both veteran Federal police officers with combined service of just over forty years. Assigned to a four-man security team tasked with the job of protecting one of their own, neither man stirred when the entrance door opened, squeaking quietly on hinges in need of lubrication. Both men died where they slept.

Lowe, the junior of the two, was a new appointee to the Australian Criminal Intelligence Commission, having been appointed to the Task Force investigating international drug syndicates just a month previously.

Lowe was the first to die. A silenced, .45 calibre, soft-nose slug crashed into his head as he lay snoring softly. Just a second later, Mitchell Simms was also shot in the head at close range.

Rodolfo Herrera stood between the two single beds and took a moment to study his handiwork. Satisfied, he stepped back to the door. Impeding his exit, Ignacio Vargas stood in the doorway, smiling widely, craning his head to look around Herrera at the two dead cops. In his hand, he held a large, serrated-edge knife, his personal weapon of choice.

"No," Herrera said. "There ees no time. We must go. *Andale*—hurry!"

The lecherous smile on Vargas's face disappeared. "No time? What ees this 'no time?' I do not need a long time."

"There ees no time," Herrera repeated. "We go, now." He stepped close to Vargas, forcing him to step backwards, out of the doorway.

"I need only a few minutes," Vargas insisted.

"They are already dead. You cannot make them more dead." Herrera pulled the door closed and stepped around Vargas.

"You wait. I will be very fast."

"I do not wait for you. Eef you want to stay, you can stay. I go now." Herrera moved to their vehicle.

"Eef you leave, I have no vehicle," Vargas complained.

Herrera paused, glanced at his watch, and looked back at Vargas. "Five minutes only. Then I leave. Eef you are not finished, I leave without you."

The smile returned to Vargas's face. "I will be very fast." He opened the door, stepped into the room, and closed the door behind him.

"*Pinche joto*—fuckin' faggot," Herrera muttered as he climbed into the driver's side of the rental vehicle.

———

Pete Tomkins had never seriously thought about dying, despite the risks associated with his job. Oh, he knew he would die one day. But he was only thirty-three years old; the day when he *did* start thinking about dying would be several decades away, hopefully.

Pete had never experienced the effect of a blow torch applied to his testicles either. Had he, he was confident this is what it would feel like. It seemed such an odd, obscure, incongruent thing to think about at this point, so seemingly out of context with what was actually happening; the mind is a complicated and mysterious organ.

Initially, there was no pain, just a sudden, powerful jolt in his groin. Powerful enough to knock his feet from under him and send him sprawling backwards to the hard, dry ground. The pain followed a few moments later. It radiated up through his groin into his belly and chest, and simultaneously down through his thighs to his legs and all the way down to his feet.

It was a paralyzing pain, so bad he couldn't seem to take a big enough breath to produce even a half-decent scream. He lay on his back in the dirt, hyperventilating with rapid, shallow gasps, his mouth opening and closing like a fish stranded on dry land. He tried to move his legs. Nothing happened. He tried to move his arms. Nothing happened. *Now*, Pete was thinking about dying. He closed his eyes, opened them, and tried to move his head, relieved to learn he could at least do that. He looked across at his partner.

Craig Dermott, Pete's Federal Police partner, also lay on his back, just a few metres from him, his arms flung straight out from his sides like a crucifix. Half his face was missing. Where his face used to be just a few seconds ago, was now a mushy mess of blood, mangled flesh, and bone. A pink, jellylike substance oozed from the ugly, gaping hole in his head and pooled in the dirt beneath him.

It should be white, Pete thought, between breaths growing rapidly shallower. That's his brain flowing out of his head, why is it pink? It should be white...or grey...not pink...brains aren't pink.

Finally, from a place somewhere deep within him, a place he did not instantly recognise, a pitiful, elongated moan, punctuated by his staccato breathing, escaped his lips and drifted away in the serene silence which was so much an intrinsic part of the surrounding countryside. A solitary tear trickled from his eye and plopped silently into the deep, fine, powder-like dust inches from his face.

In the final seconds remaining of his life, Pete thought of his family, his wife, his son, and his daughter. He was going to see them in a couple of days, when the shift-change crew arrived. He tried to turn his head away from the macabre sight of his partner. Now, his head would not move. He could no longer open and close his eyes; they remained fixed and staring at his dead partner. A darkness, quickly descending into complete blackness, closed around him, and Pete Tomkins died.

6

The house was basic and ordinary in its appearance, but the same could not be said in regards to its location. Situated on the north-eastern side of the township, it stood in the middle of a small clearing at the end of an obviously little-used, narrow, dirt track and was completely surrounded by trees. The track, seriously corrugated and unmaintained, skirted the northern end of an unsealed runway which provided access for emergency air-medical services should they be required in the absence of any sophisticated medical facilities in the town. It began where the approach road from the township ended at the airstrip and wound its way through the trees for approximately one kilometre before it culminated at the edge of the clearing. The house was not visible from the other homes in the town, or from the airstrip. To the unaware, it might never have existed.

Russell Foley stopped at the edge of the clearing and stared at the house fifty metres ahead. It was an unpretentious, prefabricated home, probably transported here in kit form and erected onsite; why, was anyone's guess. To Foley, it seemed a somewhat unusual place to build a house.

The front door was centrally located in the façade of the house, and a small, covered porch sheltered the entrance. At first glance, apart from the odd location, the house was similar to thousands of others erected in small towns all over the Northern Territory to accommodate an expanding population.

"You think this is the place?" Foley asked Sam.

"Has to be. We followed the directions."

"Looks kinda isolated."

"Maybe that's intentional," Sam suggested. "It is a safe-house, after all."

"Where are the Feds?" Foley asked, scanning the bush around them.

"In the house?"

"I thought we would have been challenged by now."

"Not if they were expecting us."

Foley shrugged. "Maybe. Stay alert. This has a feeling about it."

"A feeling?"

"Yeah. A gut feeling."

"Might be the steak sandwich coming back to haunt you."

"Humour me. Stay alert." Foley moved the transmission stick into drive, moved slowly forward across the clearing, and eventually stopped approximately ten metres from the front of the house.

Sam moved his hand to the Glock, holstered at his hip. "Place looks deserted."

"It's not supposed to be deserted," Foley said. "There are supposed to be two Federal officers here, and Traynor should be inside the house."

Both Sam and Foley stared at the house for a moment, and then cast their eyes over their surroundings.

"What now?" Sam asked, finally.

"You should get out and check the house," Foley answered.

"Me?"

"Yeah, you. I will stay here with the engine running, in case we need to make a quick getaway."

"Why would we need to make a quick getaway?"

Foley turned to Sam. "I don't know why we would need to make a quick getaway, Sam. I'm just erring on the side of caution."

"Just so I understand, you want me to get out of

the car and risk my life out there in the open, while you sit here in the safety of the car?"

"Yeah. That about sums it up."

"If someone starts shooting at me, and you make a quick getaway without me, I'm gonna shoot *you*... just so *you* understand."

"Got it." Foley smiled.

Sam reached for his door handle.

"Wait!" Foley said. "Someone is coming out of the house."

Sam looked at the house and saw the front door swing open.

A tall, big-framed man, dressed in blue jeans and black T-shirt, untucked and hanging over his belt, stood in the open doorway, the bulk of his body seeming to fill the void.

"Who's this rooster?" Sam asked.

"Jackson Traynor?"

"He's a big fucker."

"Looks like a Glock he's got there," Foley said, lowering his eyes to the gun the man held at his side.

———

People meeting Jackson Traynor for the first time generally found him to be an intimidating character. There was a presence about him like an invisible aura, sensed rather than seen, which conveyed a warning suggesting it would be wise to exercise caution before entering into a relationship with him, regardless of how casual. Like a comfortable coat of confidence and self-assurance, he carried the presence with him everywhere he went, and it was obvious even before he uttered a word.

To others, those with the advantage of knowing him beyond the first meeting, 'intimidating' was a much too severe description of his persona. Standing six feet four inches tall, and built like his body was sculptured from stone, he was, nonetheless, an imposing figure of a man, even to those fortunate enough to be considered his close friends.

Although Sam Rose and Russell Foley were first time acquaintances with Traynor, the man standing on the porch a few metres in front of them, with a 9mm Glock pistol held loosely but no doubt capably at his side, offered them no real cause for concern. They had both met plenty of characters with guns during their respective careers. The man on the porch was just another dude with a gun, albeit a bloody big dude.

"You scared?" Sam asked Foley.

"Nah!" Foley scoffed. "You?"

"I'm fuckin' shittin' myself!"

"He is one, big sucker."

"And you wanted me to get out and check the house," Sam complained.

Foley reached into his shirt pocket, removed his police identification, flipped it open, and held it up to the windscreen. The man in the doorway did not move.

"What now?" Sam asked.

"We wait."

"For what?"

Foley shrugged. "For him to invite us in for tea and scones," he scoffed. "I'm sure we will find out soon enough."

The man took a step forward onto the small porch and called out to them. "Get out of the car! Nice and slow! Hands empty!"

"We gonna take orders from this guy?" Sam asked.

"For the moment." Foley closed his ID wallet and slipped it back in his pocket. "Let's get out of the car." He unclipped his seat belt and opened his door.

"What if Traynor is dead, and that guy's a baddie?"

"He doesn't look Mexican. He's a cop, he's not going to shoot us."

"I hope you're right." Sam also unfastened his seat belt and opened his door.

"Step away from the vehicle!" the stranger ordered. "Hands away from your weapons!"

Foley lifted his hands away from his sides and took two paces away from the car. "You must be Jackson Traynor," he called to the stranger.

The man fixed Foley with steel-blue eyes. "Who are you?"

"Detective Inspector Russell Foley. My partner is Detective Sergeant Sam Rose."

"Give me the name of the man who sent you here," the man called from the porch.

"Cameron Barker," Foley said.

"What's his nickname?"

"Yap Yap."

The man appeared to relax slightly. "Where are my colleagues?"

"We never saw anyone," Foley said. "We drove straight here from Alice Springs."

The man paused and looked beyond the vehicle at the approach track. Then, he looked around at the bush surrounding the house. "You weren't challenged by two Federal police officers?"

"We saw no one."

The man looked again at the surrounding bush. "Get in the house."

"What?"

"Nobody gets this close to the house without

47

being challenged by my colleagues. You need to get inside the house...now!"

Both Foley and Sam glanced curiously at the bush beyond the clearing.

"We're here to escort you to another location," Foley said, returning his gaze to the big man on the porch.

"I know why you are here. You need to get inside the house!"

Foley looked across the roof of the car at Sam. "What do you think?"

Sam shrugged. "Maybe we should get inside the house. I could use a coffee."

"You two gonna stand there debating the issue until you get shot in the back, or are you coming in the house?"

Sam looked across at Foley. "He makes a good argument."

"Okay." Foley nodded. "Let's go in the house."

Sam addressed the man on the porch. "We accept your kind invitation. Put the kettle on."

7

The stranger ushered Sam and Foley into the house. He closed and locked the door behind them, stepped across to the nearest window, moved the curtain aside, and peeked cautiously out at the area to the front of the house, the Glock pistol still held loosely at his side.

"You Jackson Traynor?" Foley asked.

"That would be me," Traynor confirmed. He turned and faced them.

Up close, Traynor was even more impressive. Taller than both Sam and Foley, neither of whom could be considered short in stature, he held himself erect, ramrod straight, a legacy of his time in the military. His T-shirt, stretched taut across his chest and biceps, indicated he was a man more than familiar with pumping iron to stay in shape. Complementing the toned, finely-tuned physique, cobalt blue eyes, set wide below a smooth, wrinkle-free forehead, were clear, alert, and focused. A slightly crooked nose presented an air of mystery to an otherwise flawless, square-jawed face. Traynor was, by any standard, a perfect example of the quintessential Aussie male: tanned, fit, and very good-looking.

Good looks and athletic build notwithstanding, Traynor projected an image declaring loudly and clearly, he was not a man to be messed with. He who underestimated the explosive potential lingering just below the impressive exterior, did so at his own peril.

Sam Rose saw it immediately. Probably because he had met people like Traynor before in the course of his job. Not many, but enough to recognise the type. Many of those he had met turned out to be pretenders, would-be-if-they-could-be characters who, when it came to proving their true worth when the going got tough, chose to cut and run. Traynor was not a pretender. Sam did not have to know the man to see that courage and a single-minded determination pulsed through his body in accompaniment with the blood that pulsed through his veins.

"Are you sure you never saw my two colleagues?" Traynor asked Foley.

"We saw no one. Foley stepped forward and offered his hand. "I'm Russell Foley."

Traynor swapped the Glock to his left hand, shook Foley's hand firmly, and turned to Sam. "Sam Rose?"

"Yes." Sam shook hands with Traynor.

"You need to get out of here," Traynor said.

"Okay, grab what you need, and we'll get on the road," Foley said.

"You two get on the road, I'm staying."

"What do you mean you're staying?" Foley asked.

Traynor indicated the window. "Somewhere out there, my two friends are laying dead. You need to go now, or you might be next."

"What the fuck are you talking about?" Sam asked. "How do you know your friends are dead?"

"Trust me, I know."

"How do you know?" Sam repeated.

"If they never stopped you and checked your creds when you arrived, it's because they couldn't. They're dead."

"You sound pretty sure," Foley observed.

"I am sure. I know the two men who killed them. They are professional hit-men, hired by a Mexican drug lord to hunt me down and kill me...and anyone who gets in their way," he added to emphasise the point.

"Miguel Alvarez?" Sam said.

"Alvarez wants me dead. If I get to court with what I know, he stands to lose his foothold in the Australian drug trade, not to mention tens of millions of dollars in business."

"All the more reason why you should come with us," Sam said.

Foley reached in his pocket for his mobile phone. "I'll call the Ti Tree police for back-up."

"Don't waste your time," Traynor said. "I tried to call my colleagues as soon as I saw you pull up at the edge of the clearing. They're using a cell phone jammer."

"You are kidding me!" Foley said. "Who the fuck are we dealing with here?"

"I wish I was kidding." Traynor indicated the locked front door. "Somewhere out there, Rodolfo Herrera and Ignacio Vargas will be moving in on this house as we speak. You need to get out now!"

"The two men who murdered your family?" Foley asked.

Traynor paused for a short moment, as if reflecting momentarily on his lost wife and daughter. "Yes. If you don't leave now, there is a very good chance you will leave in a body bag."

"We're not leaving without you," Sam declared, adamantly.

Traynor looked at Sam, and then turned to face Foley. "You're his boss, right?"

"Officially. But Sam's never been big on the chain-of-command thing."

"Those two bastards out there raped and murdered my wife and twelve-year-old daughter," Traynor explained. "I've been hoping they would come for me. Been looking forward to it. They're outside this house right now, so close I can smell the chilli leeching from their pores. I'm not leaving, and the longer you hang around in here debating the issue with me, the less chance you have of getting out while you still can."

Foley looked at Sam. Sam offered a shrug of indifference. Foley looked at Traynor. "Three against two. Odds are in our favour if we stay," he suggested.

Suddenly, the front window exploded in a spray of glass. The three men flinched and turned away as hundreds of tiny shards of glass splayed the room. As one, they moved deeper into the room, away from the window.

"Missed!" Sam observed loudly.

"They don't miss," Traynor said. "That was a calling card. Letting us know they're here."

"How did these arseholes get weapons into the country?" Foley asked.

"Picked them up when they arrived," Traynor said. "Alvarez's cartel has links with a Middle-

Eastern crime gang in Sydney, and a couple of outlaw motorcycle gangs with associates in every state and territory, even here, in the Northern Territory."

"Is it too late to leave?" Sam asked.

"If you intend leaving the same way you arrived, it is."

"Is there any other way?"

"Follow me." Traynor moved across the room, to a short hallway.

With Sam and Foley close behind, Traynor hurried along the hallway and stopped at the door to the second of two bedrooms. He turned, confirmed Foley and Rose were behind him, and quickly entered the room. One single bed, devoid of any bedding apart from a mattress still wrapped in its plastic protective covering, stood lengthways against the back wall. The rest of the floor space was taken up with several pieces of gym equipment: a treadmill, a rowing machine, and a number of weight-lifting applications. On one side wall, a double-door wardrobe was built into an alcove. There were no other furnishings in the room. Foley and Rose paused just inside the door.

"Are we going to take a nap or work out?" Sam asked, jokingly.

Traynor fixed Sam with a look which left him in

no doubt the Federal cop was unimpressed with his attempts to make light of their situation. "If you don't do as I say, you might be taking a permanent nap."

Sam raised his hands in surrender. "Okay, okay. I get it. No more jokes."

Traynor turned his back on them and stepped across to the wardrobe.

Sam leaned close to Foley. "Grumpy bugger," he whispered. "That's what happens when you don't take the time to have a coffee."

"Shut up, Sam," Foley hissed.

"Shees! Two grumpy bastards!" Sam softly responded.

Traynor flung open the wardrobe doors. "In here," he said.

"What?" Sam asked.

"In here!" Traynor repeated, more forcefully this time. He stepped away from the wardrobe.

Foley and Sam crossed to the wardrobe. They both glanced curiously into the robe. It was empty. A little way down from the top, a shelf, also bare, ran across the full width of the robe.

Foley leaned closer and peered deeper into the interior. "You want us to hide in the wardrobe?"

Traynor stepped in front of them and leaned into the robe. He reached down, deep into the back, grasped a handle not immediately obvious, and pulled. A section of the wardrobe floor swung open, exposing a dark, empty space below.

"What the fuck is that?" Sam gasped.

"It's a tunnel," Traynor answered.

"A tunnel?"

"Yes, a tunnel. It was built here when they built the house."

"Why?" Foley asked.

"It's an emergency escape route," Traynor explained.

"Where does it lead?"

"It runs across the clearing behind the house, to the east, under the tree line, and surfaces in the woods approximately two hundred metres from here."

Sam leaned in front of Foley and peered into the dark space. "You have to be kidding!"

"Does it look like I'm kidding?" Traynor asked. "Just get in and go!"

"I'm not going down there!" Sam insisted.

"If you stay here, you die here."

Sam turned to Foley. "Russ?"

Foley shrugged. "Might be a good idea to get out of here and re-group. Call in the cavalry."

"There's three of us, for Christ's sake. None of us are rookies. We can take these pricks!" Sam reasoned.

Behind them, from the front room they had just vacated, another window exploded.

"Fuck!" Foley flinched.

"They're close!" Traynor said. "Get inside and go!"

"You first," Foley said. "Lead the way."

"I'm not going," Traynor announced.

"What was it you said, if you stay here you die here?" Foley said.

"If I die here, I'm ready for that. I've prepared mentally for that possibility. You didn't get to see what was left of my wife and daughter when those two bastards were finished with them. I did. Since that day, I have thought of little else other than killing them both. I'm staying!"

"Listen to me," Foley said, his face close to Traynor. "I understand you are the principle witness in the up-coming case against the drug cartel here in Australia. If you die before you can testify, the whole gang walks, including those two dipsticks outside. No one will pay for the loss of your family. Is that what you want?"

"No, that's not want I want," Traynor snapped. "But, I've been hiding out in this shit-hole since my family was murdered. Running and hiding from those two out there is not part of my DNA."

"It's not a part of our DNA either," Foley said. "So, here's a plan. Come with us now, and as soon as we get out of the tunnel and can get mobile phone reception, we will call for back-up. Then, we'll double back under the cover of the woods, and take these two arse-holes by surprise."

Traynor did not move. He stared at Foley for a moment, then dropped his head and stared vacantly at the floor.

"Come on, Jack," Sam encouraged. "Russell is right. You're no help to anyone dead. We'll come back and get those pricks. I promise you, they *will* pay for what they did to your family."

Traynor looked up, first at Sam, and then at Foley. "Don't bullshit me. If I come with you, we come back and get Herrera and Vargas?"

"You have our word," Foley said.

"Absolutely," Sam said.

"Wait here," Traynor said suddenly. He turned and hurried from the room.

"Now where's he going?" Sam questioned.

Foley glanced anxiously at the dark hole in the floor of the wardrobe. "To find another way out of here...I hope," he muttered.

Back in the lounge, Traynor moved quickly to a small coffee table in the middle of the room and fumbled in a drawer for a notepad and pen. He scribbled a short note, ripped the page from the notebook, and placed it on top of the coffee table.

Satisfied, he hurried back to the bedroom where Foley and Rose waited expectantly.

"Forget something?" Sam asked.

"No, nothing," Traynor answered. "Let's go. I'll lead the way." He stepped inside the robe, turned his back to the interior, and began to climb down a ladder fixed to the lip of the cavity. Just before his head disappeared into the dark depths, he looked back at Foley and Rose. "Pull the wardrobe doors and the tunnel entrance closed behind you."

8
_____

Rodolfo Herrera was a man well suited to his profession. Killing came naturally to him, almost like his life was predetermined to follow a particular path. He liked to kill. Killing did not give him a buzz or a high, like heroin or cocaine might to an addict, it was more a feeling of immense satisfaction at having completed an assignment successfully. It has to help when you are paid well for doing something you love to do.

For Herrera, killing was a way of life. It was his career, and he was damn good at it. He should be; he started at the tender age of thirteen when he shot and killed a neighbourhood bully with his father's .45 semi-automatic pistol. He knew as soon as he pulled the trigger and saw the bully fall dead at his feet that killing was what he wanted to do. Now, at forty-three, with thirty years of experience honing his craft behind him, he was considered by those in the know to be the best in the business. And killing *was* a business, at least it was in the illegal drug business.

Rodolfo Herrera also loved his nick-name. The Wolf. It suited him, he believed. He didn't know who it was who first bestowed the name upon him, and he didn't care, it was not important in the whole scheme of things, it just fit, like a one-off, well-tailored suit, designed and stitched just for him.

Herrera knew little about the habits of wolves, but he did know they almost always hunted in packs, stalking their prey, patiently waiting for the right moment to attack, and when they did, it was quick, brutal, and deadly. In some respects, Herrera and The Wolf were as one. Like The Wolf, Herrera stalked his prey, sometimes for weeks as he established a pattern of behaviour. He waited for just the right moment. When that moment arrived, the kill was also quick, brutal, and deadly. However, that was where any similarity between himself and a real wolf ended. Unlike the real wolf, Herrera hunted alone. Always had, and always would. Until now.

Now that El Chapo Guzman was no longer in control, Herrera worked exclusively for the Mexican Sinaloa cartel, headed by Miguel Alvarez. As it was with Guzman, when one worked for Alvarez one did what Alvarez ordered, especially if one wanted to remain among the living. If Alvarez ordered him to take an associate to Australia to find and kill Jackson Traynor, he would take an associate, despite his personal misgivings. He knew enough about Alvarez to know that going against a direct order from the Mexican drug lord was not conducive to a long, healthy life. Besides, with Guzman now out of the picture, Alvarez was Rodolfo's sole source of income, and it wouldn't pay to fall out with the goose that laid the golden egg. The new drug king-pin was arguably more ruthless than Guzman ever was, and a long-standing, mutually satisfactory working relationship would account for nothing if he fell out of favour with him.

The Wolf was not afraid of Alvarez; he was not afraid of anyone. It was more that he was acutely aware of his new-found power and influence. It was rumoured that Guzman tried to keep control of his drug empire from his prison cell in the United States, but things were not as easily achieved in the US prison system as they were in the notoriously corrupt Mexican system. Now, Alvarez was in command, and he ruled his new empire with even greater intimidation and threat of death than any of his predecessors.

Thanks to the efforts of those predecessors, Alvarez had enough money at his disposal to buy anything, and anyone, and the money pile just kept growing. However, control over such a rapidly expanding mountain of cash did not come without inherent risk. Both outside and inside the cartel, there was always someone willing to make a name for himself by being the one to kill Miguel Alvarez and take control of the empire. Nonetheless, Alvarez never really felt threatened. He surrounded himself with people he could trust, people just like him, people who would kill in the blink of an eye and not lose a minute's sleep over it. It cost plenty, but it was a price worth paying knowing these people would die for him and he never had to worry about looking over his shoulder.

If the rumours were correct, Alvarez moved around a lot, changing his location as often as every two or three days. Wherever he was, he had twenty-four-hour-a-day access to the very best restaurant food delivered to his door, the most modern, state-of-the-art computer system manned by the best computer geeks money could buy, and top-end prostitutes available to him at any time of the day or night. It all cost money, of course, but Miguel Alvarez had truckloads of it. Corruption in Mexico being what it was, there were plenty of folks more than willing to satisfy Alvarez's every whim, for a price.

———

Ignacio Vargas was a pig in the guise of a man, Rodolfo Herrera considered. Herrera would have preferred to travel to the other side of the world alone, but, if he had to do so with an accomplice, he would rather it be anyone else other than Vargas.

The job was to kill Jackson Traynor before he had a chance to testify against the cartel's Australian members; a straight forward assignment, he thought. No more difficult than hundreds of similar assignments he had accepted from Joaquin El Chapo Guzman over the last thirty years, and now from Miguel Alvarez. He didn't need an associate. He never asked for one and was more than a little annoyed when he was ordered to take one, particularly given the associate chosen by Alvarez was Vargas. Herrera was familiar with Vargas's reputation, and having the sadistic thug accompany him on this assignment did not sit comfortably with him.

Rodolfo Herrera was a shooter. He was not a rapist, and he was not a knifer, and wherever possible he avoided collateral victims. When they went to Traynor's house in the pre-dawn hours and found he was not at home, he left immediately, leaving Vargas in the house. There would be other opportunities to get to Traynor. His assignment was to kill Traynor, only Traynor. There was no need for the wife and daughter to die. Killing the Federal cop's family only added to the already substantial risk associated with the original assignment.

He was always curious as to why Alvarez wanted Vargas to accompany him on what was, effectively, a straightforward, uncomplicated job, albeit on the other side of the world. When he left the Traynor house that night, he *did* know why. Vargas *was* a rapist, and a knifer, a sadistic, sex-crazed, homicidal maniac who got his jollies by killing in the most, savage, brutal, depraved manner he could conceive.

Herrera should have gone back into the house and killed the mangy dog as soon as he started on the young girl. Raping her and stabbing her to death in front of her mother, and then repeating the outrage with April Traynor, was as despicable an act as he could imagine. The only thing stopping him from putting a bullet in Vargas's demented brain when he came out of the house wearing a wide, lecherous, self-satisfied smile was the risk of offending Alvarez. Instead, he turned his back and left the house and its grizzly contents behind.

Later, when Herrera asked Vargas why he raped and knifed the mother and daughter, Vargas admitted he was ordered to do so by Alvarez. If, in the hunt for Traynor, Vargas explained, they came across his family before they could get to him, Alvarez wanted Traynor to suffer in the most painful way before he himself was killed.

Herrera considered the order a betrayal of trust on the part of Alvarez. Had he known the wife and daughter were considered targets, he would have refused the assignment. It would be the first time he ever refused an assignment from Alvarez, and refusal would come with its own inherent risks, but unplanned, unnecessary killings had never been an acceptable component of his trade. In the event a 'non-target' interfered with or tried to prevent the successful execution of an assignment, killing that person, or persons, was justifiable, in Herrera's opinion. Traynor's wife and daughter were no such inconvenience. They were innocent victims, unnecessarily murdered by Vargas on the orders of Miguel Alvarez, and that was unacceptable to The Wolf.

When this job was over, Rodolfo Herrera was going to kill Vargas. The decision was not a knee-jerk reaction to Vargas's brutality; the man was a liability he was not prepared to abide. He would not do it here, in Australia, he would wait. Like a wolf on the hunt, with the scent of the prey strong in his nostrils, he would wait until they got back to Mexico. Then he would kill Vargas, efficiently, professionally, and cleanly. He would even extend Vargas the curtesy of surprise. Vargas would not see it coming. One shot. A .45 calibre round to the back of the head.

Alvarez wouldn't like it, and may well guess The Wolf was responsible, but Herrera would worry about Alvarez's displeasure when, and if, the time came. If it meant no more work came his way from the cartel boss, so be it; retirement may have to come early. At five hundred thousand dollars a hit, Herrera was a millionaire many times over. If he had to, he could retire comfortably and spend the rest of his life laying on the beach, drinking Tequila, and getting laid. Fuck Miguel Alvarez! Fuck Ignacio Vargas!

Thoughts of retirement had been at the back of Herrera's mind for a couple of years. He had enough money stashed away to keep him in tequila and hookers for the rest of his life. Perhaps it was time. Perhaps he should make Vargas his last job. A free-bie, a retirement gift to himself. He had already been paid for Traynor; another half-a-million in the pot. He was independently wealthy far beyond any-thing he ever imagined when he started out in the business of contract killing. Maybe now really was the time. By accepted community standards, forty-three was not old, but Rodolfo always knew he would retire from the killing game long before age became problematic in relation to his profession. What use was millions of dollars in the bank if you were too old to enjoy it? He would miss it though; killing was to Herrera like drugs were to the millions of wretched souls who sniffed, smoked and injected the shit Miguel Alvarez peddled on every continent in the world.

Unfortunately, The Wolf had very little going for him in the looks department and, by any stretch of imagination, he could never be considered a good-looking man. His face, round and puffy, was deeply pock-marked, a legacy of severe childhood acne. He stood just five feet seven inches tall in his bare feet and had developed a middle-age pot-belly, a legacy of too many years eating all the wrong foods and drinking way too much tequila.

Women, either aware or unaware of his immense wealth, were not attracted to him, and he learned a long time ago it was his money, and not his looks, which drew the attention of members of the opposite sex. Now, he had plenty of money. He could drink as much tequila as his body could handle, he could eat junk-food until he dropped, and women, as many as he wanted, as often as he wanted, were more than willing to slip between the sheets with him. The chances were, he could enjoy none of those things as an unhealthy old man. He should retire, and drink, eat, and fuck himself to death. At least when the time came to meet his maker, he would die a happy, contented old killer.

9

From his position, crouched low, sheltered behind trees at the edge of the clearing, Rodolfo Herrera had an unobstructed view of the house fifty metres to his front. He looked across at Ignacio Vargas, similarly crouched just a few metres to his left. The bastard was smiling! He was always smiling!

Perhaps sensing Herrera was watching him, Vargas turned his head and looked at Herrera. His smile widened. Two rows of crooked, yellow teeth, stained from years of heavy cigarette smoking and drinking cheap, red wine, filled his mouth. When Vargas smiled, it was not a comforting smile radiating warm friendliness. Rather, it was a lecherous, leering grin, where his lips flattened against his teeth, almost disappearing, giving his mouth a snake-like appearance.

If Herrera was considered unattractive, Vargas was downright ugly. The man was at least two inches shorter. His legs, disproportionately short, with thick, heavily veined ankles, were so badly bowed he waddled when he walked. Herrera had never seen Vargas run, but he suspected it would be, if not an impossibility, a most bemusing sight to witness.

The more Herrera got to know Vargas, the more he came to understand how rape became such an enjoyable pursuit for him. No self-respecting woman would ever willingly kiss that mouth!

Herrera suspected even the lowliest of hookers would baulk at indulging in her chosen profession with Vargas. When it came to conventional relationships, male-to-female, or even male-to-male, Vargas was not particular in regards to the sexuality, or the willingness, of his intended sex partner. Herrera suspected he would be an abject failure in any event. Brutal rape was probably the only way the slimy bastard could get it up!

As Herrera watched, Vargas reached behind him and withdrew a large, serrated-edge hunting knife from a leather pouch he wore concealed under his shirt. He raised the knife, waved it gently at Herrera, and smiled even wider.

"*El hijo por enfermo burro*—son of a diseased donkey," Herrera murmured to himself as he turned his focus away from Vargas and returned his attention to the house.

Held loosely at his side, Herrera raised the Ruger SR45 semi-automatic hand gun. Fitted with a Ti-RANT .45 silencer, the weapon was bulky and difficult to conceal, but the Ruger was his weapon of choice. He insisted on it when he arrived in Australia. He was familiar with it, it fit comfortably in his meaty hand, and it had stopping power. You take a hit from the Ruger SR45, you are not getting up! He was a good shot, even at the limit of the Ruger's range, and he never missed up close. He preferred 'up close' head shots. They were quick, and instantly fatal. His job was never personal; he figured there was no need for the target to suffer unduly.

He aimed at the window, to the left of the front door, slowed his breathing, held his breath, and gently squeezed the trigger. The Ruger bucked in his hand, the .45 calibre round streaked across the fifty-metre clearing at approximately eleven hundred feet per second and shattered the window. With the Ti-RANT silencer attached, the sound was minimal, and quickly absorbed by the surrounding bush.

The shot was intended as a warning. Normally there would be no warning; he would take the target completely by surprise. However, he saw the two detectives arrive at the house, and watched from the tree line as Traynor ushered them inside. They were here to escort Traynor back to Alice Springs. If they hadn't already missed the two Federal cops he dispatched earlier, they soon would. They couldn't call for help; the cell-phone jammer took care of that. Traynor would know he was out there, somewhere. Now, he had them trapped inside the house, where could they go? Their vehicle was parked in front of the house. If they came outside, he would get all three of them. Might as well make it sporting, he decided. Let them know he was out there, waiting.

He silently indicated to Vargas he should make his way to the rear of the house and prevent any exit from the back door. He watched as Vargas, grinning like an idiot, hurried away with his waddling gait, under the cover of the trees skirting the clearing.

Turning his attention back to the front of the house, he raised the Ruger, aimed at the widow to the right of the door, and fired again.

10

Sam stood at the edge of the tunnel entrance and peered into the gloom below as Traynor clambered down the ladder. "Looks bloody dark down there," he said.

"Are you scared of the dark?" Foley asked behind him.

"No, I'm not scared of the dark," Sam said, sounding affronted.

"Then, what are you waiting for?"

"I'm waiting for Jack to get down."

"Of course you are. Get down the fuckin' hole, Sam!"

"Okay, okay. I'm going! Don't get your knickers in a twist!" He turned his back on the entrance and began climbing cautiously down the ladder. When all but his head and shoulders had entered the hole he paused, looked up at Foley waiting at the top, and murmured hesitantly, "Ladder's a bit rickety."

"Thanks for the warning," Foley said, a feather-soft ripple of concern fluttering deep in his belly.

On his way down, Foley paused, reached up, and pulled the tunnel entrance door closed behind him. Suddenly plunged into a blackness impossible to penetrate, the three cops huddled close in a tight group at the foot of the ladder, their shoulders touching in the musty, damp confines of the tunnel entrance.

Impossible for any of them to see the man next him, only their bodies touching indicated to each he was not alone. There was something about complete darkness that had a way of messing with a person's equilibrium. Standing in such deep, impenetrable blackness for any length of time was, for most people faced with the experience, disconcerting. It would be easy to become disorientated and totally confused.

"I don't suppose there are any lights down here," Foley said, the unfamiliar feeling of apprehension fluttering more rapidly now.

"There is a torch. Somewhere," Traynor answered.

"Somewhere?" Foley queried.

"I've never been down here before," Traynor said by way of explanation.

"It's as black as a dog's guts down here," Foley complained. "We need a torch just to find the torch!"

"Feel around. They told me there is a ledge, dug into the wall. There should be a torch."

Foley reached out in the blackness. His hand contacted Sam.

"Shit, Russ! This is not the time to get all touchy-feely."

"Just checking you are still here."

"Where else would I be?"

"I dunno, crouched under the ladder, praying I won't leave you alone in the dark," Foley suggested.

"I thought we were finished with the jokes," Sam said. "Yours, by the way, are not at all funny."

"I found it!" Traynor announced.

Suddenly, the cramped space filled with light. Traynor shone the torch into the depths of the tunnel. At the extent of the torch beam's range, the light faded gradually into more darkness beyond. Where the three men stood, in the compact space at the foot of the ladder, they could stand upright, their heads protruding into the entrance shaft above. Ahead, the tunnel was narrow, and the roof was low.

Sam bent at the waist and peered into the gloom ahead. The tunnel's end, wherever it was, seemed a very long way away. "Not much room in there," he observed aloud.

"We'll go in single file," Traynor said.

"How far is it again?" Foley asked, struggling to control the faltering in his voice.

"About two hundred metres," Traynor answered. "I'll go first and light the way." He stooped and stepped a few paces into the tunnel.

"I didn't sign on for this shit!" Sam said. "Probably spiders, scorpions, and God knows what other creepy-crawlies in there."

"You want to stay here and wait for the baddies to find you?" Foley asked. "One of them will fuck you after he's killed you."

Sam glanced above, at the ladder rising into the fading light. Then, he pushed past Foley. "I'll go next." He followed Traynor into the tunnel.

The going was slow. It was oppressively hot, and perspiration ran freely down their faces, stinging their eyes and dripping off their chins onto the soft, damp floor beneath their feet. Walking, bent low at the waist so as not to hit their heads on the tunnel ceiling, was murder on their backs. After stumbling clumsily through the narrow shaft for about fifty metres, Traynor stopped. He turned and shone the torch behind him. Sam was close behind.

"Where's Russell?" he asked.

Sam turned and looked behind him. Foley had dropped several metres behind the other two.

"You okay, Russ?" Sam called.

"I'm fine." Foley closed the gap and stopped.

"We'll rest for a couple of minutes," Traynor said. "Catch our breath, and then continue." He squatted on his haunches, with his back against the tunnel wall. He could feel the dampness of the dirt wall soaking through his shirt, or was it perspiration?

"I don't suppose there is a cold beer or two stored down here anywhere?" Foley asked.

"No, no beer," Traynor confirmed.

"Pity." Foley nudged Sam, squatting in front of him. "You okay, Sam?"

"I could use a leak," Sam declared.

"There's a toilet in the house," Traynor said. "Perhaps you should have gone before we came down here."

"I didn't need a piss then."

"Squeeze past me," Foley said. "Go back a way and take a leak."

Sam leaned forward and looked past Foley, back the way they had come, into the deep darkness behind them. "How much further to go?" he asked, turning back to Traynor.

Traynor shrugged. "I don't know. I guess we have come about fifty metres. We might be just beyond the clearing. Maybe a hundred and fifty metres left to go."

Sam looked back again, into the darkness to

their rear. "I'll hold onto it," he decided.

"Okay, if you're sure," Traynor said. He pushed awkwardly to his feet. "Shall we continue?"

Foley was slow to rise. He climbed slowly to his feet and wiped at perspiration running into his eyes. He had never considered himself to be claustrophobic; but then, he had never been enclosed in a constricting, dark and damp, musty tunnel before. The air was stale, oppressive, thick, and heavy, and the smell of mildew was strong on the top of numerous other odours he didn't recognise and didn't want to recognise. The tunnel was narrow, and, while he knew it was impossible, it felt as though the sides were moving, closing in on him. He sensed a heart-pumping panic attack, sitting just below the surface, waiting to engulf him in a blanket of sheer, unadulterated terror. He steadied himself against the wall of the tunnel and breathed deeply.

"You sure you're okay, Russ?" Sam asked again.

"Hard to breathe in here," Foley answered. "The air is foul."

"I'm guessing it doesn't get circulated much," Sam offered. "Same air probably been sittin' in here since they dug the tunnel."

"Thanks, Sam." Foley tried to smile. "That makes me feel a lot better."

"Any time, Russ. That's what mates are for." Sam patted Foley on the shoulder.

Up ahead, Traynor stopped, and turned around. "What's the problem? Are you two coming?"

"No problem, Jack. We're right behind you." Sam looked at Foley. "You wanna swap places? I'll take the tail end if you want."

"It's okay, I'm good. Just felt a little wobbly in the legs, that's all. I'm fine now." He ushered Sam onwards, and they set out after Traynor.

11

Rodolfo The Wolf Herrera rose slowly to his feet. He looked long and hard at the house for a few moments, satisfying himself that it was safe to move. Then, he ran. Exposed and vulnerable, he zig-zagged, to his left, to his right, then to his left again, as he raced across the clearing. When he reached the detectives' car, he stopped and crouched low behind it, shielding himself from the house. He waited for a few moments, catching his breath, anticipating a barrage of gunshots from inside the house. When none came, he rose cautiously from behind the vehicle and looked at the house, the Ruger, cocked and ready, pointed at the front door.

His eyes, alert and focused, swung from the door, to both windows, and back to the door again.

He saw no movement through either of the windows, and the door remained closed. A light niggle of doubt began to flutter in his mind.

Something was wrong with the picture in front of him. He knew Traynor was in the house, he saw him from the woods just a few minutes ago. He saw him usher the two detectives from Alice Springs into the house. They had to be in there. Still, the doubt persisted. They had to know he was outside; he shot out two windows. Were they laying in ambush, waiting for him to enter the house? Suddenly, the straightforward, uncomplicated assignment he believed it would be did not look so unchallenging.

Cautiously, he stepped away from the car and crossed quickly, silently, to the small porch. He pressed his back to the wall on one side of the door and waited, listening for any sound from within. He heard nothing. He reached out and slowly turned the door handle. The door was locked. He leaned back and listened again for any sound, considering his next move. Then, he stepped in front of the door, raised his leg and kicked, hard and fast at a spot just below the door handle. The door sprang open and crashed back against the inside wall before swinging closed again. He flattened himself against the wall, waiting for the shots to come. None came.

With his free hand, he pushed the door open wider, and peeked around the corner. He saw no one as he swept the Ruger slowly from left to right across his field of vision. Satisfied there was no immediate threat, he stepped into the room and paused just inside the door. There was no one. As he cast his eyes warily around the room, he spotted the notepaper on the coffee table. He focused on it for a moment, raised his eyes and checked the room one more time, and then crossed slowly to the coffee table and picked up the note.

'I'm coming back for you—if you have a God, start praying.'

"Hmmph!" Herrera mumbled. "*Besame el culo—kiss my ass—gringo!*" He scrunched the note in his hand and dismissively tossed it aside.

The house was small and compact: two bedrooms, one bathroom, a small lounge room, and even smaller kitchen. Working very slowly and methodically, it took Herrera fifteen minutes to determine there was no one in the house. Traynor and the two Territory cops were gone. Gone where? He returned to the small sitting-room, stood in the centre of the room, and turned in a slow three hundred and sixty degrees circle, his eyes scanning the room. The house was empty. Where could they have gone? He saw the two Alice Springs detectives go inside. Where were they? Maybe they slipped out the back door before the idiot Vargas had made his way around to the rear. Mumbling expletives directly related to his dislike of Ignacio Vargas, he hurried from the sitting-room, through the adjacent kitchen, to the back door.

Herrera opened the door and stepped outside. There was nothing except fifty metres of open ground all the way to the tree line. He stood there for a few moments, staring at the distant woods. He saw movement at the edge of the tree line, and Vargas stepped out into the open.

Vargas looked across the clearing at Herrera. He lifted his arms out to his sides and shrugged. As he watched, Herrera indicated to him that he should join him at the house. Vargas paused. He looked around him, focusing on the trees to his left and right. Reluctant to move across the clearing, he hesitated. Out in the open he would be exposed, a clear target for anyone lurking under the cover of the trees. He looked again at Herrera.

The Wolf beckoned to Vargas again. "*Venir, tu el hijo de un la puta*—come, you son of a whore," he murmured.

Vargas paused. Could he trust The Wolf? He knew Herrera did not like him. Herrera was not happy when he raped and murdered the traitor Traynor's wife and daughter, and he sensed he would betray him if the opportunity arose. He could kill The Wolf himself, even considered it a couple of times. Herrera enjoyed a rock-star like reputation in the illegal drug world. Might be a real feather in his cap if he was the one to get The Wolf. Might even replace him as the go-to man when the cartel needed a rival eliminated. But then, there was Miguel Alvarez, the boss. It was on Alvarez's orders that he was together with Herrera on this assignment. Killing Herrera would anger Alvarez. Vargas supposed Herrera would like to kill him also, and perhaps the only reason they were both still alive was due to the wishes of Alvarez.

Vargas looked again across the clearing at Herrera, and then, in his awkward, bow-legged, waddling gait, he set off, tentatively, cautiously, across the open ground.

As Herrera watched Vargas walking ungainly towards the house, he switched off the mobile phone jamming device, removed his mobile phone from his pocket, and punched a stored number.

12

In an office on the first floor of the Australian Federal Police Headquarters located in the Edmund Barton Building in Canberra, the nation's capital, Superintendent Vaughn Millard's cell phone rang. The phone was a pre-paid, cheap, 'throwaway' he disposed of and replaced often. He had a telephone in front of him, on his desk, but all internal phones in the building were linked to a computerised recording device located in a special room deep in the bowels of the building. This was a conversation Millard did not want recorded. He glanced at the caller ID, frowned, and answered the phone.

"Yes," he asked quietly.

"Ee ees gone," Rodolfo Herrera announced, in a strong Mexican accent.

"Dead?" Millard said.

"No, senor. Ees not dead. Ees gone."

"Gone! Gone where?"

"Eef I knew where, senor, ee would be dead now."

"Where are you?"

"I am at the house. Ees empty."

"The house is empty?"

"No one ees in the house, senor."

"Are the two Northern Territory detectives there?"

"They came. They go inside. Now, there ees nobody."

"What about the two Federal police officers guarding Traynor?"

"They are finished, senor."

"Dead?"

"Of course, dead. They are all dead, the sleeping ones also."

"You killed the off-duty officers?"

"I am very good at my work, senor," Herrera declared, sounding offended.

If you were really that good, Millard wanted to say, *Traynor would also be dead*. Instead, he said, "Maybe Traynor and the Alice Springs cops escaped through the back door."

"No. There ees no one."

"They will be in the tunnel," Millard said, suddenly remembering the emergency escape option.

"Tunnel, senor? I know of no tunnel."

"There's a tunnel. The entrance is in a wardrobe in the bedroom."

"And where does this tunnel lead?"

"Somewhere in the trees, to the east of the house."

"Somewhere in the trees? There ees many trees. I was told of no tunnel."

"It's an emergency escape route. They will be in the tunnel."

Annoyed, Herrera paused, lowered the phone from his ear, and stared across at the woods to the east of where he stood at the back door of the house. "*Come mierda gringos!*" he muttered to himself. He put the phone back to his ear. "I weel find this tunnel," he said. "Eef I do not find the gringo, I weel leave this place."

"No!" Millard said. "You cannot leave. You must finish the job!"

"I do not work for you, senor. Already I do not like your country, and already I do not like you. Eef I do not find the tunnel and I do not find the gringo, I weel leave this place." Herrera disconnected the call.

Millard stared at the blank screen on his phone. "Fuck! Fuck! Fuck!" He tossed the phone aside and watched it slide across his desk. This was not going well. If Herrera abandoned his assignment, and

Traynor escaped, everything would turn to shit. He lowered his head and rubbed vigorously at his eyes. He was tired. Ever since both Alvarez and Salim Ghandour put contracts out on Traynor, sleep had been elusive. There was a feeling, a real, not imagined feeling, a physical twinge, gently niggling deep in his gut, telling him this was not going to end well.

The authorities knew there was a mole in the organisation; they just didn't know who, or where. The longer this matter continued, as long as Traynor was alive and capable of testifying against the cartel, the more tenuous his own position became. If this matter ever got to court, some sleazebag drug pusher would give him up in a heartbeat, just to save himself from spending the rest of his life in prison. If they found out he was on Alvarez's and Ghandour's payroll, life as he knew it would be over, and the two million dollars sitting in an off-shore account would not save him. He reached for the desk phone.

———

Two and a half thousand kilometres away, in Alice Springs in the heart of the Northern Territory, Cameron Yap Yap Barker's cell phone rang. He picked it up from his desk and glanced at the caller

ID. Vaughn Millard. This was the third time in two days Millard had called.

"Hello, Vaughn."

"Hello, Cameron. I'm after an update on your chaps in Ti Tree."

"Another update! We only spoke yesterday afternoon."

"Yeah, I know. You know how it is, Cam. The brass upstairs wants this matter done with. I'm the OIC at this end, so I'm in their sights."

"I understand," Barker said. "My chaps left for Ti Tree about three hours ago. The thing is, I can't reach them. There seems to be a problem with the phone link."

"Oh?" Millard said. Herrera would have the jammer activated, he guessed.

"I know they arrived at Ti Tree," Barker explained. "Russell Foley called me from the local roadhouse. He was supposed to call again when he got to the safe-house. But so far, nothing. I tried calling our members at the local police station, to dispatch them to the house to check, but got no answer. I'm guessing they are out of town on a job. Their patrol area covers a lot of territory, most of it is isolated and out of mobile phone range."

Millard leaned back in his chair and relaxed a little. "Traynor is not at the house," he said.

"What do you mean, he's not at the house?"

"Our security people watching Traynor contacted me, via satellite phone," Millard lied. "Traynor is not at the house. I assumed he was with your chaps, on the way to Alice Springs."

"If that were the case, your men would be with them," Barker said, his concern mounting.

"Your men arrived and entered the house," Millard said. "My chaps followed a few minutes later to finalise plans for the trip back to Alice Springs. The house was empty."

"Empty?"

"They were all gone," Millard confirmed.

"Gone where?"

"I expect they used the escape route."

"Escape route?"

"Yeah, the tunnel."

"What tunnel?"

"You don't know about the tunnel?"

"No," Barker declared. "I know nothing about any tunnel."

"There's a tunnel in the house. Constructed when they built the house. Leads out into the bush east of the house."

"And, Traynor knew about the tunnel?" Barker asked.

"Of course."

"Why would they do that? They were supposed to link up with my people and leave together. What about your chaps? Can you contact them on the satellite phone and have them check the tunnel?"

"I tried," Millard lied. "There's no answer."

"It's a satellite phone, it should work just about anywhere."

"It works. No one is answering."

"Why would they not answer?" Barker posed.

There was a pause down the line. "Maybe they can't answer," Millard suggested, finally.

"So, what are trying to say?" Barker probed.

"I'm trying to say that Herrera, and his mate Vargas, may have arrived at the house looking for Traynor."

"Tell me you're fucking kidding!"

"I wish I was."

"Jesus fucking Christ! There are seven experienced police officers up there! Traynor, his two minders, my two chaps, and your two off-duty men. I was informed by you that there are only two baddies. What the fuck is going on?"

"Unfortunately, I suspect our two Federal boys might have been eliminated. They would never leave the sat phone unattended."

"Eliminated? You mean they're dead?"

"Unfortunately, that would be my guess."

"What about your off-duty men?" Barker asked, hopefully.

"They are required to report in at every shift

change, unless something urgent crops up. I don't expect to hear from them for another six hours."

"May I suggest this might be considered as being something urgent?" Barker said with some sarcasm. "Have you tried to contact them?"

Again, there was a short pause on Millard's end of the line.

"Vaughn?" Barker pushed.

"They're not answering," Millard announced, finally.

"Jesus Christ!" Barker cursed loudly.

"It could be they are asleep," Millard offered. "They were on duty all night."

"Where are they camped?"

"They have a room behind the roadhouse."

"How many people knew where they were staying?"

"I knew. I set it up for them."

"I'll contact the roadhouse and get someone to check on them," Barker said.

"Okay," Millard said.

Vaughn Millard knew the two Federal officers watching the house were dead. He also knew the two off-duty chaps were dead. Herrera and Vargas knew where the four-man crew were staying; they knew because he told them. It was a pity; the team charged with protecting Traynor were all good men, with years of experience. The organisation could not afford to lose men of such vast experience. But, what had to be done, had to be done.

Soon, very soon, Herrera would call and confirm that Jackson Traynor was also dead. Then, he would be free and clear.

"I need to know where my two officers are," Barker said.

"And I need to know what has happened to *my* people," Millard said. "We can only hope they left via the tunnel and are on their way back to Alice Springs."

"They're not coming back to Alice Springs," Barker announced.

"What?"

"My chaps are under orders to take Traynor to a secure location if they strike trouble. Their orders are to stay there until it's safe to make their way back here to Alice Springs, or I can organise a pick-up to bring them back."

"Whose orders?"

"Mine."

"Cameron," Millard said sternly. "May I remind you that this whole business is a Federal Police operation. Your role is to facilitate our efforts at your end, not to change the plans."

"You can remind me all you like, Vaughn," Barker responded. "International drug cartels, crime gangs, and Mexican hit-men notwithstanding,

my responsibility, first and foremost, is to the safety
of my officers. I directed them to a secure location
until such time as the military can extract Traynor."

"A secure location?"

"Yes."

"And, exactly where is this secure location?"

"Aningie," Barker answered. "It's a cattle station
homestead northwest of Ti Tree. It's isolated and
safe."

"Who knows about this place?"

"Myself, my two chaps, the station owner & his
on-site caretaker, and now, you."

"No one else?"

"No, no one else," Barker confirmed.

"Good, let's keep it that way for the time being.
The fewer people who know where Traynor is the
better."

"Are you sure you can't reach anyone?" Barker
asked.

"We can't reach Traynor, or your chaps, if they
are underground in the tunnel."

"How do we know if anyone is still alive? We
can't contact anyone! For all we know, they might all
be dead!"

"If they are in the tunnel," Millard said, "your
chaps will contact you when they get clear, and
Traynor will contact me. Until they do, we can only
wait. I want you to phone me the minute you hear

from your blokes. I need to know when they are on their way to the homestead."

"As soon as I hang up from you, I will go to Ti Tree myself. If they are not there, I will continue on to Aningie, find them and sit on them until it's safe to leave. In the meantime, I'll continue trying to contact our two members stationed at the local police station."

"You need to let me know the minute you find out exactly where Traynor is," Millard impressed. "If we lose him, our whole case against the Australian arm of the cartel goes out the window."

"I understand the importance of your case. But I have two good men up there somewhere, and I can't reach them. At the moment, they are my priority."

"Just let me know, Cameron." Millard disconnected the call. Dejected, he slumped back in his chair. If Barker went to Ti Tree and found Traynor and his own two detectives before Herrera and Vargas did, it could be all over for him. He swivelled in his seat and stared absently out the window behind him at the street below.

Perhaps he should leave now, just go home, pack his bags, and leave. Although he hoped it wouldn't be necessary, he had long ago prepared for the possibility he might have to leave in a hurry. With only two more years to serve before he planned to retire, he did not want to sacrifice thirty years of superannuation payments he would have to forego if he slipped unannounced out of the country earlier than planned. However, if he had to leave, he was ready. Spending the rest of his life behind bars was simply not an option; disgraced cops do not enjoy a comfortable life among the majority of prison inmates.

He had two million dollars tucked away off-shore. There was no one in his life who would miss him. Since his divorce ten years earlier, his three kids had never so much as sent a Christmas card, or phoned him on his birthday. Now, he didn't even know where they were, and had stopped caring years ago. At his age, two million dollars would be enough to keep him in the lap of luxury for what was left of his life; a wife and kids would only complicate matters. Pity about the superannuation though. He swung away from the window. Maybe he would hang on a little longer. Maybe it would all turn out okay. He retrieved the discarded mobile phone and made another call.

———

Cameron Barker dropped the telephone hand-piece onto its cradle and leaned back in his chair. Something was definitely not right in the tiny settlement of Ti Tree. If Rodolfo Herrera and his cohort Ignacio

Vargas were already there, and it appeared they might be, Foley and Rose could be dead, Jackson Traynor also. It was not something he wanted to think about. Russell Foley and Sam Rose were not just two of the best investigators in the job, Foley was a friend, as was Rose to a slightly lesser extent. He hung onto the hope that their many years of experience and good judgement would hold them in good stead.

He pushed away from his desk, left his office, and hurried upstairs to speak with the Assistant Commissioner Southern Command. Following his conversation with Millard, he considered he should go to Ti Tree himself, as a matter of urgency.

13

The torch light began to flicker, and the immediate tunnel surrounds appeared and disappeared in spasmodic, flickering moments of dark and light. Traynor slapped the torch against his palm. Finally, the light went out and stayed out, plunging the tunnel into a complete, suffocating blackness. He stopped, and Sam crashed clumsily into his back.

"Shit, what happened?" Sam asked.

"Sorry," Traynor said. "Bloody torch is fucked. Batteries must be dead." He slapped it again, with no result.

"What's the problem?" Foley asked from the rear.

"Torch batteries are flat," Sam explained.

"Flat?"

"Yeah, Russ, flat. You know, like running out of charge."

"I know what 'flat' is, Sam," Foley huffed. "How could they be flat, we've only gone a short distance?"

Traynor turned around and spoke to Sam and Foley in the dark. "The torch has been down here for a long time. I've never been down here until to-day. Never thought I would ever be down here. Never gave the torch a second thought. Bloody batteries will go flat over time, even if the torch is not used."

"How far to go?" Sam asked.

"I reckon we are about half way," Traynor answered.

"Can we continue in the dark?" Foley asked.

"I'll have to feel my way along the sides of the tunnel," Traynor said. "It will slow us down con-siderably."

"What do you think, Sam?" Foley asked.

"Well, if we continue without a light to guide us, we might miss the exit point in the dark."

"We won't miss the exit," Foley said. "We'll hit the end wall when we reach it." He peered ahead into the darkness, towards where he knew Traynor was. "Jack, can we continue?"

"Yeah, we don't have a choice. Unless you want to go back."

"No, I don't want to go back. We've come this far, might as well keep going."

"Okay. Sam, you reach out and hold onto my belt, and Russell, you hold onto Sam. I will move forward as quickly as I dare. The going will be slow, but at least we will not be falling over each other in the dark. Everyone ready?"

"Yeah," Sam answered.

"Let's go," Foley said. *The sooner I'm out of this hole in the ground, the happier I'll be,* he said to himself.

Like a bizarre conga line, Foley grasped Sam's belt, and Sam held fast to Traynor's belt. Slowly, they inched their way forward in the pitch blackness. As they advanced, Traynor ran his hand along the side wall, feeling his way. After several minutes, with just the muffled sound of their feet scraping along the damp floor, and their laboured breathing to accompany them, he dared to increase the pace.

In the dark, Traynor did not see the large mound of dirt and rubble heaped in the middle of the tunnel floor. He stumbled into it and fell to his knees. The dead torch flew from his hand. "Shit!" he cursed loudly.

Sam, who had been holding onto Traynor's belt, almost fell on top of him. "What?" he called.

"The fuckin' roof has collapsed!"

Following close behind Sam, and gripping

tightly to his belt, Foley crashed into his partner's back. "What happened?"

"The roof has caved in," Traynor repeated. "I walked into a pile of dirt and shit."

"Where is the torch?" Sam asked.

"I dropped it."

"It has to be here somewhere," Foley said, sounding anxious. "Feel around for it."

In the inky blackness, the three men on hands and knees felt around the damp tunnel floor searching for the torch. Finally, Traynor found it laying at the base of the tunnel wall. "I've got it!" he said. He flicked the switch. Nothing happened. He slapped the torch against his hand several times. The light flickered and then a weak beam glowed dimly in the confined space. He aimed the beam at the mound in front of him. "Fuckin' hell!"

"Jesus!" Sam said as he looked past Traynor at the pile of dirt blocking the tunnel. "How the fuck are we gonna get past that!"

"Can we get around it?" Foley asked, craning his neck to look past Sam and Traynor.

Traynor splayed the weak torch beam over the mound. "No, the whole floor is covered. There's no way around it."

"Shine the torch on the roof," Sam said.

Traynor aimed the torch at the tunnel roof. Above the mound, and barely discernible in the dim light, there was a large, black hole left where the ceiling had collapsed. The hole looked deep, reaching upwards towards the surface, and the diameter of the hole appeared to be about two metres across.

In the poor light, Sam peered at the hole above. "We can't get around it," he said. "But we can get over it."

"What?" Foley said from behind him.

"We can climb over it, Russ. Look, there's a gap between the top of the mound and the hole in the roof. We can climb up there, and over the mound. The hole in the roof is only a couple of metres across. We can get to the other side and continue."

"You are kidding?" Foley said.

"No, he's right," Traynor said. "There is a gap up there. We will have to go over on our bellies, but we can get to the other side."

"Here's an idea," Foley said. "How about we turn around and go back to the house?"

"I thought you said you didn't want to go back," Sam said.

"That was before we hit this mountain of dirt. Now I'm thinking it might be our best option."

"And get our heads blown off when we pop up out of the tunnel? That doesn't sound like our best option, mate," Sam answered.

"Yeah, well, the roof is obviously unstable. We

have no way of knowing if there are more cave-ins further along. Maybe turning back is better than dying down here under a million tons of dirt."

"We'll go back to the house as soon as we get out of here," Traynor suggested. "Remember, I have two very good reasons to want those arseholes dead."

The torch beam flickered twice and then died, plunging them once again into darkness. Traynor shook the torch, slapped it, then shook it again. Nothing. A complete and utter blackness engulfed them, as though a heavy blanket through which no light penetrated had been draped over them.

"Everyone okay?" Traynor asked.

"Yeah," Sam answered.

"I will be when we get out of this fuckin' tomb," Foley muttered.

"I'll go over first," Traynor said. Without waiting for a response, he grasped the torch tightly and began climbing, scrambling clumsily on hands and knees up the face of the mound. The dirt underneath him was damp and slippery, and several times he slid backwards, losing ground. Finally, sweating profusely and breathing heavily, he made it to the top of the mound. He lay on his stomach, breathing heavily.

"You okay?" Sam called from the base of the mound.

"Just catching my breath," Traynor called back.

"Can you get through to the other side?"

"Yeah, I think so." Pushing with his feet, and pulling with his elbows and forearms, he slithered forward across the top of the mound. Then, suddenly, in an uncontrollable slide, he slid down the far side and lay in an awkward, ungainly heap, gasping for breath on the tunnel floor.

"Where are you?" he heard Sam's muffled voice from the opposite side of the mound.

"I made it!" he called back. "It's not that far. Come on over."

In the darkness, Sam turned to Foley. "You go next, Russ. I'll follow."

"I'm not going to argue with you. I need to get out of here, quickly."

Sam reached out in the darkness and found Foley's arm. "Are you okay?"

"No, I'm not okay. I feel like I'm suffocating."

"You are going to be fine," Sam tried to reassure his friend. "Don't panic. Take a couple of deep breaths, shimmy up the mound, and slide across to the other side."

"Sounds easy when you say it."

"Maybe not *that* easy, but doable."

"Okay. I'm not staying here on my own, so I guess I'll go."

Sam patted Foley's arm. "Go for it, Russ. I'll be right behind you."

14

Ignacio Vargas stopped in front of Herrera and raised the large serrated edge knife. The sun glinted off the blade. "You have found the gringos, no?" he said hopefully.

"They are not here."

"No?"

"They have escaped."

"*Hijole!*" Vargas cursed. "Escaped? Escaped where? I did not see them leave the house."

"There ees a tunnel," Herrera said. "They escaped in a tunnel."

"A tunnel? Where ees this tunnel?"

"Come! *Andale!* We weel find it." Herrera turned and re-entered the house. Vargas followed closely behind.

His weapon raised and ready, Herrera flung

open the wardrobe door. The robe was empty. He stepped tentatively into the robe and searched for the tunnel entrance. When he found it, he raised his .45 weapon in one hand and aimed at the well-disguised trap-door. With his free hand, he reached down, grasped the handle, and pulled the door open. Wary of a possible attack from below, he cautiously leaned forward over the hole, and peeked down into the inky blackness below. He could see nothing. A small amount of light from behind him penetrated weakly into the depths of the entrance. Herrera waited a few moments, allowing his eyes to adjust to the gloom. Satisfied there was no one immediately below, he stepped backwards, out of the wardrobe, and turned to face Vargas.

"There ees no one," he said.

"No one? Are you certain?" Vargas queried.

"Eef I say 'there ees no one,' there ees no one," Herrera insisted, angrily. He stepped aside and indicated the wardrobe. "Eef you wish to look yourself, you can look."

Vargas stared at Herrera for a moment and looked into the open wardrobe. He shrugged, stepped inside and looked down into the tunnel entrance. "Perhaps the gringos are still in the ground; like the *alcantarillado rata*—sewer rat, no?"

Herrera stepped into the wardrobe behind Vargas. The two men were so close their bodies touched. "Perhaps," Herrera conceded. "You go, I weel follow."

"Down there?" Vargas stared down into the hole.

"Yes, down there."

"It ees very dark, amigo."

"Ees a tunnel, not a *carretera*," Herrera responded, angrily.

"Okay, I will go." Vargas shrugged. He reached for the ladder, turned to face Herrera, and started to climb down into the tunnel. Herrera followed.

The two hit-men stood together at the base of the ladder and stared into the darkness in front of them. From above, a narrow shaft of light penetrated for just a few metres into the depth of the tunnel.

"*Mierda*!" Vargas exclaimed loudly as he peered intently into the dark distance. Then, as if suddenly realising they may not be alone, he turned and leaned close to Herrera. His voice dropped to a whisper. "You think the gringos are here?"

The Wolf turned away from Vargas's sharp, acrid breath wafting in his face. "They are here," he muttered with certainty. He pushed in front of Vargas and took several steps forward into the tunnel. Short in stature, he was able to stand upright without his head contacting the tunnel roof. He raised the .45 Ruger and, at arms-length, aimed into the dark tunnel. He pulled the trigger six times. In the confines of the narrow space, the gunshots reverberated loudly off the walls and roof of the tunnel. A small amount of damp earth dislodged from above peppering his head and shoulders. He lowered the weapon and stared into the darkness ahead.

"*Jay, caramba!*" Vargas cried. He covered his ears against the deafening sound of the gunshots echoing around the cramped space. In the silence that followed the shooting, he began to laugh maniacally. "Eat lead *baboso ojetes!*" he yelled into the black depths of the tunnel.

Rodolfo Herrera walked forward, deeper into the tunnel and stopped. Did his shots hit anyone? He listened for any sound from the darkness ahead. Should he proceed? It was dark and would only get darker the further he moved away from the entrance and the limited light filtering in from the bedroom above. The gringos had weapons. If they were up ahead, he would not see them until he was on top of them.

Ignacio Vargas was close behind him, chuckling like a lunatic. "Maybe you killed them, senor." He raised the large knife. "I will gut them and leave their intestines for *la rata and la cucaracha.*"

"No," Herrera said.

"No? What ees 'no?'" Vargas asked.

"Look there, *idiota*." Herrera pointed into the darkness. "The gringos will shoot you in the dark."

"*Idiota*? You call me *idiota*?"

"Let me pass." Herrera pushed past Vargas and walked back to the ladder.

———

Resting at the base of the mound, having followed Foley and Traynor over the top, Sam flinched at the booming sound of the gunshots. "What the fuck?"

"They're in the tunnel!" Traynor said, scrambling to his feet. "That mound of dirt probably saved us from getting shot. Let's keep moving. We can't be far from the end."

Sam and Foley pushed themselves up and wiped at the damp earth clinging to their clothes.

"How far are they behind us?" Foley asked.

"Can't tell. Gunshots would be intensified in here. I suspect they are back at the entrance. We've got a good hundred, maybe hundred and fifty metre head start on them, and they don't know about the cave-in. If we hurry, we can be out of here before they get this far."

"Will they follow?" Sam asked.

"I don't know," Traynor answered. "They will know we are armed, and if they don't have a torch, I doubt they will risk venturing too far in."

"How did they know there was a tunnel?"

"I don't know that either. We do know there is a mole in the system. We don't know where, or who. But, wherever, or whoever, someone is reporting our movements to those arseholes behind us."

"I'd kinda like to have a little one-on-one chat with that prick," Foley said.

"Get in line," Traynor said.

"Okay," Sam said. "Let's get out of this bloody hole and re-group."

"I'm with you, Sam," Foley said. "I like our chances better on the outside. At least we will be able to see trouble coming."

"Grab a hold of the man in front and let's go," Traynor said. He passed the torch to Foley, waited until he felt him grip his belt and, bending low to avoid the roof, he set out as quickly as he was able. With one hand, he touched the side wall, feeling his way forward. He waved his free hand, from left to right, outstretched in front of him, feeling for the wall that would mark the end of the tunnel. Without any light to guide them, the final leg would be slow and laborious.

"Do you think you can find the exit when we get there?" Sam called from the rear.

"It should be directly above us when we reach the end," Traynor answered.

"I hope you're right," Foley said. "Fresh air and daylight has gotta be better than sex right now."

"Obviously been a while since you had sex," Sam quipped.

"I'm not convinced this is the appropriate time for your wisecracks, Sam," Foley scoffed.

"Sorry, mate. No offence intended. Just trying to keep the mood buoyant."

"Are you two *really* good friends?" Traynor asked.

"Best friends forever," Sam confirmed, light-heartedly.

"Don't listen to him, Jack," Foley said. "He's still trying to keep things cheery. The truth is, he's an idiot. I'm the only fool prepared to work with him."

"Ooh! That hurts," Sam moaned.

They continued in silence, their footsteps and laboured breathing amplified in the confined space as they progressed slowly forward.

Suddenly, Traynor walked into the end wall. Like a concertina contracting, each man crashed into the man ahead.

"What happened?" Sam asked.

"We've reached the end," Traynor announced.

"Happy days," Foley gasped.

"Try the torch," Traynor said. "Shine it above us."

Foley flicked the switch on the torch. Nothing

happened. He slapped it against his hand. Nothing. "It's fucked," he announced, dejectedly.

"Okay, we'll have to find the exit in the dark," Traynor said. "Reach above your heads and feel around. It will be there, somewhere. Probably square, like a trapdoor."

Foley dropped the torch to the floor, and each man raised his arms and felt around the tunnel roof immediately above his head. It seemed like several minutes passed without any success. Then Foley called out.

"I got something!"

"Where?" Sam asked.

"Right above my head. I think this is it."

"Push up against it," Traynor said.

Foley braced his feet and pushed up. Small clods of damp earth dropped onto his head. "Fuck!" he cursed.

"What?" Sam asked.

"Fucking roof's falling down on my head!" Foley coughed and spat on the floor. "Got a fuckin' mouthful of dirt. Probably some earth worms, grubs, and Christ knows what else!"

"It's just dirt, built up and clogged around the edges," Traynor suggested. "Never been opened since it was put there. Keep pushing, it will give."

"Give me a hand, Sam," Foley said.

Sam moved closer to Foley, reached above his

head and placed his hands against the underside of the trapdoor. "Ready?" he asked.

"Yeah, ready."

"Push now!"

Grunting with effort, they pushed upwards together, their legs straining and their feet threatening to slip from under them. Suddenly the trapdoor moved, just a few centimetres, but far enough to allow a small shaft of daylight into the gap.

"There! It's moving!" Traynor said. "Keep pushing!"

In a rush of dirt, small pebbles, and grass, the trapdoor opened wider, reached its zenith, and then fell open with a soft thud.

"Stand back!" Traynor ordered. "They might be out there."

Sam and Foley stepped out from under the exit hole and moved a few paces back into the tunnel. Traynor stepped cautiously forward with his weapon raised and pointed up at the gap above his head. Thousands of miniscule dust motes floated in a shaft of dappled light filtering down through the canopy of trees outside. Slowly, cautiously, he stood up straight. His head protruded through the hole just far enough to expose the top of his head and his eyes. Slowly, he turned in a complete circle, his eyes scanning the surrounding bush. Satisfied there was no immediate threat, he ducked back down into the tunnel.

"It's safe," he announced. "We can climb out."

"Not a moment too soon," Foley said, his relief evident.

"I'll climb out first," Traynor continued. "Russell, you climb out next, and Sam, you follow. Give me a boost." He holstered his weapon, lifted his arms out through the hole and raised his leg.

Foley cupped his hands under Traynor's foot. "Ready?"

"Ready."

"Okay, go!" Foley pushed up against Traynor's foot. Traynor braced his forearms against the outside edges of the hole and heaved himself upwards. He scrambled awkwardly out of the tunnel and knelt on the ground at the edge of the hole. Again, he unholstered his weapon and scanned the surrounding area.

"Looks clear," he announced. "Come on, Russell, give me your hand. Sam, boost him up from below."

Soon, Foley was outside. He knelt next to Traynor and gulped huge breaths of sweet, clean air. "Thank Christ I'm out of there," he gasped. "See anything?" he asked Traynor.

"No. We must be at least a hundred, maybe a hundred and fifty metres into the woods. Everything looks okay."

Suddenly, Sam's voice came to them from below the ground. "You two gonna sit there shootin' the breeze, or help me out of here?"

Foley leaned over the hole and looked down at Sam's upturned, dirt smeared face. "We thought we might check out the woods while you wait there, in case the baddies followed us down the tunnel."

"If you don't get me out of here now, I'm gonna piss my pants, and then I'm gonna stick my gun out of this hole and start shooting!"

"Okay, okay. Keep your shirt on. Give me your hand."

Sam reached out with both hands. Foley took one, Traynor the other. They heaved together and Sam shot up out of the hole, like a cork from a bottle of bubbly. "That was fun," he said with undisguised sarcasm as he brushed at the soil in his hair and clinging to his clothes. Immediately he moved away, turned his back and proceeded to relieve himself. "No peeking," he said. He zipped up and turned back to Foley and Traynor. "What now?"

"Now we make our way back to the house," Traynor said. "I've got a score to settle."

"This is not the time for revenge, Jack," Foley cautioned. "We'll go back for the car, we need it, but we do not want to get into a gun-fight with those bastards."

"I thought we agreed we would go back to the

house and settle with those two arse-wipes. I'm more than happy to get into a gun-fight with them," Traynor declared.

"Be that as it may, our job is to get you away from here and keep you safe," Foley continued. "If they are at the house, you will get your chance. If not, we are out of here." He reached into his pocket for his phone and checked the signal. "Still dead," he announced. "We are on our own. At least until we can make contact with Alice Springs."

15

Cameron Barker sat in his unmarked police sedan and looked at the small accommodation unit, one of three identical units clustered together behind the Ti Tree roadhouse. There was a vehicle bearing Northern Territory number plates parked immediately in front of the unit, a rental car, Barker knew, used by the four-man team of Federal police officers assigned to keep Jackson Traynor from harm until his up-coming court appearance. There were no other vehicles in the vicinity, confirming what he had been told by the roadhouse manager; only the middle unit was occupied.

"Looks quiet," the man sitting next to him said.

Barker turned and looked at Sergeant John Singh, a highly-qualified crime scene investigator, attached to the Forensics section in Alice Springs.

"Not for much longer, Singo," Barker said, glancing into the rear-vision mirror.

From the direction of the roadhouse, a man walked casually towards the accommodation unit. Barker and Singh climbed out of their car and watched the man approach.

"Superintendent Barker?" The man stopped a few metres from the vehicle.

"Yes," Barker confirmed.

The man stepped closer and offered his hand. "George Bailey. I'm the roadhouse manager. I spoke to you on the phone."

Barker shook Bailey's hand. "Cameron Barker." He indicated Singh. "This is Sergeant John Singh."

Bailey and Singh shook and Bailey indicated the small accommodation unit. "I know you wanted me to check on the chaps using the room, but I never went inside. Got a bad feeling about it."

"Bad feeling?" Barker asked.

"Yeah. I dunno why. I knocked a couple of times but no one answered. It just didn't feel right, so I decided to wait until you got here."

"This is the room occupied by the Federal police officers, right?" Barker asked.

"Yes. I expect they are asleep. There was a shift change early this morning. They had breakfast and I haven't seen them since."

"Did anyone ask about them?"

"No, a vehicle arrived not long after they finished breakfast. Parked right here where you are. One man went inside and shut the door behind him. He came out a couple of minutes later, and then the second man went inside. He stayed a few minutes longer than the first guy, and then they left." The manager indicated the roadhouse building. "They never came into the roadhouse, and I never spoke to them. Saw them from the kitchen window."

"What did they look like?"

The manager shrugged. "I never paid much notice. I was busy with breakfasts. Short, stocky, both of them. One of them walked funny."

"Funny?" Barker probed.

"Yeah, kind of bandy-legged."

"Did they look foreign?"

"Yeah. Matter of fact they did, now that you mention it. I only saw them from a distance, mind you, and it was just a glimpse through the kitchen window. They looked...oh, I dunno...Asian, maybe."

"Mexican?" Barker suggested.

"Mexican! Yeah, that sounds about right."

"Okay," Barker said. "You got a master key?"

"Sure." Bailey rummaged in his pocket, removed a key hanging on a loop of string, and handed it to Barker. "What do you expect to find?"

"We don't know until we take a look inside."

"Want me to hang around?"

"No, thank you. We've got it from here."

Bailey waved a thumb at the roadhouse behind him. "Okay, I'll be inside if you need anything else."

Barker and Singh watched as the manager turned and walked back to the roadhouse. He paused at the rear door, looked back at the two cops, and then disappeared inside the building.

"I suppose we better take a look inside," Barker said to Singh.

"With all the activity outside their door, you would think they might have come out to investigate," Singh said.

"Unless they're dead."

"Do you think that will prove to be the case?"

"Yeah, I do."

"I guess that's why you brought me along."

"Dead is what you do best."

"And the perp?" Singh posed.

"Perps, plural," Barker said.

"Are they in the building?"

"I don't think so. I wouldn't be standing out here, exposed and vulnerable, if they were. Besides, the manager said they left."

"What's this all about, anyway?" Singh asked.

"We have a situation, mate," Barker answered.

"A situation?"

"Yeah. Apparently, there are two Mexican hit-men in town, looking to find, and kill, a Federal undercover cop before he can testify against the Australian arm of an international drug syndicate based in Mexico. The undercover cop is in a safe-house not far from here. The two dudes the manager just described could well be those hit-men."

Singh stared in silence at Barker for a few seconds, trying to process the information. Finally, he glanced at the building and then back at Barker. "Hit-men, international drug syndicate, undercover Federal cop, safe-house! Tell me you are kidding." He swept his arm in an embracing manner around the immediate area. "Here, in this one-horse, two-dog town?"

Barker shrugged. "Why not here? If you want an out-of-the-way safe-house, this is as good a place as anywhere. Besides. So far I've seen three dogs."

Singh turned and faced the small building. "If the two Federal chaps are in there, they might be in need of medical help. Perhaps we should have a look."

"Good idea, Singo."

"Before we do, I have one more question."

"Ask away," Barker invited.

"I'm unarmed, will you go first?"

Yap Yap Barker leaned against the bonnet of the vehicle and looked directly at Singh. "Going first is what *I* do best, Singo."

"Glad to hear that." Singh smiled.

"Ready?" Barker asked

"Ready."

Barker unholstered his weapon and stepped cautiously to the door of the unit. Singh stepped up behind him.

Having received no response after knocking several times, Barker raised the key given to him by the roadhouse manager. Cautiously, he unlocked the door, pushed it open, and stepped inside, followed closely by Singh.

Barker and Singh stood side by side just inside the entrance door and stared at the scene before them. Neither man spoke. Words seemed both inappropriate and inadequate. It was like a scene from a violent movie, only this was not fiction, and the blood was not fake.

In all his years in the job, Cameron Barker had seen many crime scenes, but nothing compared to what confronted him inside the small, stuffy, two-room building. There was no need to examine either body to determine whether they might be in need of medical assistance. They were both very obviously dead. One lay on his back, the other on his stomach, and a large pool of crimson had soaked into the pillow beneath the head of each man. The bedding had been pulled back, exposing the bodies, both clad only in underwear. Both men had been stabbed multiple times. More blood had seeped from the deep, ugly cuts and slashes and soaked into their respective mattresses. Overhead, a ceiling fan turned idly in the centre of the room, slowly circulating the sticky, humid air.

Then there was the smell. Heavy, like an invisible fog, it hung suspended in the air, seeping silently from every corner and crevice in the room. Compounded by the fact the only window in the room was closed and, prior to Barker and Singh entering, the door was also closed, the room was sealed leaving nowhere for the odour to escape. Stirred and circulated around the compact space by the overhead fan, the warm, sweet, metallic smell was not unpleasant, but nonetheless disconcerting given its presence. It washed over Barker and Singh in waves, waxing and waning with the lethargic swirling of the hot, humid air.

"Fuck!" Singh swore.

"Fuck, indeed," Barker said.

"It's a fuckin' slaughterhouse," Singh added.

Barker moved further into the room, stopped between the two beds, and cast his eyes back and forth from one victim to the other. "With all these stab wounds, I would expect there to be a lot more blood and splatter patterns on the walls."

Singh stepped forward and stood next to Barker. "The head wounds look like gunshots. The stab wounds were probably administered after they were already dead. The heart stops pumping, the blood stops flowing." He stepped back towards the door. "Who would do this?" he asked, shaking his head.

"A Mexican," Barker answered, "by the name of Rodolfo Herrera, and his mate, Ignacio Vargas, if I'm not mistaken."

———

Barker and Singh stepped out of the tiny accommodation unit, closed the door on the bodies inside, and stood together in silence, both sucking in great draughts of fresh, clean air.

Finally, Singh looked at Barker. "What's the plan, Boss?"

Barker turned and looked at the unit behind them. "There is some crime scene tape in the car. Let's get this place sealed off. I'll try again to reach the two local chaps stationed here, and then I'll phone home and get some more troops up here."

"That will take a couple of hours."

"Yeah, I know. But it is what it is. I'm going to head to the safe-house and look for Foley and Rose. I want you to stay here and start processing the scene in there." He inclined his head towards the unit. "Have you got your gear?"

"Yes. My crime scene kit is in the boot of the car."

"Good. Let's get the tape up, and then I'll see if I can find the local lads to secure the scene until we can get some help up here from the Alice."

16

Rodolfo Herrera and Ignacio Vargas moved cautiously through the trees, away from the safe-house, making for their vehicle parked hidden from view at the edge of the tree line. On the way, they paused for a brief moment and looked down at the two Federal police officers sprawled ungainly on the ground. Already the bodies were attracting frenzied swarms of flies.

Vargas smiled down at the two dead cops, wishing he had had the time to linger over their killings. The Wolf shot them both, leaving him once again deprived of the opportunity to use his beloved knife and watch the gringo cops die slowly. He would so have enjoyed taking his time with the task. Perhaps he would get another opportunity with *el perro*—the dog, Traynor.

"*Andale!*" Herrera called as he resumed walking. "We go now!"

Vargas hurried to catch up, the effort emphasising his clumsy and awkward gait. "Go? *Donde?*"

"Away from this place," Herrera answered. "We are finished here. We go home now."

"*En casa?*"

"*Si, en casa,*" Herrera said, firmly.

"*Por que?* The *cerdo* still lives."

"Soon there will be *muchos policia*. We must go!"

"Senor Alvarez and Senor Millard will not be happy," Vargas said.

Herrera stopped and looked back at Vargas. "You know of Millard?"

Vargas stumbled to a halt. "Of course." He shrugged.

"How do you know of him?"

"From Miguel Alvarez."

"He told you about *el traidor con ningun cajones*— the traitor with no balls?"

"*Si, que?*"

Herrera shook his head slowly, and then turned away and continued walking. "*Baboso ojete!*" he muttered to himself as he quickened his pace.

"*Que?*" Vargas called, hurrying clumsily after The Wolf.

———

When Herrera's phone rang, he almost ignored it. *"Vete al carajo!"* he muttered. The ringing persisted. Finally, he fumbled in his pocket for the phone, flipped it open, and stared at the caller name displayed—Millard. *"Que?"* he growled. The car began to move across the centre-line onto the wrong side of the road. He corrected with a sudden jerk. *"Malditos extranjeros*—cursed foreigners!" he cried. Driving on the left side of the road was something he thought he would never get used to.

"What?" he heard Millard ask.

"Ees nothing," he mumbled.

"Where are you?"

"On my way home."

"Home?"

"Si, home. I am finished with this place."

"Traynor is dead?"

"No, not dead, senor. I do not like this place. I go home now."

"Where are you?" Millard asked again.

"We have left that place. We are driving back to...how you say, Alice Springs?"

"No!" Millard said, loudly.

"No?" Herrera questioned. "Eet ees not the Alice Springs?"

"No! You cannot leave!"

"No? What ees this, 'no?'"

"You cannot leave. You have a job to do. You must finish it!"

"So soon you forget, senor. I do not work for you."

"I know where he is," Millard said, urgently.

"*Que?*"

"They are going to a place called Aningie. It is a cattle station...a ranch. It is to the northwest of Ti Tree. You must turn around!"

Herrera slowed the vehicle and pulled over to the shoulder of the road. He drove onto the verge, stopped, and waited a few moments.

"Are you there?" he heard Millard ask.

"*Si*, senor, I am here. Tell me about this place...Anin..."

"Aningie. It's a homestead, on a cattle station. Only one man living there...like a caretaker. It is isolated."

"How do you know of this place?"

"The police in Alice Springs told me. Traynor and the two police officers are going there. They will wait there for a military aircraft to pick Traynor up."

"The military ees going there?"

"Not yet. There is time."

"Who else knows of this place?"

"No one else. It was a last-minute decision. You can turn around and be there very soon. You can finish the job."

Herrera lowered the phone to his lap and sat quietly, pondering the information as he stared at the road ahead. He could hear Millard calling his name over the phone. Finally, he lifted the phone and spoke. "I think I am finished here."

"No! No!" Millard screamed down the phone line. "You will finish the job you have been paid to do!"

"You are a long way from here, senor. You cannot stop me."

"Oh, I can stop you," Millard announced, his voice calmer now. "I can send an alert to every airport in this country. You and your butchering friend will never get out of the country."

"He ees not my friend," Herrera said.

"Whatever! I don't give a fuck! Just get the job done!"

"It would be unwise to threaten me, senor."

"Really? Why is that?"

"I know who you are, senor. You are the *traidor rata*."

"What?"

"Eet ees Spanish, senor. In my country, you are a rat...a traitor. In my country, you would already be a long time dead."

"Are you threatening *me* now?" Millard asked.

"*Si*, if you wish to think so. Remember, senor, I know who you are, and I know where you are." Herrera paused for a moment before continuing. "Eet ees not so bad for you, I think. I understand *la carcel* —the prison in your country is like *vacaciones recurso*—holiday resort, no?"

"I don't speak Spanish."

"No matter."

"What about Traynor?"

"Ah, *si*, the other *traidor rata*. Tell me how to find this place."

"You will finish the job?"

"*Si*, I will finish the job, and then I will leave this place."

Having committed Millard's directions to memory, Herrera disconnected the call and tossed the mobile phone onto the dashboard of the vehicle. "*Bastardo!*" he cursed loudly.

Quitting a job before it was finished was a foreign concept for Rodolfo Herrera, but now, sitting in the vehicle, parked on the verge of a long, straight, almost deserted highway in the middle of a foreign country, he found himself seriously questioning his decision to continue with the assignment. If he quit before the job was done, the problem would be getting out of the country. He had never met Vaughn Millard, but he knew he was a corrupt cop. Even worse, he was a corrupt cop in a position of power.

Herrera did not trust Millard. Indeed, putting his trust in anyone was as foreign a concept as was quitting. He had long ago learned that trusting others, particularly given his career choice, was unwise at best and downright foolish at worst. Common sense suggested he should continue heading south, get the first available flight out of Alice Springs and leave this cursed country behind him. But he knew Millard would make good on his threat and have him stopped before he got close to leaving and spending the rest of his life locked away in a prison in an alien land, in any land, was simply not an option.

"*Que?*" Vargas asked.

"We go back," Herrera answered.

"*Es bueno.*" Vargas smiled.

17

Foley, Rose, and Traynor paused and squatted on their haunches twenty metres from the edge of the clearing. In silence, they studied the safe-house. There was no movement.

Finally, Sam spoke. "Looks quiet."

"They might be inside the house," Foley offered.

"We need to split up," Traynor declared.

"Split up?" Foley questioned.

"Yeah. If they are in the house, we have a better chance if we approach from three different directions."

Foley looked at Sam. "What do you think?"

"Jack's right. If we cross the clearing together, and they are inside the house, we would make an inviting target."

"Okay." Foley turned to Traynor. "How do you want to do this?"

Traynor got to his feet. "I'll go to the right and cross the clearing from that side. One of you take the left, and the other straight ahead from here."

"Sam?" Foley asked.

"I'll take the middle."

"Spread out," Traynor said. "About fifty metres between us. Get to the edge of the tree line and wait. When you see me leave the trees, we all go together, low and fast. Okay?"

"Okay." Foley nodded.

"Got it," Sam said.

They rose to their feet and unholstered their weapons. Foley glanced at Sam. "You okay?"

"Yeah, I'm fine. This is fun, isn't it?"

"Just like old times, Sam." Foley smiled. He glanced at Traynor, nodded, and moved away to his left, making his way cautiously through the trees.

Traynor moved to his right, and Sam lowered himself once more into a crouch, alternately watching the house to his front, and the respective progress of Traynor and Foley.

Several minutes later, when the three men were in position, Traynor burst from the tree line, followed immediately by Foley and Rose. The three men, crouched low with their respective firearms held at the ready, ran fast towards the house. Should they be fired upon, there was nowhere to hide. It was a long fifty metres.

Short of breath, Sam stopped just to the left of the back door. He leaned with his back against the wall and waited for his breathing to steady and his racing heartbeat to slow. He glanced first to his right, and then to his left. Foley and Traynor were in position at either end of the house. He gave them both a thumbs-up.

Traynor signalled for Sam and Foley to enter the house through the back door, and he would move around the house and enter through the front door. If Herrera and Vargas were in the house, they would have them in a front and rear pincer movement. There would be no way out.

———

The house was empty. In the bedroom, where the tunnel began, the wardrobe doors stood open wide and the tunnel trap-door was flung back exposing the dark interior. Traynor, Foley, and Rose stood in front of the robe, staring at the tunnel entrance.

"Do you think they are still in there?" Sam asked, the question not directed at anyone in particular.

Traynor shrugged. "No, I don't think so. They don't know how long the tunnel is. They know we are armed and it's dark inside. Would you follow three armed men in there?"

"Point taken." Sam looked at Foley. "What's the plan, boss?"

"Same plan we started with. We get out of here. Get to Aningie station and make contact with Yap Yap."

Traynor turned to Foley. "Aningie station?"

"It's a cattle station northwest of here," Foley explained.

"What's there?"

"Nothing, that's the whole point."

"I understood your job was to get me back to Alice Springs."

"It was, initially. The plan has changed."

"Who changed it?"

"Our boss, Cameron Barker," Foley explained. "He figured if the two dudes trying to kill you found this place, they would also know about the plan to get you into protective custody back in the Alice. They will have considered that, and we don't want to run into an ambush on the way back. We are going to Aningie and wait for a military chopper to pick you up."

"How many people know about this Aningie place?"

"The three of us, our boss, and maybe your boss."

Sam joined the conversation. "What about the two Mexican pricks? Where are they?"

Foley shrugged. "I don't know. Maybe they have given up and left."

"I very much doubt that," Traynor said.

"Why?" Foley shrugged. "They're not here. We assume they are not in the tunnel. They must consider reinforcements will be on the way. Why wouldn't they just give it up and get out while they still can?"

Traynor paused. "Maybe," he said, finally. "But I don't think so. I've never met either one of them, but I know all about them. Herrera is not the quitting type. He has never yet failed to complete an assignment."

"There has to be a first time," Foley offered.

"Maybe they're out in the woods, searching for us," Sam suggested.

Foley looked at Sam. "We approached the house from deep in the trees, from three different sides. They were not there. I think they have cut their losses and left." He looked from Sam to Traynor. "Our vehicle is still out front. Even on the off-chance they are still here, either in the tunnel, or out in the trees, we can drive out of here and be on the way to Aningie station before they realise we have left."

"I don't like leaving if they are still here some-where," Traynor said. "I owe those bastards for the loss of my family."

"Jack," Foley said, "we are cops. We all know there is no room for revenge in our job. If you are right, and your two colleagues are laying dead out there, somewhere, Herrera and Vargas will never get out of the country. You have been in the job long enough to know their faces will be on every airport watch-list in the land."

"That won't make them dead," Traynor answered.

"No, it won't," Foley agreed. "But you've also been in the job long enough to know our job is to find and arrest the bad guys, not kill them."

"Hmph!" Sam scoffed.

"What?" Foley glared at Sam.

"Nothing, boss. Just clearing my throat."

"I don't want to leave here without first looking for my friends," Traynor said.

"There's no time, Jack," Foley said.

Traynor looked around at the surrounding bush. "I don't like leaving them. They're alone out there, somewhere. They have families. We can't leave them out there."

"We can't take them with us," Foley said. "You said yourself, you believe they are dead."

"I'm certain of it. But that doesn't mean we should just leave them. I have a military background; we never leave our fallen mates behind."

"We are aware of your background, Jack," Sam said. "We don't like leaving them any more than you do. But we don't know where Herrera and Vargas are. They could be watching us right now. We need to leave here, and we need to leave now."

Traynor remained silent, his eyes scanning the distant tree line. If Herrera and Vargas were out there, he wanted them badly. The urge to hunt them down and kill them was strong. Common sense told him that leaving would be the smart, sensible thing to do. However, right now, smart and sensible were not words that dominated his thought process. Right now, he was angry. He knew, by their absence, that his two colleagues were dead. If they were alive, they would be here. He guessed his two off-duty colleagues were also dead.

Rodolfo Herrera was a cautious individual, and it would be totally out of character for him to walk away from an assignment unless he considered the risk of completing it too great. The hit-man might want to walk away, maybe even seriously thought about it. He must know the place would soon be crawling with Northern Territory police and leaving while he still could might have been his best chance of avoiding capture. But he would not, of that Traynor was certain.

There was something, some indefinable thing deep inside Traynor, instinct perhaps, insisting Herrera and Vargas were still around, maybe even closer than he, or the two detectives accompanying him, imagined. He heard Foley speak, and turned to face him.

"Sam's right, Jack. Your mates will be taken care of, but right now we need to get away from here."

Leaving dead or wounded comrades behind on the battlefield was an abhorrent concept to Traynor. Ingrained in his psyche from the first days of his military training, and reinforced later at the police academy, abandoning your mates who were, either by injury or death, no longer able to fend for themselves was totally unacceptable. Leaving Pete Tomkins and Craig Dermott behind, perhaps Mitch Simms and Trevor Lowe also, clawed at his gut like an insistent, nagging pain that would not go away.

"Come on, Jack. Let's go!" Foley insisted.

Traynor looked at Foley, then at Sam, turned away and walked briskly from the room. He hurried along the short hallway, into the lounge and then out the front door. Foley and Rose followed close behind.

At the car, Traynor stopped and stared across

the clearing, into the woods, making a silent promise to his fallen mates that he would come back for them. He opened the rear door of the car and, as he climbed in, he said to Foley and Rose, "Let's go, before I change my mind."

18

William 'Bill' Kirkwood was, for the most part, a contented man. It was not, however, a contentment reached as a result of his achievements in life. In reality, up until he arrived at Aningie Station, Kirkwood's life consisted mostly of a never-ending succession of failures. It seemed, at least to him, that whatever he attempted, he was forever falling short of the mark.

It was an unfortunate fact of life that most people placed certain expectations on others, and Bill Kirkwood was one of those who it was assumed by those close to him would attain a greater status in his life. Regardless of how achievable those expectations might have been, Bill never seemed to be able to reach them. It wasn't that he didn't try; he could never be called an unmotivated, indolent individual, it was just that, despite his best intentions and effort exerted, results for Bill never amounted to anything greater than average at best.

Fail often enough, for long enough, and the consistent under-achievement more often than not leads to the gradual erosion of self-worth. For Kirkwood, that degradation was the catalyst for a not-so-gradual decline into a world of booze and self-loathing.

Now, however, at fifty-six years of age, and carrying the burden of a past which could only be described as unremarkable, Bill Kirkwood was finally at peace with where he fit in the universe.

A recovering alcoholic, he had lived at Aningie Station for four years, and had been sober for every day of those years. His sobriety was just one of the successes that contributed to the peace of mind he now enjoyed. He knew that living in this remote, isolated place was another contributing factor. He was alone, and there was no peer pressure influencing him to enjoy a drink or two, as there always seemed to be in his past life. And, there was no booze out here, and nowhere nearby where he could get it. He could drive to Ti Tree, of course, but the only licenced premises in Ti Tree was the roadhouse, and that had a no take-away alcohol policy due to problems in the past with some of the inhabitants of the two closest aboriginal communities, both of which were declared 'Dry Areas.'

Perhaps the single most important factor in his new-found contentment was that he was no longer married. Where life's failures and poor choices were concerned, marriage was Kirkwood's crowning glory. The flotsam and jetsam of four failed marriages littering the highway of his life behind him was testament to that. If there was one positive to be found from any of his marriages it was that there were no children condemned to a lifetime ruing they were the offspring of an alcoholic, unachieving father.

Women and alcohol—the downfall of many a good man, some would say. Not in Kirkwood's case, however. Bill was his own worst enemy. Nothing of his miserable life before he came to Aningie Station could be blamed on women or alcohol. The truth was, he was a weak individual, both physically and emotionally, and rather than strive to overcome those impedances he simply accepted that he was a sub-standard example of Australian manhood.

Relentlessly bullied at school, he was always the last to be picked in any school sporting team, and often overlooked altogether. In conjunction with the perceived constant teasing by many members of the school's female students, Bill's early years were, to him, nothing more than a window looking out upon more of the same awaiting him for the rest of his life.

Only now, now that he had walked away from the last of his four best-forgotten marriages, quit the demon drink, and arrived in this serene and peaceful place, did he finally feel that he was in control of his life for the very first time.

Physically, he still resembled the skinny-legged, bony-framed, bespectacled kid from his youth, only much older. But now, physical appearance aside, he was for the first time in his life totally in control. Now, there were no school-yard bullies picking on him and no giggling, pre-pubescent girls pointing at him and sniggering behind hands adorned with garishly painted fingernails. There were no work-place colleagues purposely avoiding him during lunch break, and no constantly complaining wife waiting at home all day just to nag the crap out of him as soon as he set foot in the door. William Kirk-wood was finally at peace with the world.

Stepping casually out of the front door of the large homestead, he crossed the wide, covered ve-randa and rested his coffee mug on the railing. He removed his glasses, breathed on the lenses, and wiped them over with the tail of his shirt. To his right, several wide, wooden steps led to an expan-sive, open area overlooking almost a million acres of cattle grazing country. He held his glasses out in front of his eyes, satisfying himself they were clean, and replaced them.

The expansive veranda was three metres wide and surrounded the whole homestead, capturing any breeze on offer and providing welcome shade from the hot, intense central Australian sun. As he did every morning, Bill sipped his coffee, and walked slowly along the veranda, stopping every few metres to take in the outback vista, often taking fifteen or twenty minutes to complete a circuit of the homestead.

He never got tired of looking at the country surrounding him. The homestead faced north, and way off in the distance, forty kilometres to the northeast, a small, dark, dome-shaped hill protruded almost insignificantly against the horizon where the clear, unadulterated blue of the skyline met the darker, ochre shade of the Tanami desert.

Approximately eighteen kilometres north of Ti Tree, Central Mount Stuart, named by John Mc-Douall Stuart in April 1860 as he led a small party of intrepid explorers on his first south-to-north crossing of the continent, is the closest significant land feature to the geographical centre of Australia.

Other than its proximity to the centre of the continent, there was nothing about the hill that would attract anyone's attention. It was just a large hill, Kirkwood thought; calling it a mountain had to be somewhat of a misnomer. From what he recalled from his reading, something he had plenty of time to do these days, Australia had over six hundred and thirty mountains higher than Central Mount Stuart. Up close, however, a large, vehicle pull-off area accommodated cars, tourist buses, caravans, and motor-homes while a never-ending flow of travellers took the opportunity to read a large information display board and take happy snaps of a hill in the heart of the country.

Bill considered it incongruous that just forty kilometres away from where he stood in what he considered to be peaceful solitude there were people, scores of them coming and going over the course of each day, who found it fascinating to mill around, "oohing" and "aahing," as they jostled for the best view of what was, essentially, a featureless hill. Few, if any he believed, would have any idea of the vast expanse of peace, serenity, and silence which lay beyond the object of their fascination; there was no accounting for the naivety of the single-minded tourist, he thought.

Kirkwood blew gently on the surface of his hot coffee, sipped cautiously, and smiled. Finally, his life had purpose and meaning.

19

---

on Williams and Luke Boyd were freelance hit men, killers for hire. While drug dealing, extortion, motor vehicle theft, and numerous other illegal activities were all part of their everyday routine, more as a way of keeping busy and earning a few dollars between jobs than for anything else, killing for money was the cornerstone of their financial pursuits.

Both habitual criminals, Williams and Boyd were well known to police, and had been in and out of prison many times since their respective teenage years. To date, despite their extensive history of offending, neither had been convicted of anything serious enough to incur a particularly lengthy term of imprisonment. The maximum either of them had ever served in any one stretch was eighteen months.

Generally, their respective sentences were served without major incident and their behaviour while inside was considered by prison authorities to be of an acceptable, if not exemplary, standard. What prison authorities, and by extension the police, did not know was that prison was where both men arrived at the conclusion that the shit-pot offences accounting for their periodic terms of incarceration were considered minor by hardened criminal standards. Both Williams and Boyd believed they were capable of greater things and those expectations could be realised far sooner by working together.

They met in prison when they were both still young men and formed a close relationship which continued on the outside. The bond between them was strong and now, almost twenty years later, they were practically joined at the hip. Respected, admired, and even feared by many members of the criminal underworld, they had earned their place among the elite of the nefarious, secretive world in which they moved. Finally, they belonged. This world was their family, something both men found sadly lacking in their respective childhoods.

Williams and Boyd had earned a reputation as the best option when it was deemed necessary to eliminate a transgressor. There were tacit, unwritten rules in the world in which they lived and forgiveness was not a common emotion within the criminal element of society, particularly the illegal drug business.

Sometimes it became necessary to demonstrate to a rival criminal organisation that attempting to move in on territory controlled by others would not be tolerated and would be dealt with in the only way these people knew and understood. On very rare occasions, as in the case with Jackson Traynor, an infiltrator, a rat, an undercover cop had to be dealt with.

Killing cops was a dangerous business, accompanied by substantial, inherent risk. While there were many in the criminal world who relished the thought of cops dying, there were very few individuals willing to murder a member of the wide police family. Such occasions were rare, but when they arose and it was deemed necessary, Don Williams and Luke Boyd were the 'go to' men. They loved their work, they were good at it, and they revelled in the status within the criminal world that such a role attracted.

Physically, neither man was tall, but they were both big, broad-chested, strong individuals. It was evident, even to the casual observer, that they both spent a lot of time working out. It showed in the stretch of their shirts and jackets across their respective chests. Weightlifting was a popular way to pass the time, or at least combat the tedium of months locked behind prison walls.

There were any number of psychologists who would declare that, for most of the characters who chose to become members of a criminal organisation, the weightlifting, body sculpting thing was more about intimidation compensating for the lack of intelligence and self-esteem than it was about anything else. Those very same psychologists might even say the affection and loyalty displayed by a member to his colleagues, may well be an indication of a loveless childhood. It is highly unlikely, however, that anyone employed in the psychology profession who held such views would ever express it directly to a member of such an organisation.

Then there were the psychologists who prescribed to the theory that all criminal gang members were simply misunderstood individuals from economically handicapped, dysfunctional families who needed little more than understanding, love, and nurturing. That may well be the case for a small number of the hundreds who opted for the criminal lifestyle, but it certainly wasn't the case in regards to Don Williams and Luke Boyd. They were just plain evil, and no amount of psychological evaluation was ever going to change that.

———

Sitting on a well-worn chair, on the narrow, covered porch of a bunk-house style accommodation block behind the Aileron roadhouse, Don Williams reached for his phone, flipped it open, and looked at the caller ID.

"Yeah?" he answered, his voice deep and croaky, a legacy of too many years of heavy drinking and smoking.

"Williams?" Vaughn Millard asked.

"You know who it is, you called me!" Williams rasped.

"Where are you?"

"Same fuckin' place we've been for the last three days. Fuckin' cockroach infested dump in the middle of fuckin' nowhere."

"You and your friend are on," Millard said.

"About fuckin' time! Where?"

"Aningie Station, a little way northwest of Ti Tree."

"Are you sure Traynor is there?"

"Traynor, two plain clothes cops from Alice Springs, and two Mexican arseholes."

"Mexican?"

"Yeah. Sent out here by Miguel Alvarez, to get Traynor."

"No one said anything about a couple of Mexicans."

"You can take that up with Ghandour, after the

job is done. Oh," Millard added, "there is also a lone caretaker at the station."

"Six? When we accepted this job, there was only Traynor and a couple of his copper mates babysitting him."

"It's complicated," Millard offered.

"Complicated?"

"Yes. Are you up for it, or not?"

"That's a dumb fuckin' question," Williams said. "You do understand that the price for six has to be higher than the price for one?"

"Something else you can take up with Ghandour," Millard suggested.

"Oh, I will, you can bet on it. Where exactly is this Aningie place?"

"I don't know, exactly. Not far from Ti Tree. You are in a roadhouse, buy a map. Just get it done." Millard disconnected the call.

Williams stared at his phone for a few moments, closed it, and stuffed it back into the pocket of his vest. He looked at his colleague.

Boyd was seated on the top step of a set of three at the front of the narrow porch. He alternately dragged deeply on a cigarette and drank from a can of beer. Four empty cans, and numerous cigarette butts, littered the ground at the base of the steps.

"What?" Boyd looked at Williams.

"Time to go," Williams said, getting up from his seat.

Luke Boyd was not one to ask a lot of questions. He was not a leader, he was a follower. He and Williams had worked together for a long time and he had come to know that, where Williams was concerned, it was best just to go with the flow. They were a good team. They worked well together. Why complicate it with peripheral bullshit like who leads and who follows?

Their combined score so far was seven kills. From the tone of Williams' conversation on the phone, that score looked like it was about to almost double. That was certainly going to enhance their reputation as the best in the business, Boyd guessed. He drained his beer, tossed the empty can amid the others at the base of the steps, and rose to his feet.

"Okay, let's go to work," he said.

They rode abreast. The twin Harley Davidson Soft Tail Fat Boy motorcycles were identical, right down to the colour. The air-cooled, high output, twin cam 103B engines burbled in harmony as they rode north along the Stuart Highway, heading towards Ti Tree. They stuck rigidly to the posted speed limits; getting pulled over for exceeding the limit was a risk they could not afford to take, particularly since they were both armed with concealed handguns.

Every so often, one of the riders would politely drop back behind the other, to allow a fellow road user, also heading north, to overtake. As soon as the vehicle moved on ahead of them, they resumed the two-abreast formation and continued north, passing through Ti Tree without stopping.

Occasionally, they would momentarily take their eyes from the road ahead, look across at each other, and nod their helmeted heads. It was like an un-spoken salute at one hundred kilometres an hour, an acknowledgement of their partnership. They knew where they were going, and they knew what they had to do when they got there. They were here to kill a cop. It would be their first cop killing, but neither of them felt any different about that than any other job they had carried out together. Apart from ridding their iniquitous world of one of those they hated most, it was just another job. It was what they did best.

20

Ti Tree police station was a small, two-man station located on the service road, one hundred and fifty metres north of the Ti Tree Roadhouse. Staffed by officer-in-charge, Senior Constable Jim 'Chook' Fowler and his partner Mathew 'Mickey' Rooney, the building appeared deserted. The station four-wheel-drive Toyota was gone, and when Cameron Barker tried the door, he found it locked. He stepped to a window, peered inside, and confirmed the one-room building was empty. He moved away and walked to the rear of the building where he knew there was a small cell block, used for holding prisoners for up to twenty-four hours before releasing them, or transporting them to Alice Springs to face court. The cells were also empty. As he turned and started back to his vehicle, a woman Barker recognised as Jim Fowler's wife approached from the residence next door.

"Hi," she called. She stopped a few paces in front of Barker. "I'm Gail Fowler, can I help you?"

Barker offered his hand. "Hello, Gail. I'm Superintendent Cameron Barker from Alice Springs. I was looking for Jim and his partner."

Gail Fowler lightly shook Barker's hand. "The lads are not here. They left this morning to go out to Willowra."

"Willowra? That's out past Aningie Station, isn't it?"

"Yes. It's an aboriginal settlement, way out west of Aningie. It's about a four-hour return drive."

"Trouble?" Barker asked.

"No, just routine. They visit all the outlying settlements and cattle stations at least once a month: vehicle registrations, firearm licenses, that sort of thing. Sometimes it's just a PR thing. Many of the people who live out there don't get the opportunity to come into town all that often. Jim and Matt should be back soon, they've been gone all day. Is there anything I can help you with?"

"Are you able to reach them?"

"Not by phone," the woman answered. "Not until they get closer. And the radio in the vehicle is useless way out in that country. Is it urgent?"

"It might be. One of my chaps is at an accommodation unit behind the roadhouse. Would you send them to liaise with him as soon as they get back?"

"Okay. I'll keep trying the phone and the radio. Is there anything I can do in the meantime?"

"Thanks, but no. Just keep trying to reach Jim."

"Of course."

"Thank you, Gail." Barker offered his hand once again.

"You're welcome," she said, taking Barker's hand. As she watched him walk hurriedly to his vehicle, a hint of concern fluttered gently in her chest.

———

From the approach road leading to the woods and ultimately the safe-house, Cameron Barker saw no sign of the Federal police rental car, and no sign of the vehicle used by Foley and Rose. He stopped where the road entered the tree line, got out of his vehicle, and cast his eyes over the surrounding woods. The silence here was palpable. He turned slowly, pausing occasionally, straining to hear any sound. Strangely, he could not even hear the sounds of birds in the trees. There were a lot of trees, there should be birds, he reasoned. His eyes wandered slowly over the surrounding woods, searching deep into the trees. Then he saw it—a glint of sunlight on metal deep in the trees to his right. An uncomfortable feeling of uneasiness, not totally unfamiliar given his line of work, settled over him. He rested his hand on the butt of his holstered weapon, and moved cautiously forward, into the trees.

He found the rental vehicle parked and locked, one hundred and fifty metres to the south of where he left his own vehicle. There was no marked road here, just wheel tracks left when the vehicle was driven on a tight, meandering course through the trees and parked where it would be out of sight. Why, he wondered? Why would the Federal officers drive their vehicle so deep into the trees? Warily, he approached the car and walked around it, stopping momentarily at each window to peer into the interior. Satisfied there was nothing untoward, at least in regard to the vehicle, he shifted his focus once again to the surrounding trees. Now, inexplicably, like the flick of a switch, his sense of uneasiness moved into high alert as he moved slowly forward, deeper into the trees.

It was the faint humming that directed him to Pete Tomkins and Craig Dermott. Their bodies were sprawled ungainly on the ground twenty-five metres from their vehicle. The blood from their wounds had soaked into the hard, dry ground beneath their bodies, and hundreds of flies buzzed and droned over their respective, lifeless faces. Immediately Barker knew there was no need to check for signs of life. Both men were very obviously dead. Their respective injuries suggested each was killed by a single shot from a high-powered weapon.

"Jesus fucking Christ!" he murmured, turning away from the grizzly scene. He reached in his pocket for his mobile phone and called John Singh.

"John Singh," the forensic expert answered.

"Singo, it's Yap Yap here."

"Where are you?"

"Close to the safe-house."

"Have you found Foley and Rose?"

"No, not yet."

"You sound a bit strange," Singh said. "Everything okay?"

"No," Barker answered. "I found the second two Federal chaps."

"Why am I getting the feeling this is not good?"

"They're dead. Both of them."

"Oh, shit!"

"Both shot with what looks like a high-powered weapon, and left in the dirt, in the middle of the woods," Barker continued.

"Anyone in the safe-house?"

"I don't know. I haven't been there yet."

"Any luck with the local chaps?"

"I spoke to Chook Fowler's wife. They're on routine patrol a couple of hours west of Ti Tree. Been out all day. She expects them back at any time. I've

asked her to send them to you as soon as they return. When they arrive, I want you to send them out
here." He paused and looked back at the two bodies.
"How are you going there?"

"I'm still working the scene. It's a fucking mess.
Gonna take a while."

"Okay, mate. Stay with it. Ring headquarters and
activate the mobile crime scene unit and as soon as
Chook Fowler and his partner arrive, send them out
here to secure the site. The crime scene unit should
be here in a couple of hours. As soon as it arrives,
send a couple of them out here to work this scene
and then direct Chook and his mate out to Aningie
Station."

"Will you be there?"

"I am going to the safe-house, to look for Foley
and Rose, and Jackson Traynor. If they are not there
I will go out to Aningie Station. Before I leave here
I'll wrap some tape around a couple of trees at the
murder site so the crime scene chaps can find it."

"Okay, boss. I hope Foley and Rose are okay. You
take care."

"I'll be fine, Singo. I'll talk to you later." He disconnected the call and immediately heard the
sound of a vehicle coming from the woods. Through
gaps in the dense trees, he saw glimpses of a car approaching the exit of the tree line. Coming from the
safe-house, he guessed. Hurrying from the woods,

he ran quickly towards the point where he left his own vehicle.

———

"Look, there's a car parked there!" Sam exclaimed.

"I see it," Foley said. He slowed the vehicle as they neared the exit from the woods.

"It's one of ours," Sam announced.

"Are you sure?" Traynor asked from the rear seat.

"Yeah, I'm sure."

Foley slowed further. Suddenly, he recognised the vehicle. "It's Yap Yap's car."

"There, there he is!" Sam indicated the man running towards them.

Foley, Rose, and Traynor got out of their vehicle and watched Barker approach.

Barker reached the vehicle and leaned heavily against the front passenger side door. Breathing heavily, he paused, head bowed, and sucked in as much air as his lungs could hold.

Foley stepped up alongside his immediate superior. "You okay, boss?"

"I...I will be. Just give me a second." He took another few deep breaths of air and turned to face the Federal cop. "You must be Jackson Traynor, right?"

Traynor stepped forward and offered his hand. "Yes, I'm Traynor."

Barker shook hands firmly with Traynor. "I'm Cameron Barker. Nice to meet you, finally. I'm sorry it couldn't be under different circumstances."

"When did you get here?" Foley asked Barker.

"A while ago. I brought John Singh with me. He's back at the roadhouse." He turned back to Traynor. "They call you Jack, or Jackson?"

"Everyone calls me Jack. Everyone except my mother."

"I've got bad news for you, Jack," Barker announced grimly.

"My whole life the last couple of years has been bad news," Traynor responded with a shrug. "I guess I can handle more of the same."

"We're all cops here, so I won't sugar-coat it. Your colleagues have been murdered."

Expressionless, Traynor stared at Barker. "Simms, and Lowe? At the roadhouse?"

"All of them."

"What?"

"All of them. There's two more back there, in the woods." He indicated the trees from where he had emerged moments earlier.

"Pete Tomkins and Craig Dermott?" Traynor lowered his head.

"I'm not aware of any of their names," Barker said. "I'm sorry."

Traynor turned and looked back towards the woods, in the direction Barker indicated. He started to move away from the car. "I need to see them."

"That's not a good idea," Barker said. "It's not pretty."

Traynor stopped and faced Barker. "Dead people never are. And I've seen plenty. Those men were my friends. I need to see them."

"We need to get you out of here," Barker insisted. "There's nothing we can do for them now. The two local chaps will be here soon, and I have a crime scene unit on the way from Alice Springs."

Foley turned to Barker. "Just a couple of minutes, boss. Jack needs to pay his respects."

Barker looked from Traynor to Foley, and then back to Traynor. "Okay, a couple of minutes, that's all, while we put some tape around the trees near the site so the forensic chaps can find it. A couple of minutes, then we have to get out of here."

21

Rodolfo Herrera slowed and entered the Central Mount Stuart vehicle rest-stop viewing area adjacent to the Stuart Highway. A couple of dozen curious tourists, having briefly interrupted their journey to observe and photograph the mount several hundred metres to the west, gathered in small groups around the western edge of the parking area. Some gathered in front of a large information board displaying historical facts relating to the mount while others snapped photos of the hill in the distance. A well-worn walking track from the viewing area to the base of the large hill led those who wanted a closer look, or perhaps the opportunity to climb the landmark, a chance to get up close and personal with the popular attraction.

"What ees this place?" Ignacio Vargas asked Herrera.

"I do not know," Herrera said dismissively.

"Why do we stop?"

"I need to read the map," Herrera answered. He stopped on the highway side of the parking area, as far away from the milling curiosity seekers as possible. A road map, purchased at Ti Tree, lay casually discarded on the dash. He reached for it, unfolded it in his lap, and searched for the road to Aningie Station.

"*Jay, caramba!*" Vargas exclaimed. "*Muchos extranjeros!*" He stared out at the tourists across the carpark. As he watched, three very pretty young women, all similarly dressed in brief shorts and light cotton tops, moved away from the information board and headed for a small, compact vehicle parked nearby. "*Muchos* pretty senoritas also," he added as the young women, laughing and talking animatedly among themselves, walked jauntily to their vehicle. "*Jay caramba!*" he murmured lustily. "*Muchos* pretty senoritas."

"*Concentrar*," Herrera said with authority. "This is not the time for senoritas."

"Perhaps we could make time. Do you not see them? They are very pretty, no?"

Herrera looked up from the map, glanced briefly at the three women climbing into their vehicle, and tossed the map casually aside. "We go now," he announced.

"*Hurra*! We follow the senoritas," Vargas said excitedly.

"No, *idiota*. We go to kill the gringo *cerdo*." He swung the vehicle around and headed back across the carpark in the direction they had come.

Vargas turned in his seat and stared back at the small car containing the three women as it moved away from the viewing area, heading in the opposite direction. Dejected, he turned and looked across at Rodolfo Herrera. "Again, you call me '*idiota*.' You *insultar* me too much, amigo. *La lengua es fuerte*—your tongue is sharp."

"I am not your amigo. My job is to kill *la rata policia*. Then we go home. *Eso es todo*."

Vargas slumped in his seat. "*Jay caramba!*" he murmured dejectedly.

———

From an old, well-worn but comfortable chair on the front veranda of the homestead, Bill Kirkwood noticed the dust cloud in the near distance north of the homestead. It was late in the afternoon and, as he followed the progress of the cloud, he decided it was a vehicle approaching. Apart from his employer, who came perhaps three times a year, visitors were a rarity out here. It had to be the police, he assumed. His boss had informed him via the satellite phone that several police officers would be coming to Aningie and would be staying for a short while. He didn't know how many were coming or why, but, despite being more than comfortable with the solitude Aningie offered, it would be nice, he supposed, to have a bit of company for a change.

Occasionally the two local coppers from Ti Tree, Chook Fowler and Mickey Rooney, dropped by on a courtesy call on their way to somewhere else, but they only ever stayed long enough for a coffee and a quick chat. While Bill had some reservations about people staying longer than that, he was slowly warming to the prospect of having a couple of house guests for a day or two. He rose from his chair, stepped to the front of the veranda, and watched the approaching vehicle with interest.

Shimmering in a heat haze on the distant horizon, the vehicle slowly took shape as it approached. Eventually, he could see it was not a four-wheel-drive but a conventional car. In all the years he had lived at Aningie Station, Bill had never seen a conventional vehicle this far away from the main highway. *Can't be the police*, he decided. The police would know better than to come out into this country in a conventional vehicle. *Must be lost. Bloody tourists!*

How hard can it be to stay on the bitumen? he wondered.

The driveway into the homestead was five kilometres long, and the Stuart Highway was another thirty-five kilometres to the east, all rough, corrugated, dirt road even the hardiest of four-wheel-drive vehicles struggled with. Had to be lost, he decided. Or plain bloody stupid!

A small, four-door Mitsubishi Mirage slowed to a crawl and stopped about twenty metres from the front of the veranda where Bill stood. There were two men inside the vehicle, and neither made any attempt to get out. They sat, staring out through the dusty windscreen, watching him watching them. A strange feeling of uneasiness descended around Bill as he stood looking at the vehicle and its occupants. *Why don't they get out? What are they doing way out here, so far from the highway?*

"You fellas lost?" he called loudly. The two men in the car did not respond.

Bill stepped closer to the edge of the veranda. "You're a long way from anywhere," he yelled. "Are you lost?"

The driver's side door swung open slowly, and a short, stocky man climbed out of the car. From where Kirkwood stood, twenty metres away, the man looked foreign, Mexican maybe, he thought.

The man stood next to his open door and stared silently at him.

"Gidday, mate," Bill called to the stranger. "I reckon you must have taken a wrong turn somewhere. Where ya headed?"

Then the passenger side door opened and the second man climbed out. He was shorter than the driver and, by his stance, he appeared to be badly bow-legged. Another Mexican, Bill thought. The feeling of uneasiness was stronger now.

"You blokes need help?" Bill asked, his eyes swinging from the driver to the passenger, and back again. "Got car trouble?"

Slowly, both men moved away from their vehicle and approached the veranda. The passenger walked with an awkward, hobbling gait, and he was smiling, something Bill found strangely incongruent. There was something about the way the man smiled that sent a tiny shiver of fear down Kirkwood's spine. It was not a smile that radiated friendliness. It was a more sinister look than friendly, much more. Bill took a pace backwards, closer to the homestead door.

"Wait!" the driver called, stepping closer to the veranda.

Kirkwood paused. The driver reached behind his back and produced a gun. Suddenly Bill regretted the pause. He should have trusted his gut feelings. He should have fled into the house. He had a rifle, an old Remington .308 he kept in a broom cupboard in the laundry. The rifle wasn't his, it was there when he came to Aningie, but he knew how to use it. On the rare occasions he came across injured stock while on his service-round of the station bores, it was necessary to dispatch the beast as humanely as possible. He had used it a few times and, while it was not something he enjoyed, it was his job, and he hated to see an injured animal suffer. Instinctively, he glanced behind him, judging the distance between himself and the door.

"Don't!" the driver called.

"Wh-who are you? What do you want?" Kirkwood stammered.

The driver stepped to the foot of the steps leading up to the veranda. He raised the gun and aimed at Bill's face. "What ees your name, senor?" he asked in a heavy accent.

"Kirkwood. Bill Kirkwood."

"Who else ees een the house, senor Kirkswood?"

"Kirkwood," Bill corrected.

"What?"

"My name is Kirkwood, not Kirkswood."

"No matter, senor Kirkswood. Who else ees een the house?"

"Nobody. I'm here alone."

Reluctant to take his eyes from the man holding

the gun, Bill noticed in his peripheral vision the passenger moving forward. He glanced at the second man as he waddled ungainly forward and stood next to the gunman. He held a knife, one of the biggest knives Bill had ever seen, and his eyes were involuntarily drawn to it. The blade was long and wide, and one edge was adorned with ugly serrations which sent an icy shiver down his spine.

"What do you people want?" Bill asked, his eyes darting from the knife to the gun. "I have no money here."

The gunman smiled. "We do not want money, senor."

"What then?"

"We weel wait. Perhaps you have coffee?"

"Wait for what?"

"You are expecting a visitor, no?"

"Yes...yes," Bill answered hurriedly. "The police. The police are coming. They will be here at any moment."

"Ay, that is good." Herrera smiled. He indicated with the gun that Kirkwood should lead the way into the house. "We weel wait," he added.

22

Luke Boyd and Don Williams manoeuvred their motorcycles to a stop on the Aningie Station approach road, two hundred metres short of the homestead. In the hot, still, humid air, the twin Fat Boy engines burbled quietly in the distinctive Harley Davidson manner. Boyd and Williams sat astride their respective machines, their legs spread wide with their feet pressed hard against the dusty ground, preventing their bikes from toppling sideways. They looked at the homestead ahead, specifically focusing on the small Mitsubishi sedan parked in front of the building.

Almost like it was a well-rehearsed, coordinated dance movement, both men removed their helmets and sat them on the fuel tank between their legs. Beneath their helmets they wore identical, colourful bandannas wrapped around the lower half of their faces as a precaution against the dust that swirled, and finally settled, around their respective machines as well as for protection against swallowing bugs as they rode.

Don Williams pulled the bandanna away from his mouth and spat a glob of saliva into the dirt at his feet. "This is not a road," he complained, his eyes locked on the homestead and vehicle up ahead. "It's a fuckin' goat track." He lifted his helmet, and with his gloved hand wiped at the dust that had settled on the highly buffed and sparkling fuel tank.

"What's with the Jap shit-box?" Boyd posed, nodding at the Mitsubishi.

"Won't be cops. No self-respecting copper would drive one of those."

"Might belong to the caretaker dude."

"Nah." Williams gestured at the rough, desolate country around them as far as the eye could see. "This is the fuckin' outback. He would have a four-wheel-drive."

"Maybe it belongs to the two Mexican pricks," Boyd offered.

"That would be my guess."

"I'm beginning to dislike this assignment more and more," Boyd said. "We're good, but, two against six? That's a big ask, even for us."

Williams shrugged. "I can't see any other vehicles. Unless the cops have parked around the back somewhere, there might not be six here. Just the Mexicans and the caretaker."

"What's with the Mexicans anyway? Four hired guns just to take out one cop! Sounds like overkill to me."

"Well, that's what we get when you got a chilli-munching Mexican shit on the other side of the world trying to run things over here in our country, and a garlic-munching Lebanese here who thinks *he's* the boss of the world, both trying to work in partnership when they don't even like each other."

"So, how do you want to do this? If the cops aren't already here, they will be soon enough."

Williams looked across at Boyd. "You wanna pull out?"

Boyd shrugged. "Probably the smart thing to do. If Traynor and the Territory cops are coming, they won't be far behind us. But if we leave, it will be the last job we get from Ghandour...or anyone else, after he puts the word out."

Williams spat on the ground again. "Fuck Ghandour. Fuckin' greasy, Middle-Eastern toe-rag. Fuckin' prances around the place with all his fuckin' bling on every fat finger and swingin' around his even fatter neck. I'd like to put one between his eyes just for the hell of it."

"Might have to get in line," Boyd suggested.

"What do you want to do?" Williams asked.

"Neither one of us has ever been the cut-and-run type." Boyd looked to the distant west, shading his eyes from the afternoon sun sinking slowly towards the horizon. "It's getting' late. If we're gonna do this, we should do it before it gets dark."

"Okay. We'll ride around the back and see if the cops are here. You ready for this?"

"Yeah, let's do it."

The two bikers reached out, touched fists, and replaced their helmets before moving forward. They rode slowly, never taking their eyes from the house. As they rode, they skirted wide around the small Mitsubishi sedan, maintaining what they considered to be a safe distance between themselves and the house.

———

Rodolfo Herrera heard the motorcycles before he saw them. He moved to the large window of the front room facing the approach road to the large homestead. He pulled the drapes aside and looked out. Two motorcycle riders had stopped approximately two hundred metres from the house. The riders sat astride their bikes, removed their helmets and sat staring ahead at the house. They were too far away to tell, of course, but it was like they were staring directly at him.

Behind Herrera, the homestead caretaker, Kirkwood, sat in an old, worn armchair, facing the front door. Vargas stood behind him, with one hand pressed firmly against his shoulder and the other holding the large, serrated-edge knife pressed against the side of his neck.

"Wha-what do you people want?" Kirkwood stammered.

Herrera dropped the curtain, turned his head slightly from the window, and said to Kirkwood in a quiet, but commanding voice, "We have visitors, senor Kirkswood. You will be quiet. If you make the warning, senor Vargas will cut off your head and throw it out the front door."

Vargas chuckled quietly and pressed the knife a little harder into Kirkwood's throat. A thin trickle of blood ran down the caretaker's neck and disappeared beneath his collar.

"I'm not afraid to die," Kirkwood said, struggling to keep his voice from faltering.

Herrera turned away from the window and looked directly at Kirkwood. "Some men, men like you, are brave at first. Until they feel the knife enter the neck. Then, senor, the bravery does not matter. Then, eet ees too late to be the hero." He smiled at

Kirkwood and turned his attention back to the window.

"Who comes?" Vargas asked Herrera.

Herrera lifted the curtain aside again. "Two gringos. On motorbikes. Friends of yours, senor Kirkswood?"

"Kirkwood! I told you before, my name is Kirkwood," the caretaker insisted. "And no, they are not friends of mine. It might be the police. I told you they were coming. You should leave while you still can."

"No, it ees not the *policia*," Herrera said.

"What do they want?" Vargas asked.

Herrera turned and scowled at Vargas. "How can I know. Eef they come into the house you can ask them." He turned back to the window in time to see the two riders moving in a wide arc, closer to the house. "They come now," he announced. He stepped away from the window. "Watch the gringo," he ordered Vargas.

———

Williams and Boyd stopped at the rear of the homestead, between a large shed and a set of steps leading up to the wide veranda of the house. Side by side, their bikes idling beneath them, they watched the back door leading to the interior of the homestead. The door opened, and a short stocky man of Mexican appearance stepped out onto the veranda and halted at the top of the steps.

Williams leaned slightly towards Boyd and said softly. "That would be one of Alvarez's boys."

"Looks harmless enough," Boyd responded.

"Don't bet on it. Looks can be deceiving."

Boyd looked at the man's hands. "He's unarmed."

"Don't bet on that either."

"What do you want?" Rodolfo Herrera called from the veranda.

"Same thing you want, I expect," Williams called back.

"What is your name, senor?"

Williams indicated Boyd. "Bill," he lied, "and Ben." He tapped himself on the chest. "You are from Mexico, right?"

"*Si*, I am from Mexico."

"You are a long way from home," Williams said.

"Why are you here?" Herrera asked.

"We are here on business."

"Business? What ees your business een this place, senor?"

"I told you, our business is the same as yours." Williams turned off his engine, kicked the bike stand down, swung his leg across his bike, and dismounted. As he did so, Herrera reached behind his back and produced a semi-automatic hand gun from his waistband.

"I was mistaken," Boyd said softly to Williams. "He *is* armed."

"He's here to kill a cop," Williams murmured with a knowing shrug. "He's too fat and slow to do it with his bare hands." He lifted his hands from his sides to indicate he presented no threat to the Mexican. He took a couple of paces forward, towards the house. Behind him, Boyd also killed his engine and dismounted from his bike.

"You should stop there, senor," Herrera warned.

Williams stopped, Boyd stepped up alongside him. Both men stared at Herrera. The gun in the Mexican's hand was raised and pointed at the ground immediately in front of them.

"We mean you no harm," Williams said.

"Yes, we fuckin' do," Boyd whispered beside him.

"If you go from this place now, I weel not kill you," Herrera said menacingly.

"I think we should talk," Williams said.

"There ees nothing to talk about, senor."

"You are wrong. The police will be right behind us."

Rodolfo Herrera turned his head and looked towards the far end of the veranda. When he turned back to face Williams and Boyd, both men had semi-automatic pistols aimed directly at him.

"*Ay caramba!*" Herrera exclaimed. "You are very fast."

"We've been doing this for a long time, mate. Do you really think we would have come here unarmed?"

Herrera shrugged. "No, I suppose not, senor. But then, I did not know you were coming. I do not even know who you are."

"I told you, he's Bill, and I'm Ben. We are here for the same reason you are here."

Herrera paused, as if considering his options. He could turn and rush back inside the house, but he knew he would never make it before being shot in the back. These two hombres were good; he had been in the killing business long enough to determine that much about them. "Perhaps you are right, senor," he said with a shrug. "Perhaps we can talk."

Williams and Boyd moved to the foot of the steps leading up the veranda, stopped and looked up at Herrera.

"We all know the police are on their way here," Williams said. "Two more guns has to be to our advantage."

Herrera hesitated and then nodded. "After you, senor," he said, stepping aside and indicating the door.

Williams and Boyd exchanged glances. Boyd

nodded almost imperceptibly and then looked at Herrera. "Who's inside?"

"My traveling companion, and an old man, senor. That ees all."

"Okay," Boyd continued. "Here's how we are going to do this. I'll go first, you follow me, and my friend will follow you. If you decide to shoot me, he will put one in the back of your head. You'll be dead before my body hits the ground. You got that?"

"You make eet very clear, senor," Herrera answered. "Shall we go?" He stepped further aside to allow Boyd to go before him.

23

"What is that place?" Jackson Traynor asked as Foley slowed and turned off the Stuart Highway.

"Central Mount Stuart," Foley said. "Supposed to be the geographical centre of Australia."

"Supposed to be?"

"Yeah. When it was first discovered, back in the 1860s, the explorer John McDouall Stuart named it, figuring it was the centre of the continent, but modern surveying technology has proven it's not. It's close, but it's not exactly in the centre."

"Pretty good estimate for that era, nonetheless." Traynor looked at the gathering of tourists lingering around the rest-stop area. "Busy place," he noted.

"Bloody tourists," Sam responded sarcastically. "They'd take photos of me if you put a notice around my neck announcing I'm of historical value."

"Yeah," Foley scoffed. "Like that's ever going to happen. Don't mind Sam," Foley said to Traynor. "He's the quintessential pessimist. When it comes to tourist attractions in the Territory, he wouldn't recognise one if it bit him on the arse."

Traynor laughed.

"That's not funny, Jack," Sam said, sounding offended.

"It is a little bit funny," Traynor said.

"Okay, gentlemen," Barker said, interrupting the moment. "That's enough levity. We are about forty klicks from Aningie Station. Perhaps we should use the time to focus on what we might find when we arrive."

"What *are* we expecting, other than the caretaker?" Traynor asked.

"Hopefully nothing," Barker answered. "But we do know the two Mexicans are looking for you. It might be wise to assume they are there already, waiting for us to arrive."

"How would they know we are going to Aningie?" Sam posed.

"We know there's a mole somewhere in the Federal Police ranks," Barker explained. "As far as I know, only my contact with the Feds in Canberra is aware Jack will be at Aningie. However, if there is a leak, we should assume the Mexicans are waiting."

"If they are waiting," Sam continued, "it doesn't look good for the caretaker."

"You're right," Barker said. "He is our most immediate concern. Let's hope he isn't among the growing list of deceased."

———

Foley slowed and stopped the vehicle. "There," he announced, pointing ahead. "In the distance."

A few moments silence followed as the four cops focused on a dark shape against the horizon, perhaps two kilometres ahead of the vehicle.

"Is that the homestead?" Sam asked.

"I believe so," Foley answered.

"How do you want to approach this, boss?" Sam asked Barker.

"Cautiously would be my advice. There should be a pair of binoculars in this vehicle. Let's have a look."

Sam opened the glove compartment and removed a small pair of binoculars. He wiped the lenses quickly on his shirt, raised them to his eyes and focused on the distant homestead. "There is a small vehicle parked in front of the house," he announced. "Conventional, not four-wheel-drive."

"The caretaker's car?" Foley suggested.

"Or a rental," Barker said from the back seat.

"If it's a rental, it won't belong to the caretaker," Foley said.

"Okay," Barker said. "If it is a rental it might indicate the Mexicans are, in fact, already here. We'll have to move quickly. It's getting late and I don't want to get involved in a shoot-out in the dark."

"Do you think it will come to that?" Sam asked.

Barker turned to Traynor. "Jack, you know these Mexicans, what are your thoughts?"

"I've never met them, but I know all about them, particularly Rodolfo Herrera. He will not surrender. If they are at the homestead, he will fight. It's me he's after, and he will have already been paid handsomely to kill me. He will want to finish the job."

"Okay," Barker said. "We need a plan of approach. Any ideas?"

"Let me out here," Traynor said.

"What?" Barker asked. Sam and Foley turned and looked at Traynor in the back seat.

"What do you mean 'let you out?'" Foley asked.

Traynor nodded towards the distant homestead. "How far is that, two klicks?"

"All of that," Sam agreed.

Traynor began to explain. "I can get to the house without being seen."

"How do you propose to do that?" Barker asked.

"I'm military trained. Trust me. They'll never see me coming."

"And then what?" Barker asked.

Traynor shrugged. "I'll work that out when I get there and see the lay of the land."

"The lay of the land?" Foley said incredulously. "The lay of the fuckin' land! Look out there, Jack." He indicated the desolate country around them. "There's nothing out there but spinifex grass and gibber stones. There's no cover."

"Russell's right, Jack," Barker said. "You're gonna stand out like dog's balls out there. They'll see you coming before you get halfway."

"I served in Afghanistan. Even less cover over there. Nothing but sand and more sand. Fuckin' towel-heads never saw me coming; and there was a lot more of them than there is in that house."

"And," Sam asked, "what are we supposed to do in the meantime?"

"Drive to the homestead. This is a cattle station, isn't it? There has to be at least one shed somewhere, probably behind the house. Drive past the house and get behind the shed."

"And hide?" Sam said.

Traynor reached across the seat and patted Sam on the shoulder. "Let's not say 'hide,' Sam. It sounds so...I don't know...*cautious*?"

"Cautious is good in situations like this," Sam suggested.

"I haven't known you chaps long. But you don't seem to me to be the type to hide from anyone. Let's say 'take cover.'"

Foley looked questioningly at Barker. "Boss?"

"Well," Barker began somewhat hesitantly. "We don't even know if the Mexicans are there. If they are, and we go storming in all guns blazing, they will surely kill the caretaker, if they haven't already. I suggest we move in slowly, blue light flashing, let them see us coming. Take a wide berth around the house and hope Jack is right and there is a shed behind the house we can use for cover. If they are not there, what harm can it do? If they are, maybe we can keep them occupied with negotiations while Jack is moving in. Our first priority has to be keeping the caretaker alive."

"These people will not negotiate," Traynor reminded them.

Barker shrugged. "It is what it is, Jack. Gotta be better than sitting here doing nothing."

Traynor moved to open the door and climb out of the vehicle. Barker grabbed his arm. "Jack, let's not have any heroics when you get to the house. If you make it without being seen, see if you can find out who is in there and where they are located.

Then join us behind the shed and we'll discuss our next move."

"Heroics?" Traynor asked.

"Yeah, Jack. You know what I mean. We are all very sorry about your family, but this is not the time for revenge."

Traynor paused and looked at Barker, gave an almost imperceptible nod, and climbed out of the vehicle.

24

In the front room of Aningie Homestead, Don
Williams and Luke Boyd and Rodolfo Herrera
stood side by side in front of the caretaker. Positioned deliberately about a metre apart so the caretaker's focus swung erratically from one to the other,
they glared threateningly at him.

Behind Bill Kirkwood, the second Mexican, the
short stocky one with the bandy legs, held a large
knife pressed against his neck. He fought against the
urge to stand and fight the intruders, knowing to do
so would inevitably get him killed. He was not a
young man anymore; far too many years of booze
and poor eating habits had left him incapable of
anything more than token resistance. From somewhere deep inside, he mustered strength to not appear afraid. His eyes were clear and focused, a

benefit of sobriety, he figured. He stared back at the three men in front of him with what he hoped was a steely determination, albeit at odds with the situation he found himself in.

Williams spoke, finally. "You would be the caretaker."

Kirkwood looked at the man in the middle and offered a shrug of silent indifference. If he spoke, he knew he would tell them to fuck off, out of his house and out of his life. Best not to say anything, he reasoned. The gesture caused the knife at his neck to dig in ever so slightly deeper and the trickle of blood down his neck increased proportionately. He shifted his gaze and glanced around the room. By any standards, the scene was bizarre. Four professional assassins, two Mexicans and two Australian bikers, three hand guns, and one very large, ugly looking knife between them. The bikers not trusting the Mexicans, and the Mexicans not trusting the bikers. Four pairs of wary, untrusting eyes all focused directly on him. It could easily have been a scene from a Quentin Tarantino movie, Kirkwood decided, except this was real. Almost like a wild west standoff. One mistake, one itchy trigger finger, and the ensuing shoot-out was going to be chaotic. There would almost certainly be no survivors. It was a big room, the biggest in the homestead, but it suddenly felt very small. The tension in the air was palpable, so dense he felt if he was able to concentrate, he was certain he would hear a soft sparking in the air, like the sound of high voltage power lines arcing in an atmosphere heavy and damp with humidity.

"What is your name?" Williams asked Kirkwood.

"His name ees Kirkswood," Herrera said.

Williams glared at Herrera. "I was asking him," he said indicating the caretaker.

"It's Kirkwood," the caretaker said. "Bill Kirkwood. Not Kirkswood. I've told this fuckwit several times," he looked directly at Herrera, "it's Kirkwood!"

"What ees this fucksweet?" Herrera asked.

"Take a look in the mirror, you moron," Kirkwood answered dismissively.

"Okay, okay!" Williams said loudly. "Let's all settle down." He looked at Kirkwood. "You are not really in a position to be throwing insults around, Bill."

"You think? Look at me. I'm an old man. I'm unarmed. I've got a fuckin' great knife at my throat, and three guns in the hands of edgy, nervous punks hell bent on killing someone. I can smell the sweat and fear from here. One misinterpreted move by any one of you and we are all going out in a blaze of gunfire. I decided when these two Mexican arseholes arrived that I was probably never going to get out of here alive. That assessment was confirmed when you and your drop-kick mate arrived. If I'm gonna to die today, I'm gonna die cursing you all to Hell and back."

Standing next to Williams, Boyd glared at Kirkwood. "You calling me a drop-kick?"

"Well, if the shoe fits."

"What?"

Kirkwood looked back at Williams. "Is he the brains of your outfit?"

Boyd raised his pistol and took a step towards Kirkwood. "You fuckin' piece of shit!" he said menacingly.

Suddenly, Herrera raised his weapon and aimed at Boyd. Williams raised his and aimed at Herrera. Vargas, standing behind Kirkwood, flinched involuntarily and nicked Kirkwood's neck again with the knife.

Williams reached out and grabbed Boyd's arm. "Whoa...whoa! Wait!" he called loudly. Boyd paused, Williams released his arm and raised his hand in the air. "Wait! Stop!" he said to everyone in the room. "Stop! Let's all settle down!" He lowered his weapon so it pointed at the floor. "Relax," he said a little quieter. "Let's all just relax. We are not here to kill each other." As he looked from Herrera to Vargas and back to Herrera, he saw Herrera lower his weapon slightly. Without taking his eyes from Herrera he addressed Boyd. "Lower the gun, mate."

"You have to be kidding!" Boyd said.

"Kirkwood is right, Luke," Williams said. "If we all start shooting we are all going to die."

Boyd lowered his weapon and glared at Kirkwood. "Before I leave here today, I'm gonna kill you, you fuckin' prick!"

"Look around, Einstein," Kirkwood said. "You're gonna have to get in line."

Williams faced Kirkwood. "Bill," he said quietly. "See what happens when you start insulting people. You are at a distinct disadvantage here. You need to settle down. I don't believe you want to die today."

"What do you want?"

Williams inclined his head towards Herrera and Vargas. "I expect we want the same thing they want." He shifted his gaze to Herrera. Suspecting he might be the spokesman for the two Mexicans, he glanced down at the pistol Herrera still held half raised. "Now you, lower your gun."

Herrera hesitated. Then, slowly, warily, he lowered the pistol until the business end pointed at the floor in front of Williams.

"Thank you," Williams said with a nod.

"Who are you, senor?" Herrera asked.

"I told you before, our names are not important."

"Who sent you to this place?"

"Not the same people who sent you, I'm guessing."

"You are here for the *rata policia*?"

"*Rata policia*? What is that?" Williams asked.

"How do you call it here in your country...police rat?"

"Oh...I see. Yes, we are here for the rat police officer."

"It ees under control, senor. You should leave this place," Herrera said.

"I don't think so."

"We have travelled a long way, senor. You should leave this place."

"You know what...*senor*," Williams said, emphasising the '*senor*.' "I don't care how far you have travelled. We are not leaving until the job we were sent to do is done. You might want to get used to that."

Suddenly, Boyd's eyes were drawn to the large window offering a view over the approach road to the homestead. "No time for anyone to leave now," he announced. "Looks like the *rata policia* are here."

Vargas removed the knife from Kirkwood's neck and turned towards the window behind him. Herrera and the two bikers all looked across the room.

Outside, an unmarked police car, identified by the blue light flashing on the dashboard, approached the house at speed. Instead of stopping, or even slowing, the car raced on a track that would take it wide of the house. Then it was gone. It disappeared from view around the eastern end of the homestead leaving only a cloud of dust in its wake.

"*Mierda!*" Vargas yelled. "*La policia esta aqui!*"

"*Carajo!*" Herrera cursed. "*A donde fueron*—where did they go?"

"*No se,*" Vargas answered. "*A la espalda, creo que*—to the back, I think. *Conducir muy rapido*—they drive very fast."

"*Hijueputa!*" Herrera hissed. "*Policia bastardo!*" He turned back towards the rear of the room, looked past Williams and Boyd at the kitchen at the rear of the house. Then he addressed the two bikers. "Perhaps, senors, we should put our differences aside... for the moment."

"We kinda figured you might see it our way," Boyd said.

Williams looked at Vargas. "Bring the caretaker," he ordered.

"*Que?*" Vargas said with a shrug.

"*Traer el prisionero,*" Herrera interpreted.

"*Yo no trabajo para los perros del extranjeros,*" Vargas said with determination. He lifted the knife and waved it at Williams and Boyd.

"What did he say?" Williams asked Herrera.

"He said he does not take orders from you, senor."

"We are all here for Jackson Traynor," Williams said. "They give us Traynor, we give them Kirkwood. They will want to see he is alive. So, either your ugly mate brings him outside or my friend and I will take him." He indicated Vargas. "And, if Pancho there gets in our way, I will shove that knife up his fat arse."

Herrera turned again to face Vargas. "*Traer al prisoner, Ignacio. Por favour, no pasa nada.*"

Vargas hesitated. He glared first at Williams and Boyd and then he looked at Herrera. With eyes filled with contempt, he waved the knife at Williams and Boyd. "*Cuando temenos la rata, mueren, esta bien*— When we have the rat, they die, okay?"

"*Si, esta bien.*"

"What's he babbling about?" Boyd asked Herrera.

"No need to worry, senor. Everything ees okay."

"About fuckin' time. Let's go."

———

Herrera, Boyd, and Williams stood abreast on the wide veranda at the rear of the homestead. In front of them, at the leading edge of the veranda, Vargas sheltered behind Kirkwood's much taller body, like a shield should the police decide to shoot from their cover of the shed. He held tightly to Kirkwood's belt and pressed the knife to the side of his neck. As he pressed his body against Kirkwood's back, his breathing became short and rapid as he felt himself becoming aroused. He licked his lips and chuckled softly.

"What's so funny?" Kirkwood asked.

"I am thinking, senor, of the pleasure I weel have with you," Vargas whispered. He pushed his groin harder into Kirkwood's back.

Kirkwood instinctively tried to pull forward only to feel the knife blade dig deeper into his neck. "You will have to kill me first, you faggot!" he hissed.

"Of course, senor. That ees my way."

25

Foley drove fast, maintaining a distance of approximately fifty metres from the eastern end of the large homestead. The vehicle bucked and skidded dangerously over the rough, stony ground, and he wrestled furiously with the steering, desperate to maintain control. Beads of perspiration ran freely down his forehead and into his eyes making it difficult to see but he dared not remove a hand from the wheel to wipe his brow.

As he passed the end of the house, a shed came into view. Separated from the house by about thirty metres, the shed was huge, spanning almost the entire length of the homestead.

"There!" Sam said. "There is a shed! Can you get around behind it, Russ?"

Foley changed direction and the rear of the vehicle began to fish-tail. He turned the wheel into the slide and steered a course which would bring them closer to the shed. "Yeah, I can get behind it," he yelled above the roar of the engine. "If I don't lose control and wind up through the side of it first."

The vehicle raced past the end of the building, missed sideswiping the back corner by a whisker, and skidded to a halt in a cloud of dust a few metres from the rear of the large, galvanised iron storage shed.

For a few moments there was silence inside the vehicle, save for the sound of the now idling engine.

Sam reached across and patted Foley on the shoulder. "Good work, Russ," he said with a smile. "We made it."

"Must have been all the praying I was doing." Foley looked at Sam and then into the rear vision mirror at Barker in the back seat. "You okay, boss?"

"Fine," Barker nodded to Foley's reflection in the mirror. "Might need to change my Jockey shorts though."

All three men took a moment to study their surroundings in silence.

"Did you see the bikes?" Barker asked.

"Bikes?" Foley questioned.

"Yeah, two motorbikes, parked between the house and the shed. What is that about?"

"Dunno, boss," Foley answered, rubbing and

flexing his aching wrists. "I was too busy trying to keep this thing on its wheels to look at the scenery."

"Let's get out of the car," Barker said. "There's a door here, we can get inside the shed and make our way to the front."

A single door, in the middle of the rear wall of the shed, stood open.

Barker climbed out of the vehicle, followed by Sam and Foley. Each man drew his service weapon and stepped closer to the shed. Barker stood on one side of the open door, Foley and Rose on the other. Barker leaned forward and peeked around the edge of the door.

"What have we got, boss?" Sam asked.

Barker leaned back and looked across the gap in the door at Foley and Rose. "Looks like a machinery shed and workshop of some kind. There's bits and pieces of equipment everywhere, and a vehicle up the far end."

"No one in there?" Foley asked.

"Too hard to tell with all the stuff in there. But I don't think so. There looks to be an access door on the other side, opposite this one, and I think the western end of the shed, where the vehicle is, is open, no end wall."

"How do you want to handle it?" Foley asked.

"Standard procedure. We go in fast and low. Sam, you go left and Russell, you go right. I'll go straight through the middle. Clear the shed and we'll gather at the front wall, nearest the house. Okay?"

"Okay," Foley said.

"Copy," Sam echoed.

Barker darted low and fast into the shed, followed immediately by Foley and Sam. Inside, Sam and Foley moved towards opposite ends of the shed, while Barker moved in a straight line towards the front of the shed facing the house. They moved quickly, crouched low, their eyes scanning everything to their front and sides, their respective weapons sweeping the line of vision across their path.

The shed was filled with all types of machinery and mechanical equipment essential for the efficient running of a large cattle station. If something broke down out here, one could not just run down to the local workshop to get it repaired. Northern Territory cattle stations were vast, isolated properties and equipment breakdowns had to be handled on site as quickly as possible. There was no emergency road-service to come to your aid out in this country, at least not quickly, and out here, time was money.

They moved quickly but cautiously through the shed, working towards both ends and across the centre. It took several minutes for them to determine they were alone in the shed. A Toyota Land Cruiser, tray-back, four-wheel-drive was parked just inside the western end of the shed which was, as Barker had originally observed, open to the elements. The Toyota carried a decal on the driver's side door declaring it was an Aningie Station vehicle.

Barker, Foley, and Sam moved to the front of the shed and gathered on each side of a closed door.

"Everyone okay?" Barker asked.

"Yeah, good," Foley said.

"I'm good," Sam said.

Barker nodded towards the Toyota at the end of the shed. "That's a station vehicle. So it seems the caretaker has a couple of visitors."

"More than a couple," Sam said. "We've got a small rental car in front of the house and two motorbikes outside this door. I think we've got us a welcoming party."

"Don't be expecting wine and canapes," Foley said.

"Canapes?"

"They're little pre-dinner snack—"

"I know what canapes are, Russ," Sam huffed. "What, you getting all hoity-toity now?"

"Focus, gentlemen, focus," Barker reprimanded. "We need a plan. Any ideas?"

"Well," Foley began, "they must know we're

here. I'm guessing the rental car belongs to the Mex-icans, but it's the two bikes that concern me. Who belongs to them? Could it be we have four baddies in the house?"

"They could be friends visiting the caretaker," Sam offered. "Caught in the wrong place at the wrong time."

"It's possible, I suppose," Barker said. "But I don't think so. Too much of a coincidence."

"Maybe we should just ask them," Foley said.

A small window on each side of the front access door offered a good view of the rear of the home-stead thirty metres away. Barker sheltered on one side of the window to the left of the door, while Foley and Sam stood, one on either side of the window on the right. Barker turned his body slightly, peeked briefly out through his window, and then withdrew almost immediately.

"Fuck!" he cursed softly.

"What have we got, boss?" Sam asked.

"Four baddies," Barker answered. "At least four that I can see. At least three handguns and one very large knife. The dude with the knife has it at the throat of an older bloke, I'm guessing that will be the caretaker."

"Four baddies?" Foley said. "Where did four come from?"

"I only took a short look. The man with the

knife, and one of the others, look Mexican." Barker shrugged. "The other two look Caucasian."

"That might explain the motorbikes," Sam said.

"And your contact with the Feds said nothing about four perps?" Foley asked.

"No," Barker confirmed. "Nothing."

"Traynor's going to walk into a whole mess of shit," Sam said. "We need to warn him."

"How do you suggest we do that?" Foley asked. "We don't even know where he is."

"If Jack's as good as they say he is," Barker interrupted, "he'll be okay. Our immediate concern is to get the caretaker out of there alive."

"Do you have a plan, boss?" Foley asked.

"Yeah, sort of. As much as I hate to negotiate with arseholes, talking might be our best option. We need to give Traynor all the time he needs to get to the house and do whatever it is he does."

Suddenly, a loud, commanding voice came at them from across the open ground between the house and the shed.

"Hey, you in the shed! Step out here where we can see you!" Williams called.

"Yeah," Sam said softly, "like that's ever going to happen." He leaned forward and took a tentative look through the window. "Three of them are standing together, a metre apart. The dude with the knife is in front of them, sheltering behind the caretaker."

"What are our odds?" Foley asked.

"There's only the two motorbikes between us and the house. There's no cover. We would never make it across the open ground. Besides, they would kill the caretaker if we tried," Sam said.

Foley looked across at Barker. "I guess negotiating is our best option."

The loud voice came again. "Hey, pigs in the shed! You need to get out here where we can see you, and you need to do it now!"

"Who are you?" Barker called back.

"Never mind who I am. And you can forget about the official police negotiation shit! Just get out here, or the old dude dies."

"What is it you want?"

"You know what we want, arsehole. We want Traynor!" Williams stepped forward, past Vargas, and stood next to Kirkwood. He raised his handgun and placed it against Kirkwood's temple. "Take a look out the window, shit-for-brains!" he called.

Barker glanced across at Foley and Rose. He lifted his head and cautiously peeked through the window.

Williams saw the movement and smiled widely. "I'm gonna blow this prick's brains all across the yard if you fuck with me! Send Traynor out!"

Barker pulled back from the window. "One of them, one of the biker dudes, is holding a gun to the caretaker's head."

"Have you got a plan B?" Foley asked.

"No. There's no plan B. I figured I'd keep talking while you two work on a plan B."

Sam nudged Foley. "That's why he's the boss," he said quietly.

Barker turned back to the window. "Traynor's not here," he yelled.

"I can count, pig!" Williams yelled. "There are three of you in there! One of you is Traynor. Send him out or the old man dies!"

"There is no need for anyone to die," Barker answered. "I told you Traynor is not with us."

26

Jackson Traynor ran hard, fast, and low. He was fit, strong, agile, and an experienced runner. He figured the distance he would have to cover at around three kilometres. On flat, even ground, and on a direct route, he knew he could reach the homestead in less than twenty minutes. But he was not on a direct route, and he was not on flat, even ground. He had to weave around tufts of sharp, spiny spinifex grass, and flat, sharp-edged gibber stones shifted under his feet as he ran making it difficult to maintain his footing. His path took him in a wide berth to the west of the house and the twenty minutes he originally estimated was now going to be at least thirty.

Like the battle at Shah Wali Kot, Afghanistan all over again, he was exposed and vulnerable. There was no cover. No trees, not even a stunted bush to take cover behind should he draw fire from the house. But this was not Afghanistan, and Traynor was no longer a soldier. Nonetheless, the feeling was the same. Not fear exactly; there was no room for fear. He knew it was there somewhere deep inside, and it would surface later, after the job was done, just as it had in Afghanistan. For now, it would remain deep inside, suppressed by a pure heart-racing, adrenalin-pumping determination to reach the objective and not die in the process. Also, as he had done following the battle of Shah Wali Kot, he would deal with the fear when it finally arrived.

Anyone inside the house looking out towards the front of the homestead would see him. All he had was his speed, faith in his ability, and an unquenchable desire to kill the men responsible for the murder of his family. Hopefully, he would also have the element of surprise.

The arrival of Barker, Foley, and Rose at the house would attract the attention of whoever was inside. If they were focused on the Territory cops at the rear of the house, they would not be looking out the front. If the cards fell the right way, he would be able to get a look inside, maybe even get inside, and check on the caretaker. Poor bastard might already be dead, he thought. Herrera and Vargas were killers. Brutal, sadistic killers. The chances of the caretaker still being alive were slim at best, he decided. Nevertheless, he had to get to the house undetected and check for himself. The intention spurred him on and he pushed harder.

———

Don Williams hesitated. Something made him look down at the Mexican holding the caretaker. "What the fuck are you doing?" he hissed.

"The faggot is dry humping me, that's what he's doing!" Kirkwood said.

"He's what?" Williams asked, incredulously.

"Get this fuckin' bastard away from me, or kill me now," Kirkwood demanded.

Williams moved the gun from Kirkwood's head and placed the barrel in the Mexican's ear. "What the fuck are you doing?" he asked again.

"*Jay, caramba!*" Vargas cried. He flinched and pulled away from Kirkwood.

"Get the fuck back there!" Williams ordered. He turned to Herrera. "Keep this fuckin' horny goat herder under control or I will kill him myself!" he spat.

Herrera shrugged indifference. "Eet ees of no concern to me if he dies, senor."

Williams re-positioned the barrel of his weapon

against the side of Vargas's head and, using it as a lever, he steered him away from the caretaker.

Vargas stumbled backwards and joined Herrera and Boyd. "What ees this 'goats harder,'" he mumbled, rubbing vigorously at his ear.

"It's goat herder, you dick, not goats harder." Boyd scowled at the diminutive Mexican. "You do have goats in Mexico, don't you?"

With a look of confusion, Vargas turned to Herrera. "*Debemos matar a todus los perros de la policia—*we must kill all the police dogs," he said. "*Y ese hijo de puta,*" he said, indicating Williams.

"*Ir dentro de—*go inside," Herrera said. "*Ver que nadie se acerca—*see that no one is coming."

Vargas hesitated. He looked questioningly at Herrera for a moment, scowled at Williams, then at Boyd, and then, mumbling incoherently, he turned away and re-entered the house.

27

Traynor reached the western end of the homestead without being detected by anyone inside the house. Crouched low below the decking of the wide veranda surrounding the house, he waited for his breathing and heartbeat to return to normal following his run to reach the homestead. He held his handgun, a Sig Sauer P226 semi-automatic, in a two-handed grip and looked back and forth from the rear end of the veranda to the front, and then back again. He cautiously raised his head and peeked over the base of the veranda.

There were no steps onto the veranda at this end of the house and he would have to climb over the veranda railing if he was to access the interior of the homestead. There were two windows in the end wall, one towards the back of the building and another closer to the front. Both appeared to be closed. With his breathing and his heart rate now close to normal, he crouched back down, taking a few moments to consider his options.

Then, he heard voices. They came from outside the house, from the back veranda, he decided. Raised voices, calling back and forth between two people. As he listened he recognised Cameron Yap Yap Barker's as one of the voices. The second voice he did not recognise. It came from someone on the veranda, just around the corner from where he crouched.

Carefully, he moved to the end of the veranda and, keeping low to the ground, he dared to sneak a look around the corner. He saw no one. A large shed, approximately thirty metres behind the house and open at the end closest to where he lay, ran almost the whole length of the homestead. Barker's voice came from inside the shed.

Halfway between the shed and the house, two Harley Davidson motorcycles stood parked side by side, both identical. Traynor leaned back and considered the motorcycles. What were they doing way out here in this isolated place? Who did they belong to?

Jack had learned a very long time ago to trust in his instincts; it was something that came natural to him after his time in both the military and the Federal Police Force. His instincts had saved his life more than once on the front line in Afghanistan. Instinct, premonition, precognitive thought, whatever one labelled it, Traynor knew the two Harleys parked at the rear of the house were not as innocuous as they might otherwise seem.

He moved back to his original position, stood, and quickly and silently scaled the veranda railing. On the veranda he paused, studying the wooden decking beneath his feet. It looked old and weathered. The last thing he wanted was for a loose floor board to creak loudly when he moved. If there were suspect decking boards here, they would be in the centre where there was less support beneath them, he guessed. Careful not to lose his balance, he stepped wide, over the centre of the veranda and pressed himself against the end wall of the house.

Here, he hesitated and listened again to the voices coming from the rear of the house. Then he thought he heard two people talking in a foreign language. Mexican, he decided, Spanish, maybe. It had to be Herrera and Vargas. The bastards were here, just a few metres from where he stood. The urge to step around the corner of the house and kill the two men responsible for murdering his wife and daughter was strong. He leaned back against the wall and closed his eyes. He had to suppress the urge. As hard as it was not to step around the corner and start shooting, he had to get control of his emotions.

Finally, watching closely where he placed each footstep, he dared to move quietly to the end of the veranda. Again, he leaned back against the wall and waited. With his senses on high alert, he leaned forward and sneaked a look around the corner.

There were five people on the front of the veranda. One of them, a big man, stood at the very edge of the veranda facing the shed. He held a gun to the head of a short man of Mexican appearance. The Mexican held a large knife at the neck of an elderly man, and behind them stood two others, another man of Mexican appearance and a man who could easily have been a twin of the big guy with the gun in the Mexican's ear. Traynor pulled back out of sight.

The elderly man had to be the caretaker, he guessed. The two Mexicans would definitely be Herrera and Vargas. Who were the two white dudes, he wondered? He thought about the two Harley Davidson motorcycles parked between the house and the shed. They had to belong to the two strangers, he decided. But who were they? Where did they fit into this? Something familiar, a faint, distant memory perhaps, fluttered in his mind. Something he heard once, a long time ago in the course of his duty as a Federal police officer. Was it twin Harley Davidson motorcycles? Was it the two men who rode them? Whatever it was, he knew it was not good.

From his brief glimpse of the scene around the corner, the big bikie and the Mexican to whose head he held a gun, were obviously not friends. So, what should he assume from the scenario on the rear veranda? There appeared to be four adversaries, not two as he was led to believe. Two Mexicans, Rodolfo Herrera and Ignacio Vargas, and two unknown biker types. It also appeared that the bikers and the Mexicans, although apparently tolerating each other's presence, were not best buddies. What did all that mean? Were there four hit men? There had to be!

Then the penny dropped! Salim Ghandour! The two bikers had to be Ghandour's men. There was no other explanation. Salim Ghandour was widely suspected within the drug enforcement section of the Federal Police Force of having rival crime gang members killed. So far he had never been charged with such; he was too smart for that. Who actually did Ghandour's dirty work for him was not known but there was a very strong suspicion that two people were involved. The two bikers on the back veranda of the homestead were Ghandour's men, Jack Traynor was now certain of it.

How did they know to come to Aningie Station? Leaving the safe-house in Ti Tree and coming to

Aningie was a last-minute change of plans. How could the two bikers have known? How could any of them have known?

Suddenly, he heard the two Mexicans talking to each other in what he assumed was their home tongue. Then he heard someone leave the veranda and enter the house.

He moved silently back to the closest window and peeked inside. Dirt and grime, built up over years, covered the outside of the window making the interior look dark and cloudy, like looking at the room beyond through a thin, sepia film. The caretaker was obviously not particularly house-proud, Jack thought.

The room was empty save for a large wardrobe against the far wall opposite the window. The wardrobe suggested he was looking at a bedroom, at least what was intended as a bedroom. There was nothing else in the room, no bed, no other furnishings of any kind. It had to be a bedroom, Jack guessed.

He looked down at the base of the window and noticed a small gap just a few centimetres wide, and he slipped the fingers of his free hand into the gap. Slowly, silently praying the window would not squeak, he lifted. Nothing happened. The window would not budge. He tried again. Nothing. The window was stuck fast. If he forced it, it was going to make a noise. He leaned back against the wall and rested for a moment.

Wondering if the second window further along the wall might be the same, he stepped cautiously across to it, and peered in. In respect of the dirt and grime, this window was the same. This place was in urgent need of a woman's touch.

Under the window, a queen-size bed with the bedding casually pushed aside filled almost half of the room. A wardrobe, similar to the one in the empty room next door, stood against the wall at the end of the unmade bed. This had to be the caretaker's bedroom. A door in the wall to the right of the wardrobe stood open. Beyond the door, Jack could see a small section of what appeared to be a hallway connecting the bedrooms to the rest of the house.

There was no gap at the base of this window. Aningie Station was situated on the eastern fringe of the Tanami Desert. This was desert country. The nights were freezing cold, too cold to sleep with the window open. He placed the palm of his free hand against the pane, hoping the caretaker did not lock the window at night. He pushed up. The window moved silently up a few centimetres.

He paused, looked across at the open door, and waited. No one came. With a quiet sigh of relief, he holstered his weapon and, using both hands, he slowly, carefully, pushed the widow open, never taking his eyes from the open door. When he lifted his hands from the window, it slid down a couple of centimetres and then stopped. Must be held open by the build-up of grime, he thought.

Cautiously, he stuck his head through the open window and looked around the room. A small bed-side table sat on each side of the bed. On one of them, there was a small reading lamp and an open magazine. With the bed positioned beneath the window, gaining access to the room was not going to be easy. What if the bed squeaked? What if he knocked over a bedside lamp while climbing in?

He turned side-on to the window, lifted one leg and placed it through the opening and onto the bed. Bending low, he manoeuvred his upper body inside, supported his weight on the bed and followed with his other leg. He found himself in an awkward posi-tion on his knees on top of the bed and he waited for a few moments, his eyes focused on the open doorway.

Finally, he sat on the bed, swung his legs over the edge and carefully climbed off. Now, he was on the side of the bed opposite the doorway. He unhol-stered his weapon and slowly, one cautious step at a time, moved around the end of the bed and stepped across to the open door.

There was a hallway beyond. Directly opposite, on the other side of the hallway from where he stood pressed against the inside of the door jamb, there was another open door. The room within, at least what he could see of it, appeared to be empty. This would be the first room he looked into from the veranda, he guessed. He leaned forward and peeked around the corner, into the long hallway. There were three more doors along the length of the hall. Another bedroom, a bathroom, and a toilet, perhaps. At the far end of the hallway was what appeared to be a large, open room, the back of a sofa visible from where he stood. This would be the main living-room of the homestead, Jack figured. This was a big house. The hallway was long and wide and the room at the end seemed to be a long way away. He pulled back inside the bedroom and leaned against the door jamb.

There was someone inside the house, Jack knew. But where exactly, he did not know. Who was it? From his position in the bedroom at the end of the long hallway, he could hear voices, muffled and indistinguishable, from the men still outside on the back veranda. Was there only one person inside?

His heart started to pump hard inside his chest. It was not an unfamiliar feeling to Jack; he had felt this way many times over his lifetime. That pulse pounding, adrenalin pumping, nerve tingling energy surging through his body he always felt right before going into battle. For some, it might be a terrifying feeling; for Jackson Traynor, it was not. He never felt afraid immediately before engaging the enemy. He had trained long and hard for just this sort of thing.

When going into combat was inevitable and retreat was not an option, the many months of intense physical and emotional training kicked in. The mind focused. The body, honed and sculptured as a result of a physical training regime that brought over ninety percent of those who tried out for the Commandos to their knees, was wound tight, coiled like a viper ready to strike. There was no fear. There was no time for fear, just the pounding, pumping, tingling surge of energy.

Jack took another peek around the door jamb. The hallway was clear. He stepped around the corner and pressed his back against the wall. He held the Sig semi-automatic in a two-handed grip, high in front of his face, the business end pointed at the ceiling. His eyes remained fixed and focused on his objective. He took a deep breath and slowly, silently moving sideways, he started inching his way towards the large room at the end of the hall.

28

Vaughn Millard's throw-away mobile phone lay on his desk. Switched to silent, it suddenly began to vibrate on his desk-top. He hoped the caller would be either one of two people, Rodolfo Herrera or Don Williams, with the news he was waiting to hear: Jackson Traynor was dead. He snatched up the phone and flipped it open. The display indicated an unknown caller. He stared at the phone as it vibrated in his hand. Finally, he pressed to accept the call and answered. "Millard," he said.

"Is it done?" a voice he did not immediately recognise asked.

"What?"

"Is it done?"

"Who is this?" Millard asked.

"Hakim Ghandour," the voice said. "Tell me it is done."

Hakim Ghandour was the only surviving son of Salim Ghandour, the head of the Middle-Eastern crime gang operating out of Sydney. Salim was the boss, but Hakim was the head of the family's drug importation and distribution operations. Both Salim and Hakim were prime targets of the Federal police task-force charged with the job of bringing the Ghandour family to justice and their illegal drug operations to a halt. The father and son were currently on bail awaiting their upcoming court appearance at which Traynor was to give evidence which would see the family business disintegrate and Salim and Hakim sent to prison, hopefully for the rest of their lives.

"I don't know," Millard said.

"You don't know?" Hakim asked.

"That's right, I don't know."

"When do you think you will know?"

Millard ignored the question. "Your father must be getting a little anxious, Hakim. His number one son ringing me personally. I don't know whether to be honoured or concerned. How did you get this number, anyway? Does Salim know you are calling?"

"Never mind how I got the number. You should know by now we can get anything we want. And don't worry about my father. You are the one who needs to be concerned. If Traynor gets to court with what he knows, you will not see your next birthday."

"Are you threatening me, Hakim?"

"If you want to call it a threat, call it a threat; I prefer to call it a promise."

"If Traynor spills his guts in court, Hakim, both you and your father will see all of your future birthdays in prison."

"Your job is to ensure that never happens," Hakim said with a threatening tone.

"So, fuck off and let me do my job!" Millard hissed.

"It would not be wise to piss my father off," Hakim responded, the threatening tone more evident now. "May I remind you that you have been paid very handsomely for many years in return for your cooperation. My family wants this business over and done with."

"We all want it over and done with, Hakim."

"So, what do I tell my father?"

"Tell him I'm working on it. Tell him I don't know if Traynor is still alive. The people sent to take care of it are out of telephone range. They will contact me when it is done, and then I will contact you."

"What do you mean 'out of telephone range?'"

Hakim sounded surprised. "Ti Tree is not Mars!"

"Traynor is no longer at Ti Tree."

"What?"

"He has been taken from the safe-house to an-other location."

"Another location? Where?"

"An isolated cattle station, northwest of Ti Tree. There is no mobile phone reception out there."

"The cops took him there?"

"Yes, a couple of cops from Alice Springs. I am told a military helicopter is to pick him up from there and take him to a secure location."

"They are sending the military?" Hakim asked. "When?"

"I don't know when."

"Jesus Christ! This is all turning to shit! What the fuck *do* you know?"

"Don't get your panties in a bunch, Hakim. There are people out there now taking care of it."

"Williams and Boyd?"

"Yes, to name a couple."

"A couple? Are there others?"

"Yes."

"Who?"

"Alvarez sent a couple over from Mexico," Mil-lard answered.

"You have got to be kidding!" Hakim said.

"Like you and your old man, he also wanted

Traynor taken care of," Millard explained. "Perhaps he is losing faith in Salim and you to get the job done."

"My father told you *we* would provide the personnel to get Traynor."

"He told *me*. But obviously he didn't tell Miguel Alvarez. Besides, what difference does it make? Four professionals have gotta be better than two. They should all be at the cattle station by now."

"They fuckin' better be, Millard. They better be! If Traynor gets on that helicopter, we are all fucked!"

"He won't get on the chopper, Hakim."

"If he does, there will be nowhere you can hide," Hakim spat.

"Still with the threats, Hakim?"

"I told you, they're not threats, they're promises!" Hakim disconnected the call.

Vaughn Millard sat for a few moments staring at the dead phone. Finally, he flipped it closed and tossed it aside on his desk. "Fuckin' Lebanese arsehole," he murmured. "Alvarez shoulda sent the fuckin' Mexicans after *you*."

Maybe Hakim was right, he thought. Maybe it really was all turning to shit. If Traynor wasn't dead yet, and the military chopper got to him before the four hit-men did, they would never find him. It would be over for all of them. If Jackson Traynor got to court and brought down Salim Ghandour and his drop-kick, coke-snorting son, the gutless pricks would drop his name in a heartbeat if it meant a reduced prison sentence. Maybe they would drop his name anyway, even if doing so had no effect on any sentence the court might impose. Or they would simply kill him. Not them personally, that would be difficult from prison. But Salim Ghandour was a man of influence; you didn't get to be the biggest drug king-pin in the country without gaining a little influence along the way. Even from his prison cell, Ghandour would still control certain people, people like Don Williams and Luke Boyd for instance. Millard never considered himself a coward, but Williams and Boyd were two dudes he did not want to have looking for him.

Perhaps it was time to seriously consider getting out while he still could. He had money, more than enough to keep him in relative comfort for the rest of his life. He had a false passport; he got that from one of Ghandour's associates several years ago, when he first hooked up with the family. All the necessary preparations were in place for a hasty departure, had been for a long time. He could be gone from the country just as soon as he could get home and pack some clothes.

He glanced at his discarded phone. Perhaps he should try Williams again. Or Rodolfo Herrera. He wished he knew what was happening at Aningie

Homestead. Surely four professional killers could do what was required. How hard could it be? Why hadn't he heard anything yet? Maybe he should wait a little longer, give them time to get back to where there was mobile phone service. Yes, he would wait. He leaned back in his chair. *I'll give them until the end of the day.*

———

Hakim Ghandour turned away from the large, panoramic window overlooking the pristine, azure waters of Sydney Harbour and casually tossed his phone onto a deep, plush, velvet covered lounge chair, one of a matching pair positioned regally on either side of the window. He looked across at the sleeping girl laying naked on his king-size bed in the middle of the room, her long, dark hair splayed haphazardly across her pillow. She was quite beautiful, he thought. He couldn't remember her name, but what the fuck? He wasn't going to see her again after today anyway.

Hakim was no stranger to beautiful women, and there was no shortage of them in the social circles in which he moved. He could, and did, have as many as he wanted, whenever he wanted. Mostly, he knew women were attracted to him because of his money, and he had plenty of it. But, he also knew he was not

completely undesirable to the opposite sex in regards to his looks. He kept himself in shape with
hour-long daily work-outs in a personal gym located
in the basement of his luxurious home, and his
swarthy, olive skin tone, maintained with an almost
obsessive ritual of moisturisers and skin-tightening
lotions, presented an image that would be the envy
of the most in-demand male model.

Hakim's home was the epitome of Middle-
Eastern opulence. For one man living on his own,
folks could easily be forgiven for considering the
ten-room mansion to be over-kill. The house was
one of three purchased eight years earlier for a rumoured fifty-three million dollars by Hakim's father,
Salim, the head of the Ghandour family. All three
houses were sited next to each other in a gated
family compound on the western side of South
Head Peninsula in the affluent, prestigious Sydney
suburb of Vaucluse. The compound overlooked
Sydney Harbour and commanded uninterrupted
views of the Sydney Harbour Bridge and the Opera
House.

The middle house of the three, and by far the
largest, belonged to Salim. Hakim's house was on
the right, closest to the Tasman Sea away to the east,
and the house on the left belonged to the late
Ahmed Ghandour, Salim's eldest son and Hakim's
brother. Ahmed's house was vacant, left exactly as it

was the day he died. His mother insisted it remain that way as a memorial to her son.

Ahmed was killed in a drive-by shooting believed to have been ordered by a rival crime boss and carried out by a professional hit-man brought in from interstate. To date, no one had been charged with the killing and Salim was of the firm belief that the police didn't really care who killed his son. To the cops, Ahmed was one more scum-bag drug dealer off the streets. If the police couldn't, or wouldn't, find who killed his eldest son, Salim would, by whatever means and at whatever cost. To Salim, his wife, Assi, and Hakim, Ahmed was their beloved son and brother. Someone had to pay for his murder, and someone would.

Hakim stepped across to the middle of the room and stopped at the edge of the bed. He looked down at the naked girl laying on her stomach. A small amount of drool from the corner of her mouth had left a tiny damp spot on her pillow. Hakim reached down and gently pushed a wayward strand of hair away from her face. The girl stirred, her eyes fluttered and, squinting against the light flooding into the room through the large window, she peeked up at Hakim. She rolled seductively over onto her back, moaned sleepily, and offered Hakim what might have been an attempt at a smile.

Hakim allowed his gaze to wander up and down

the girl's body. She certainly was a looker, he thought. He shrugged indifferently and shifted his gaze to the large, round, bedside table and to the line of white powder sitting there. Wearing only a pair of body-hugging, black briefs, he looked down at his rapidly growing excitement, picked up the glass straw, leaned over the table and inhaled the whole line, his third since he brought the girl home from the nightclub. Then, in one swift movement, he removed his briefs, turned back to face the girl and paused, allowing her to gaze hungrily at his nakedness. Hakim smiled, flashing his profession-ally enhanced, perfectly straight and brilliantly white teeth, and climbed onto the bed, a trace of white powder still clinging to the side of his nostril.

29

Salim Ghandour's expansive, private study was located in the basement of his luxurious home. The room was, by any standard, huge. It covered over half the total floor area of the basement, the remainder taken up with a luxuriously appointed bathroom complete with gold basin and shower fittings.

The study was lavishly furnished with solid, oak-panelled walls, a matching oak floor-to-ceiling bookcase ran almost the length of one wall, and thick, rich, deep burgundy carpet imported from Turkey covered the floor. A soft, plush, three-seater, leather Chesterfield settee sat in the centre of the room. A matching wing-chair on either end of the settee completed the ensemble. Salim's desk, large enough for three men to sit behind, imported from

Russia and also made of oak, sat at the rear of the room, directly opposite the double, solid oak doors. On one side of the room, opposite the bookcase and bathroom, and running the full length of the wall, a huge wet-bar offered the privileged few who were invited to imbibe an array of alcoholic beverages more comprehensive than many small hotel bars. A faint odour of furniture polish, and money, hung in the air.

Only one chair sat behind Salim's desk, a high-back, ridiculously expensive, Chesterfield office chair purchased at the same time as the settee suite. Despite the presence of the settee and its attendant twin chairs, those who entered Salim's personal sanctuary never sat without first being invited to do so. Sitting without invitation was considered by Salim to be disrespectful. Should a visitor transgress, they only ever did so once. A look of silent scorn was always incentive enough for the offender to immediately stand and excuse themselves. It quickly became understood in the circles in which Salim moved, that should one be summoned to the cellar, as his study was referred to behind his back, one should expect to stand for the duration of the meeting.

So defensive was he in regards to his private sanctuary, no one ever entered Salim's study who was not first invited by him personally to do so, even members of his own family. That's the way it was with Salim Ghandour. He was the master of his domain. What he ruled over, he considered his kingdom and he ruled with an iron fist and a loaded gun. Should you insult him, disrespect him or, God forbid, cross him, you had better be prepared to pay the consequences.

The patriarch of the Ghandour family was extremely wealthy; the illegal drug importation and distribution business had been good to him for many years and showed no signs of slowing down. As long as there remained an insatiable appetite for recreational drugs in the country, Salim Ghandour was only going to get wealthier—unless someone stopped him.

For all intents and purposes, Salim was a hardworking, respectable businessman who made, and continued to make, his vast fortune from a string of nightclubs, topless bars, and high-end escort agencies located in every capital city in the country. Of course, one had to be as dense as a house brick not to understand that Salim's business holdings in the guise of escort agencies were nothing more than brothels for rich men. But escort agencies were legal enterprises and the books, expertly doctored as they were, indicated nothing illegal transpired behind their doors; and so it was with all of his business enterprises.

Like the vast majority of Australian business-
men, Salim paid the appropriate taxes commensu-
rate with the declared income from his extensive
business holdings. However, although suspected by
the Australian Taxation Office but never proven, the
gulf between Salim's declared income and his actual
income was as wide as the Grand Canyon is to a
crack in a patch of sun-scorched earth. By even the
most diligent of observers, Salim appeared to be exactly what he claimed to be, an honest, hardworking, successful Australian businessman, proud of his
Lebanese heritage and extremely grateful for the
opportunities presented to him by his adopted
country.

Appearances however, can be, and in Salim
Ghandour's case were, deceiving. Salim was about
as dishonest and as crooked a character as anyone
would ever meet. His business enterprises were a
front, a means to launder the millions he made from
the illegal drug trade. The police knew it, the Australian Taxation Office knew it, the government
knew it, and the vast majority of the general public
suspected it. However, proving it was another matter
entirely, and as long as that remained the status quo,
Salim's wealth would continue to grow.

As for his bail, well that was just a minor bump
in the road for Salim. One million dollars cash for
himself and another million for his son, Hakim. He

would make that back in just a few days. Not that it really mattered; Salim Ghandour was that wealthy he would never miss two million dollars. It was never about the financial penalty for Salim, it was about the inconvenience, and the stain the publicity left upon his reputation as a responsible, hard-working member of society.

There was an outcry of course, driven mostly by the media who had a love/hate relationship with Salim. But Salim was never one to cry foul over what he considered to be biased reporting. He rarely ever read a newspaper or watched television anyway, and the media was always going to sensationalise their stories because that's what sold newspapers and drove television ratings. It was all bullshit according to Salim. Shit, he had enough money to buy every media outlet in the country should he choose to do so. Fuck the media! Fuck the courts! Fuck their bail! These were the mantras Salim Ghandour lived by.

The biggest problem Salim had was where to hide his undeclared income, and there was plenty of it. He couldn't put it in the bank; that would be like walking into the Australian Taxation Office and saying, "I'm a crook, I have hundreds of millions of dollars in cash hidden in a warehouse in the suburbs."

Salim bought real estate in several countries, countries that wouldn't know Salim Ghandour from

Santa Claus. He set up dummy corporations in dummy names and invested in dummy enterprises as a means to launder the torrent of cash flowing in from his illegal drug dealings and still he couldn't spend it all. So the bulk of it actually *was* stashed in a warehouse in the suburbs of Sydney.

Only three people ever knew of the existence of the warehouse, himself, his son Hakim, and his late son Ahmed. Now, following the murder of Ahmed, only he and Hakim knew. The police assumed there had to be millions in cash hidden somewhere but, much to their frustration, they never found it when they raided the Ghandour estate. They found nothing because there was nothing to find. Salim was way too smart to get caught with evidence in his home, or indeed in Hakim's or Ahmed's homes. They came at dawn, over twenty of them, and eleven hours later they left, frustrated and empty handed.

It wasn't the raid so much that concerned Salim. They had come before and would undoubtedly come again. It was inconvenient and intimidating not to mention time consuming putting everything back together after the cops left. They seemed to take great pleasure in turning furniture upside down, opening containers, emptying cupboards, and leaving without putting it all together again. It was particularly upsetting to see them enter Ahmed's empty home, ransack it, and then leave it that way. Salim's wife cried a lot when they raided Ahmed's home; she liked to keep it just the way it was when her beloved son died and she went in almost daily just to make sure everything was the same as when she left it the previous day.

The crying made Salim angry. The police didn't care that Ahmed was dead; they didn't even seem to spend a lot of time looking for his son's killer. To them, Ahmed was just another scum-bag drug dealer who they no longer had to concern themselves with. Still, they ransacked his home every time they came and every time they found nothing, and every time Salim's wife cried.

Salim held Jackson Traynor directly responsible for his wife's tears. He held him responsible for the inconvenience of the raids on his estate and he held him responsible for the threat which now hung over his empire.

He trusted Traynor, loved him like a son. Traynor had been to Salim's home many times, had been welcome in his very private study, had been invited to sit in the plush, leather settee and drink from the well-stocked wet-bar, and had been welcomed many times to sit at the family table. Traynor betrayed that trust. He betrayed the love and friendship extended to him by Salim and his family. In

Salim Ghandour's world you do not betray a man's trust and expect there not be consequences.

Traynor had to die. It was not something that Salim anguished over. There would be no second chances, betrayal did not warrant a second chance, and there would be no grieving when it was done. It was what it was. The contract was offered and accepted. Now it was just a matter of waiting until it was done and Salim hoped that it would be sooner rather than later. If he were to have any regrets at all, it would be that he would not be there to look Traynor in the eye and pull the trigger himself. But that was not his way. Expensive as it was, assassination was best left to others, those far more qualified than him.

He leaned back in his comfortable chair and drew deeply on the six-inch, forty-three-gauge, Cazadores, his favourite choice of cigar, fully imported directly from Cuba. He lifted his head and exhaled a thick plume of strong cigar smoke towards the ornate ceiling.

A light knock on his door interrupted his few moments of contemplation. "Come in," he called softly.

Hakim Ghandour opened the doors and stepped into his father's office. He stood behind the Chesterfield settee and looked at his father. "I'm sorry to interrupt, father."

"What is it, Hakim?"

"I have spoken with Millard."

"Traynor is dead?" Salim asked hopefully.

"Millard doesn't know."

"What do you mean he 'doesn't know?'"

"Traynor is not at the safe-house in Ti Tree."

"Where is he?"

"A couple of cops from Alice Springs picked him up and took him to a cattle station north west of Ti Tree," Hakim explained.

"Why?"

"It seems the safe-house may have been compromised."

"Compromised? Of course it was fucking compromised! Millard compromised it himself. That's how we knew Traynor was in Ti Tree, for Christ's sake! Why doesn't he ring Williams, or Boyd, and find out what is happening?"

"Apparently there is no telephone reception at the cattle station. He is waiting for Williams to contact him."

"Allah, why do you forsake me?" Salim hissed, angrily.

"That's not all, father," Hakim added nervously.

"Why am I not surprised?"

"There are two other hit-men."

Salim lowered his eyes and placed his cigar down in a large marble ashtray on his desk. Then he looked up into his son's eyes. "Who are they?" he asked, quietly.

"I don't know." Hakim shrugged. "Millard didn't say. He just said they were sent by Miguel Alvarez."

"Alvarez?"

"Yes. He sent them over from Mexico."

Salim pushed away from his desk and leaned back in his chair. "So, let me see if I've got this right. There are four hit-men gunning for Traynor. They have followed him to some stinking cattle station in the middle of fuckin' nowhere, and we have no idea if they have found him or not. How am I doing, son?"

"There's still more."

"There's always more, Hakim," Salim said, shaking his head. "There is always fucking more. Tell me."

"According to Millard, the cops are expecting a military helicopter to arrive and pick up Traynor."

"And take him where?"

"Millard doesn't know. A secure location, probably a military base in Darwin."

Salim rose from his chair and walked slowly to the window overlooking a small section of the beautifully manicured gardens of his family estate. He stood in front of the window in silence, his back to his son, and stared out over the expanse of his domain.

Hakim knew better than to interrupt his father when he was in such a mood. Better to stay silent and wait until he was spoken to. He stared at his father's back, moved his feet restlessly, and waited.

With his back to his son, Salim continued. "Who do we have in Alice Springs?"

"There is no one, father. Obviously, Williams and Boyd were there, but we have no one else."

"We have people in Darwin, I know we do," Salim said, more to himself than to his son.

"Yes, we have people in Darwin. Some of our product comes into the harbour by boat from Indonesia."

"Speak to them," Salim ordered. "Explain the situation. Make sure they understand that, if Traynor gets on that helicopter, he is not to arrive in Darwin alive. They will know what to do."

"How will we know if he gets on the helicopter?" Hakim asked.

Salim turned back to face Hakim. "We all better hope we find out, son. Because if four professional killers can't do what they have been paid a small fortune to do, and Traynor gets to Darwin, life as we know it will be over."

"I'll get right on it, father."

Salim walked around his desk and moved across the big room. He stopped in front of the Chesterfield settee, looked across the top of it at Hakim and quietly addressed his son. "We have other people with the Federal Police on our payroll—we have no further use for Millard."

"I understand." Hakim nodded. "I'll take care of it."

Salim walked around the settee and stood directly in front of Hakim, their faces just inches apart. "Son," he began, "I'm not sure you fully understand the consequences facing our business, our family, if Traynor makes it into the courtroom."

"I understand, father," Hakim responded. "I do understand."

"Until this is over, stay off the product, and kick the spaced-out, bimbo, wannabe supermodels out of your bed."

Hakim lowered his eyes. "Yes, father," he mumbled.

"I mean it, Hakim," Salim insisted sternly. "You need to focus. Everything we have worked all our lives for is at risk. Now that your brother is gone, I rely on you to step up and fill the role he held in the business."

Overcome with shame, Hakim wanted to crawl under the carpet. "I understand, father," he mumbled even quieter.

Salim reached out and patted Hakim on the shoulder. "Good...good." He smiled. "Now, dinner. Here...tonight...eight o'clock. Your mother wants a family dinner. You know how she likes to cook for her family."

"Of course." Hakim turned to leave the room.

"Hakim," Salim said to his son's back.

Hakim stopped and turned back to face his father. "Yes?"

"Come alone, it's just the three of us. Be clean, and sober."

Hakim knew it wasn't a request, it was an order. "Of course, father." He walked from the room and pulled the heavy, double doors closed behind him.

———

Hakim Ghandour was intimidated by his father. He loved Salim; there was never any doubt in his mind in regards to the love he felt for both his parents and his late brother, Ahmed. But he felt his father was constantly comparing him to his older brother. Like he didn't quite measure up to the man Ahmed was.

As was the case with many family businesses, and particularly in traditional Middle-Eastern family businesses, there was a succession plan in place. When the head of the family, be it the patriarch or the matriarch, was no longer in charge due to death or retirement, the eldest child took over the day-to-day running of the business. As the eldest son, that was always going to be Ahmed Ghandour.

Ahmed was being groomed by his father for the eventual role of head of the family. He was a fast and enthusiastic learner. Salim doted on him, encouraging him at every opportunity, never failing to congratulate him on his progress.

Ever since Ahmed was killed, and Hakim became the next-in-line to ascend to the leadership of the Ghandour family, he felt he might get to experience some of the same adoration his dead brother enjoyed. He was still waiting. Instead, what he did feel was irrelevance in comparison to Ahmed. He envied Ahmed's success and secretly coveted the attention and overtly demonstrative gestures of pride bestowed upon him by their father.

Ahmed was never a drinker and he never touched drugs. He was the son every parent dreams of, respectful, loyal, ambitious, and clean-living. Hakim loved his late brother, but that didn't mean he didn't think he was a smarmy daddy's boy.

30

Before moving forward, Traynor looked down at the floor, looking for anything that might make a noise and give him away if he stepped on it. The floor was made of timber, a series of tongue-and-groove boards running lengthways along the hall-way, locked together, and nailed to timber joists beneath the house. The floorboards were old, probably been there since the house was built, he thought. They would creak in places where age had warped them and the nails had gradually loosened over time.

Jack moved forward slowly. This is where his military training once again came to the fore. As he moved, he placed each foot down on its outer edge and then slowly rolled the foot flat so his weight pressed down on the floor in gradual increments. The hallway was long and it was very slow going.

He paused after every step and glanced at the open doorway and the room beyond the end of the hallway. Someone was in the room; he could hear someone muttering softly. Maybe there was more than one person in the room. He cocked his head and listened intently. He was unable to discern what was being said, but the language was foreign. Spanish? Yes, it was Spanish, he decided. It had to be the Mexican he saw go back into the house from the rear veranda. He was talking to himself! Mumbling incoherently in his home tongue! Not a good sign, Jack thought; a lunatic Mexican killer talking to himself!

There was another door a few metres along the hallway from where he approached. The door was open, and when Jack reached it, he paused again, and took a tentative peak into the room. It looked like it was another bedroom but was being used as some sort of storeroom; cardboard boxes and piles of disused household items lay scattered around the floor.

He slipped silently past the open door and continued his agonisingly slow advance towards the end of the hallway. There were two more doors ahead of him, on the opposite side of the passage, a bathroom and a toilet, Jack guessed. The main door at the end of the hallway leading to the large room beyond opened inwards, towards the interior of the hallway. Jack slipped past the bathroom and toilet doors and edged himself behind the hall entrance door. Praying it would not squeak on old hinges, he pulled the door back against his body. He pressed himself into the tight corner and waited for his heart to stop racing.

Many years ago, the military taught Jack and his commando colleagues how to remain still and silent in an ambush position for many hours if required. They also taught him various methods of killing an enemy with his bare hands. It was a long time ago, but he never forgot; he didn't think he would ever forget something like that. He had killed enemy soldiers more times than he cared to think about, but never with his bare hands. Killing enemy soldiers silently with just your hands was more a close-contact, jungle warfare thing than it was a house-to-house clearance thing like it was in Afghanistan.

Technically, the Mexican in the next room just a few metres from where Jack stood was not an enemy soldier and the homestead was not the jungle. Vargas was, however, one of the men who raped and brutally murdered his wife and daughter and that was all the justification Jack needed to determine the arsehole had to die. And he was just the person to see that he did, and soon.

While shut away in a safe-house under twenty-four-seven security since the murders, Jack had come to the conclusion that he was probably never going to see the two men responsible for killing his family face justice and that angered him. Now, he knew he was close to seeing justice done, his way.

He was a cop now, a good one he liked to think, but if Herrera and Vargas were ever to face court for their crimes, a life in prison, particularly the relative comfort of an Australian prison, was never going to satisfy him. It was never going to atone for the loss of the two people he loved more than life itself.

There was such a thing as a justifiable killing, like killing someone to save yourself or another person from being killed. But killing someone out of vengeance was not, and never would be, considered justifiable, at least not by the Australian legal system. Right now, however, while hiding behind a hallway door on a remote cattle station in the middle of the Australian outback, Jackson Traynor was not concerned about what might or might not be considered justifiable. Just a few metres away, Ignacio Vargas, a sadistic, brutal, sex-crazed killer, the man who raped and butchered his beautiful wife and his precious twelve-year-old daughter, was so close he could almost smell him.

Jack silently holstered his weapon, leaned back

against the wall and inhaled a long, deep, silent breath.

————

Ignacio Vargas could not stay still. Pent-up frustrations pushed and prodded at his gut, screaming for release. He paced the floor of the kitchen area, walked into the large lounge room adjacent, and crossed to the open front door looking out over the wide veranda and the approach road beyond. Only the rental car he and Herrera arrived in stood in front of the house. He looked away to the north and saw no vehicles approaching, not even a dust cloud in the distance indicating a vehicle might be heading towards the house. He hurried back to the kitchen which opened onto the rear veranda of the homestead where Herrera and the two gringo killers were attempting to negotiate with the police in the shed.

They were never going to hand Traynor over, Vargas thought. The police in this country were not like those back home. In Mexico, there were many police officers willing to cooperate with Miguel Alvarez providing the price was high enough; the late Pablo Escobar was testament to that. Escobar had police, politicians, and local government officials on his payroll for years. If he couldn't entice them to aid him, he had them killed, or he had their family killed. Miguel Alvarez was the new Pablo Escobar. Just like Escobar, Alvarez had more money than many small countries and he would kill anyone he considered a threat to his making even more millions. Some he killed simply because he didn't like them. It was this most basic, uncomplicated approach to running his vast drug empire that made Miguel Alvarez a hero in Vargas's eyes.

Ignacio hoped to actually meet the man he admired most in the world someday. Perhaps soon, he thought. When this was over and the rat cop Traynor was dead, he would be the toast of the international drug syndicate. Alvarez would love him, might even invite him to stay at his secret estate, one of several hideaways he owned hidden deep in the hills behind Mexico City. It was a pity Herrera would be invited there as well, he thought. Maybe Herrera might be killed in the battle that surely loomed just beyond where Vargas paced the kitchen floor. He paused and smiled at the prospect.

First, he had to kill Traynor. The cops were never going to hand him over, despite the numerous threats to the caretaker. *I'm gonna slice that old el bastardo up too*, Vargas decided.

He would get Traynor himself. Herrera and the two gringos could negotiate all they liked but the police were never going to agree to their demands to surrender Traynor. He would do it himself. He was the best knife-man in the business; he had proved it many times. Fuck getting caught up in a shoot-out. Many, many men and a couple of disease-ridden, drug-addicted whores had fallen to his skill with the knife. It would not be difficult. Traynor would never see him coming. He would be on top of him before he knew what hit him. Vargas felt himself once again becoming aroused at the thought. He rubbed at his crotch, lifted the long-bladed, serrated-edge knife in front of his face, and smiled at his distorted reflection in the shiny blade. "*Pronto, mi uno bonito, pronto*," he whispered.

———

Traynor stood silently listening for sounds from the lounge room. He heard Vargas shuffling back and forth from the kitchen to the lounge room, and back again, sometimes mumbling incoherently to himself. The bastard was quite mad, Jack thought.

The hallway was wide, and when the door behind which he waited was opened all the way to its limit, it touched the wall without contacting him. A plan began to form in his mind. On his left side, attached to his belt, he wore a leather pouch containing a spare magazine for the Sig Sauer 9mm semi-automatic pistol. Silently, he opened the pouch and removed the spare magazine. Muffling any sound by holding it tight against his body, he slipped one round out and replaced the magazine in its pouch. Then he waited.

Eventually, Vargas came back into the lounge room and crossed to the front door. Must be checking for police back-up, Jack thought. He listened to the Mexican mumbling quietly for a few moments and then he pushed the door aside just enough to get his arm out and tossed the 9mm round as far along the passage as he could. It clattered to the wooden floor almost reaching the far end of the hallway.

————

Vargas started at the sound and spun around towards the open hallway door. "*Que carajo fue eso?*" he muttered. The noise seemed to come from the hallway. Was there someone else inside the house? Cautiously, he stepped across to the open door, paused, and peered into the gloom along the length of the wide corridor. He saw no one, at least not in the hallway. He could see doors on both sides of the long corridor. Was there someone hiding in one of the rooms? What was the noise he heard? It was an old house; maybe it was just the sound of old timbers creaking. Maybe not. Maybe it was something else. Something sinister. Perhaps he was not alone in the house. "*Pinche bastardo*," he mumbled softly.

He reached out and pushed on the open door only to find it was tight against the hallway wall. He raised the knife, held it in front of his body, and stepped cautiously forward into the hallway. He stopped, cocked his head and listened. All he could hear was the sound of muffled voices coming from outside on the back veranda. He took another step forward into the hallway and paused again. His eyes darted nervously from doorway to doorway along the length of the passage. Eventually, becoming a little more satisfied the noise he heard was benign and unthreatening, he stepped forward again... once...twice.

Startled by a soft rustle of movement from behind, he started to turn and saw just a glimpse of movement as a strong arm flashed in front of his face and closed around his throat. Then another arm hit him hard in the back of the neck and locked with the arm in front. A vice-like grip closed against his throat, shutting off any sound and all air. He could not breathe. He could not call out. With his free hand, he clasped at the arm around his throat, struggling to pull it away and break free of the hold, but it was useless. Whoever had him around his neck was very strong. He tried to speak. Only a muffled groan came from his throat. Suddenly, his legs were lifted from the floor to a point where they hung, kicking furiously at thin air.

"You have only seconds left to live!" a warm, soft voice whispered against his ear. "How does it feel, arsehole?"

Vargas tried again to speak. No sound came other than more grunting. He could not breathe and felt himself beginning to panic. He was choking. He kicked wildly, trying to strike the man behind him, but his short, bandy legs swung about ineffectively, striking nothing but air. He clawed furiously albeit vainly at the arm around his neck. His face was burning and his eyes began to water. He tried to suck life-giving air through his nose but nothing got past the restriction in his throat.

"My name is Jackson Traynor," Jack hissed. "Before you die, I want you to know who is killing you. You raped and murdered my wife and my daughter. I have longed for this day. How does it feel, knowing you are about to die?"

Vargas tried again to inhale air through his nose and mouth. Nothing happened. The air would not pass beyond the back of his throat. Then, from somewhere amid the confusion and panic surging through his mind, he understood. The man who held him, the man who was slowly suffocating him, was Jackson Traynor.

Slapping and clawing at the arm around his

throat, his hand holding the knife flailed wildly, in-effectively, slicing at the air in front of his face. As he felt his life rapidly slipping away, he focused on the knife. It was his only hope. Mustering all his will power, he swung the blade wildly backwards but hit nothing. The arm around his throat tightened even more. Now his hand grasping at the arm at his neck, and his fingers clutching the knife, were rapidly growing numb. He tried to flex his fingers on his free hand and could not feel them.

"Drop the knife, arsehole!" the voice behind him hissed.

Vargas tried again to thrust the knife backwards. This time he attempted to lift his arm and stab blindly behind his head, hoping to strike Traynor in the face. His arm rose only as high as his chest. All feeling in his fingers clasped around the hilt of the knife was gone. The knife fell from his fingers and clattered to the floor at his feet. He tried to look down but could not move his head, up or down. In desperation, he clutched with both hands at the arm squeezed tightly at his throat. He clawed, scratched, and slapped at the arm but it only squeezed tighter. Ignacio Vargas had never begged for anything in his life; now he wanted to. He was dying, and he was afraid. He tried again to speak. This time not even a muffled groan escaped his lips. He felt himself fading into unconsciousness.

"You are dying, arsehole!" the voice whispered in his ear. "Can you feel it? Your lungs are almost out of air. This might be a good time to make your peace with God. But, not quite yet."

Suddenly, Vargas felt the arm around his throat ease just a fraction. Just enough to allow him to suck a small amount of air into his lungs. Then it tightened again, crushing his larynx.

"Her name was Jessica!" Traynor hissed. "She was twelve years old. My wife's name was April! You butchered them, you son-of-a-bitch! Now, you have to pay for what you took from me! The very last thing you are going to hear is their names." Jack squeezed tighter, his right wrist locked tightly in his left hand. The Mexican's legs stopped kicking and now swung limply in front of him.

"Are you listening, arsehole?" Traynor whispered close to Vargas's ear. "Don't die yet!" He leaned his head closer until his lips almost touched the Mexican's ear. "Their names were Jessica and April! Jessica and April!" he repeated. He squeezed tighter. "Now you can die!" Suddenly he twisted Vargas's head sharply sideways and he heard a loud crack. Vargas's body went limp in his arms. The Mexican was dead, his neck snapped like a dry twig. Jack lowered the body to the floor and stepped a pace away from it.

Vargas's left leg twitched once, twice, and then lay still.

"Fuckin' arsehole!" Traynor said to the Mexican's body. He kicked the corpse, turned his back and moved to the entrance of the main lounge room. He paused at the doorway and leaned against the jamb, sucking large mouthfuls of air into his lungs, and waited for his racing heartbeat to slow. He looked into the large room beyond, satisfying himself that there was no one else inside the house.

On an island bench separating the lounge from the kitchen, a satellite phone caught his eye immediately. He took a cautious step into the lounge and paused again, casting his eyes around the room. Voices from the veranda outside reinforced his assessment that he was indeed alone. He decided to risk crossing the room and taking the satellite phone. He unholstered his weapon, moved swiftly across the room, and picked up the bulky phone. With a cautious glance towards the back door, he moved quickly back to the hallway, stepped around the body of Ignacio Vargas, administering another kick in the process, and then hurried along the passage to the room where he first entered the house.

Having climbed back out through the bedroom window, and then over the veranda railing, he crept to the end of the veranda and paused. Raised voices still negotiated back and forth between the men on the veranda and Barker, Foley, and Rose in the shed. He focused on the distance between where he crouched and the shed, calculating his chances of making it across the open ground without getting shot by one or more of the killers on the veranda. He was a fast runner, he was fit, and under any other circumstances he would not even think about it, he would just run. It was only about thirty metres, he guessed, and should take no longer than a few seconds. But, for those few seconds, he would be exposed and vulnerable.

He did, however, have the element of surprise. The men on the veranda believed he was in the shed with the others. Surprise was good; it worked against the Taliban in Afghanistan. That was several years ago, but, if anything, he was fitter now that he was back then. *Don't spend too much time thinking about it,* he said to himself. *That's when things turn to shit. Just get up and do it. It's only thirty metres. Do it! Do it now!*

Clutching the satellite phone tightly in one hand, he checked his weapon was secure in its holster, rose to a sprint position and darted from the cover of the house.

31

Don Williams glimpsed movement in his peripheral vision, off to his right, towards the end of the long veranda. "What the fuck...?" he cried. A man sprinted from behind the end of the house towards the shed. He raised the gun and fired at the running man. The shot went wide and then the runner was gone, disappeared behind the far end of the shed.

Bill Kirkwood flinched as the gun fired in front of his face. "Jesus fuckin' Christ!" he yelled. He clasped his ear and staggered backwards as the roar of the weapon temporarily deafened him.

"What was it?" Luke Boyd asked.

"Someone ran behind the shed," Williams answered.

"From where?"

"From the end of the fuckin' house."

"Who ees it?" Rodolfo Herrera asked.

"I don't fuckin' know," Williams said with undisguised contempt. "He didn't stop and present his ID," he added sarcastically.

"*Que*?" Herrera asked.

"Jesus Christ!" Kirkwood rubbed furiously at his ear. "You fuckin' nearly killed me!"

Williams tapped Kirkwood on the forehead with the barrel of his weapon. "Quit whining, old man. You're still alive...for the moment."

"Was it a cop?" Boyd asked.

"That would be my guess," Williams answered.

"What the fuck was he doing behind the house?"

"Maybe he was *in* the house."

Boyd looked across to the back door. "*Inside*?" he queried.

Williams shrugged. "I don't know, maybe."

"*Que*?" Herrera said again.

Williams turned his attention to the Mexican. "Why don't you shut the fuck up with the '*que?*' bullshit. Speak fuckin' English. This is Australia, you moron."

"Moroon...what means this moroon?" Herrera asked.

"It means idiot," Williams answered.

Herrera raised his weapon and pointed it at Williams. "*Idiota*? You call me *idiota*?"

Suddenly, Herrera froze as Boyd placed the barrel of his weapon against the back of his head.

"*Jay, caramba!*" Herrera cried in surprise.

"Pull the trigger and you won't even hear the next shot!" Boyd warned.

"Don't ever pull a gun on me again, Mex," Williams said. "If you do it will be the last move you ever make."

"You threaten me, senor?"

"Yes, you can bet your Mexican arse I threaten you. The next move is yours."

Boyd pushed the barrel harder into the back of Herrera's head, leaned forward and said with menace, "Don't do it, Pancho!"

"Pancho? My name is Rodolfo, senor."

"Pancho, Rudolf, whatever. Don't do it!"

Herrera slowly lowered his weapon. "Okay, okay. Everything ees okay."

"Good," Williams said. "Now, why don't you go inside and check on your friend." He indicated the end of the veranda. "I'd like to know where that cop came from."

"He ees not my friend," Herrera said adamantly.

"Check on him anyway," Williams ordered.

Herrera did not like taking orders from anyone, least of all the two gringos. However, starting a gun-fight with them here on the veranda of a house in the middle of nowhere would not be such a smart thing to do, he decided. Right now, leaving this place far behind him seemed more attractive than it ever did. Just the same, it would be nice to kill them both before he left. He shrugged indifferently. "Okay, senor. I weel go inside." He turned away and stepped across to the back door of the house.

———

"Jesus!" Sam flinched at the sound of the gunshot. He looked across at Barker. "What's going on? Please tell me they haven't shot the caretaker."

"No," Barker answered. "He's okay. One of the others fired wildly towards the end of the house."

"What at?" Foley asked.

"I don't know," Barker said. "I can't see."

Sam noticed movement from the open end of the shed, behind the station vehicle. He turned towards the vehicle and raised his Glock. "We've got company," he warned.

Foley and Barker raised their weapons and turned towards the end of the shed just as Traynor stepped out from behind the Toyota.

"Easy, chaps," Traynor called. "Don't fuckin' shoot me. That's their job." He thrust his thumb in the direction of the house.

"Jack!" Barker called. "Was that you one of them shot at?"

"He missed." Traynor smiled. He walked to where Barker, Foley, and Rose stood.

"Glad to hear it," Barker said, lowering his weapon. "Is that a sat phone?" he asked, indicating the satellite phone Traynor carried.

"Yeah."

"Where did you get it?" Sam asked.

"In the kitchen."

"In the house?" Foley said incredulously.

"Yeah, it was just sitting there on the bench top." Traynor smiled.

"You went inside the house?" Barker asked.

"Yep."

"How did you do that without getting caught?" Sam asked.

"It wasn't hard." Traynor shrugged. "Climbed in through a bedroom window. All but one of them were outside on the veranda."

"What about the Mexican inside?" Barker asked.

"Ignacio Vargas. He never saw me."

"You climbed through a window, walked into the kitchen, took the sat phone, climbed out again, and he never saw you?" Foley said.

"No."

"Where is he now?" Foley asked.

"In the hallway."

"What's he doing?" Foley asked suspiciously.

"Nothing. He's dead."

Foley looked at Traynor, then at Barker, then at Sam, and then back at Traynor. "Dead?"

Traynor nodded. "As a door-nail."

"How did he die, Jack?" Barker asked suspiciously.

Traynor smiled. "Tripped, took a tumble, and broke his neck."

"A tumble?"

"Well...yeah...sort of."

"I'm not sure we want to know any more details," Barker said.

"Might be for the best," Jack agreed.

"I'd like to know," Sam said. "How did you manage all that?"

"The military taught me well, Sam. I'm very good at what I do."

"Okay...okay," Barker said. "We can discuss the Mexican's bad fortune later. Right now, we have an innocent man out there with a gun to his head. We need to think about him. It's getting late and there are way too many guns being waved about for us to be stumbling around in the dark trying to free him."

"Who are the other two dudes on the veranda?" Traynor asked.

"Don't know," Barker answered. "There's a

couple of motorcycles parked between us and the house. I don't think they belong to the caretaker."

"I saw them," Traynor said.

"They look like Harleys," Barker said.

"Harley Davidsons?"

"Yeah."

"Fuck! Williams and Boyd!"

"What?" Barker asked. "You know those blokes?"

"Not personally. But, I know of them."

"Do tell," Barker invited.

"They work exclusively for Salim Ghandour," Traynor explained.

"Hired guns?" Foley asked.

"Assassins would be a better job description for those two arse-wipes. They too are very good at what they do. If they are here, there will be more killing before this day is over. You can bet your house on it."

Rose turned to Foley. "This is turning out to be an interesting day," he said.

"And getting more so as the day progresses." Foley nodded.

32

Rodolfo Herrera re-entered the house through the back door, quickly crossed the kitchen and entered the large loungeroom. Ignacio Vargas was nowhere in sight. He moved to the open front door and looked out onto the front veranda. Vargas was not there. He turned and walked to the centre of the room. "Vargas, *d'onde estás*?" he called softly. He received no answer. Growing concerned, he looked across to the hallway door. It was only slightly ajar. He was certain it was wide open before they all went out onto the rear veranda. Perhaps Vargas was in the bathroom, he thought. He moved across the room and stood before the partially closed hallway door. "Vargas," he called again. "*Estás allí*?" He received no response. Now, his concern deepened. He raised his pistol and, with the barrel, gently pushed on the door. It opened a short distance and then stopped. He pushed again. Something was preventing the door from opening all the way. With his free hand, he pushed harder and the door would not open any further than half way before meeting solid resistance.

With his weapon held in front of him, he stepped closer to the door and dared to sneak a look around it into the hallway beyond. "*Ay caramba!*" he gasped as he saw the body of Ignacio Vargas lying face up on the floor, his head on an angle at odds with the rest of his body.

Rodolfo Herrera knew immediately that Vargas was dead. It was not something that frightened him, or even caused him any grief. Vargas was a fool; an *idiota*. Herrera was not sorry the madman was dead and he certainly would not miss him. If someone else had not killed him, he would have done it himself before he returned to Mexico. He would have left his twisted, misshapen corpse abandoned in the desert to wither under the hot Australian sun until his bones were bleached white.

While Vargas's death did not concern Herrera, it did indicate someone else had been in the house, someone other than the caretaker and the four of them sent to kill Traynor. A cop, perhaps. Were there more police than those in the shed, he wondered? Perhaps they were still inside.

He looked suspiciously along the hallway, noticing for the first time several doors on either side of the long passage. He held his weapon in a two-handed grip in front of him, constantly moving it from left to right and back again across the width of the passage. If there was someone else inside the house, they could be in any one of the rooms in front of him. Silently, he stepped around Vargas's body and slowly, cautiously edged along the hallway, his back close to the wall.

He searched every room, even opened wardrobes and looked under the beds. Whoever had been inside the house, whoever killed Ignacio Vargas, was gone. In the master bedroom, he noticed the open window and immediately realised this is where the intruder entered and then left after killing Vargas.

Satisfied the intruder had left, he hurried back along the hallway to the kitchen and then out to the back veranda.

Don Williams turned and glared at Herrera as he came outside. "Where the fuck have you been?" he asked.

Herrera glared back at Williams. "Inside the house, senor."

"Where is your friend?"

"I tol you, senor, he ees not my friend."

"You know what, Mex, I don't give a flying fuck if he's your friend or not. Where is he?" Williams asked again.

Herrera shrugged. "Senor Vargas ees no more."

"What do you mean 'no more?'" Boyd stepped closer to Herrera. "Has he left?"

"Si, he ees gone."

"Gone where?" Boyd pushed.

Herrera shrugged again. "To God, senor," he said indifferently.

"He's dead?" Williams asked.

"Si. He ees dead."

"You killed him?" Williams asked.

"No, senor, I did not keel him."

"How did he die?" Boyd asked.

"A broken neck, I think."

"A broken neck? Who did that? Is anyone else in the house?" Williams asked.

"There ees no one else."

"Traynor," Boyd murmured.

"I agree," Williams said. "Had to be the bastard we saw run from the end of the house."

"Traynor was een the house?" Herrera asked.

"He's in the shed now." Boyd nodded, indicating Williams. "That was the dude my friend fired at."

Herrera stepped forward to the veranda railing, leaned out, and looked towards the end of the house. "There ees nobody else?" he asked, turning to face Williams.

"No," Williams said. "There's no one else. They are all in the shed."

"You missed him, senor," Herrera said. "I theenk you are not so good a shot as I am."

"Here's a tip, *senor*!" Williams spat. "Climb back in that piss-fartin' Japanese shit-box you came here in and get the fuck out of here."

Herrera looked confused. "What means this 'pees-fartin' sheet-box?'"

Suddenly, the tension level in the air shot into the stratosphere. Boyd took one step closer to Herrera. "It means you should leave and go back to where you came from," he said with undisguised threat in his tone.

"You want me to leave thees place?"

Boyd looked at Williams. "I think Pancho's finally got it," he said, sarcastically.

"About fuckin' time." Williams turned his attention back to Bill Kirkwood, placed his weapon close to the side of his head, the muzzle almost touching a spot just above the caretaker's ear. He called loudly to the occupants in the shed. "Hey, you in the shed! Can you hear me?"

"We hear you," Cameron Barker called back.

"Who was that?" Williams called.

"Who was who?" Barker asked.

"Don't fuck with us!" Williams threatened. "The dude who ran from the house, was that Traynor?"

"I told you, Traynor is not here!" Foley answered.

"And you are a lying sack of shit!" Williams yelled. "Traynor! Jackson Traynor! Are you in the shed?"

Traynor stepped forward and Barker restrained him by grabbing his arm. "Don't go out there, Jack," he warned. "The bastards will shoot you on sight."

"I'm not going to hide here in the shed and watch them kill another innocent person!" Traynor declared adamantly.

"Yap is right, Jack," Sam said. "If you go out there you'll die and they'll kill the caretaker anyway. They're not going to leave any witnesses behind."

"What do you suggest we do?" Traynor asked, the frustration evident in his voice.

"Wait them out," Barker answered. "There is a military chopper on the way. If it's not already en-route, it will be soon."

"What about the caretaker?"

"He's their only bargaining chip. If they kill him before they have you, they have nothing to deal with."

"The chopper could be hours away," Traynor said. "It's going to be dark soon. We need to do something."

"The darkness will work in our favour," Foley

said. "We know where they are but, if they can't see us, they won't know exactly what we are doing."

"I have an idea," Barker said. "Pass me that sat phone."

Traynor passed the satellite phone to Barker who walked away towards the rear of the shed.

33

Sergeant John Singh had been moving back and forth between the first crime scene at the road-house and the second in the woods bordering the safe-house. Currently he was supervising two of his forensic specialists hovering studiously over the bodies of the two Federal police officers shot in the woods. When his phone rang, he fished it from his pocket and walked a few paces away from where his investigators worked at photographing, measuring, and taking notes of their observations.

"John Singh."

"Singo, it's Cameron Barker."

"Hey, boss, I've been trying to call you."

"There's no phone reception out here. I'm using the caretaker's satellite phone. Is everything all right there?"

"Yeah. I just wanted to let you know that I have organised a vehicle to collect the bodies and transport them to Alice Springs."

"Good. What about Task Force?"

"Should be on their way here as we speak. Probably be another hour or so."

"Okay, send them straight here to Aningie Station when they arrive."

"Will do, boss. Everything okay out there?"

"Not exactly. We have a stand-off. Three perps in the house holding the caretaker hostage. Foley, Rose, and Jack Traynor are with me, in a shed about thirty metres from the house."

"Three perps?" Singh asked curiously.

"Yeah. There were four but one has been eliminated."

"You got one of them?"

"Not me, Singo. Jack Traynor took care of one of the Mexicans."

"Onya, Jack!" Singh said loudly. "Where did the other two perps come from?"

"Like the Mexicans, they are hired killers. Apparently these two are Salim Ghandour's personal hit-men."

"What a fuckin' mess!" Singh exclaimed. "Are you chaps okay?"

"Yeah," Barker answered. "For the moment. Our main concern is for the caretaker. Right now, he is standing on the back veranda of the house with a gun at his head."

"What can I do?"

"Tell Task Force to get their fuckin' skates on. We're bottled up here."

"Okay, boss. I'll get straight on it. Anything else?"

"Have you caught up with the two local chaps?"

"Yeah," Singh said. "Fowler and Rooney, they're here with me now."

"Send them out here, Singo. Tell them to set up a road block at the entrance to Aningie Station. The perps have one car and two motorcycles. If they make a run for it, Fowler and Rooney may be able to stop them."

"Two motorcycles?"

"Yeah, they belong to Ghandour's men. Tell Fowler and Rooney to make sure they are well armed. These pricks are not going to give up without a fight."

"Okay, boss. You blokes take care."

"Will do, Singo. Talk to you soon." Barker disconnected the call. He walked further towards the back of the shed, glanced quickly back at his three colleagues, and then dialled another number on the satellite phone.

———

Singh placed his phone back in his pocket and looked across to where Senior Constable Jim 'Chook' Fowler and his junior partner Constable Mathew 'Mickey' Rooney waited at the edge of the tree line.

Both Fowler and Rooney were experienced officers and had, at times during their respective careers, been present at murder scenes, but nothing quite like this. This was confronting: two murder scenes and four dead Federal cops. Murder never happened in the tiny village of Ti Tree, at least not in the time Fowler and Rooney had been there. Mostly their duties revolved around the occasional drunk and disorderly local resident, a rare motor vehicle accident on the Stuart Highway which ran through the centre of the township, and regular courtesy calls to the outlying cattle stations and aboriginal settlements within their patrol area. They stood together at the outer limit of the taped-off area around the scene and watched as Singh approached.

"We are out all day on routine patrol and we come home to this," Fowler said. "What the fuck happened, Sarge?"

"It's a fucking mess," Singh said.

"Is this all about the Federal guy from the safe-house?" Fowler asked.

"Yeah, Jackson Traynor. Unfortunately, it is."

"Okay. What do you want us to do?"

"You know Aningie Station, right?"

"Yeah. We were there this morning. We call in there about once a month to check on the old chap who looks after the place."

"I just spoke to Superintendent Cameron Barker. He's out there now with Inspector Russell Foley, Sergeant Sam Rose, and Jackson Traynor."

"We've met Traynor," Fowler said. "What are they all doing out at Aningie?"

"Trying to stay alive it seems."

"What's going on?" Mickey Rooney asked.

"Four hit-men were sent up here gunning for Traynor. At least two of them are responsible for all this shit." Singh indicated the bodies of the two Federal cops. "Somehow, they found out Traynor went to Aningie and they followed him out there."

"To kill him?" Rooney asked.

"That's what hit-men do, Mickey."

"Four hit-men!" Fowler said. "This is some pretty heavy shit."

"Apparently there are only three of them now," Singh said. "Traynor got one of them."

"That's one for the good guys," Rooney said.

"Why did Traynor go to Aningie?" Fowler asked. "We understood Foley and Rose were supposed to escort him back to Alice Springs."

"That was the original plan. It seems the killers

got wind of the plan so Barker changed it. Apparently, a military chopper is coming from up north to fly Traynor to a military base in Darwin."

"How did the baddies find out Traynor was at Aningie?" Rooney asked.

"I don't know for certain. Apparently, there is a leak in the Federal police organisation."

"A dirty cop?" Fowler said disgustedly.

Singh nodded. "That's how it appears."

"Okay," Fowler said. "What do you want from us?"

"Barker wants you to go back out to Aningie and set up a road block at the entrance road in case the baddies decide to make a run for it."

"Okay, we can do that."

"Gotta be more exciting than hosing piss and vomit out of the cells every morning," Rooney scoffed.

"You chaps got plenty of firepower?"

Fowler nodded. "Yeah. We've got our issue side-arms and a .308 Remington we use for shooting injured stock."

"Good. Get the .308 plus extra ammo for your personal weapons." Singh paused before continuing. "And pray you don't have to use any of it."

"You think we *might* need it?" Rooney asked.

"I hope not. But we are dealing with professional killers. If you are unlucky enough to meet them, they are not going to shake your hand and invite you to have a beer. Wear your Kevlar, stay alert and be prepared for anything."

"Hope for the best and prepare for the worst," Fowler added. He clapped his partner on the shoulder. "Okay partner, you ready for this?"

"Yeah," Rooney answered. "I'm not jumping up and down with enthusiasm, but I'm ready."

34

Cameron Barker rejoined Foley, Rose, and Traynor at the front of the shed. "Task Force is on the way," he announced to the small group. "Should be here soon."

"Can the caretaker hang on?" Sam asked.

"I think he will be okay as long as Jack is in here with us," Barker said. "If they kill him they have nothing."

Foley turned to Sam. "The point is, can *we* hang on? Standing around in this shed doing nothing is starting to get to me."

"It will be dark soon," Barker said. "We can use that to our advantage. And remember, there are only three of the bastards now, thanks to Jack. Let's put our heads together and work on a plan of action."

"They won't stand out there on the veranda after it gets dark," Traynor said. "They will be exposed, backlit by the lights inside the house. They're killers, but they're not stupid."

"If they go inside, it will give us the chance to move without being seen," Foley said.

"How did these arseholes know we were coming here to Aningie?" Sam asked.

"I think I can answer that, Sam," Barker said. He turned to face Traynor. "How well do you know Vaughn Millard, Jack?"

"He's sort of my boss," Traynor answered with a shrug. "I met him when they put me in the witness protection program. Why?"

"He's the OIC of Witness Protection. Right?"

"Yeah, but I don't know him well. I dealt mostly with his subordinates."

"Could he be the leak?"

Traynor paused momentarily considering the suggestion. "It's like I said. I haven't had a lot to do with him personally. We know there is a leak in the job somewhere, but I'm not privy to the investigation into who it might be. Why would you suspect him?"

"I'm not sure. But Sam asked how those blokes out there knew we were coming to Aningie. I spoke to Millard and told him we were bringing you here and we both agreed that, given there was a leak in your organisation, no one else should know about the plan. I assure you I told no one other than Sam and Russell. So that leaves Millard."

"Maybe he discussed it with others in his command," Traynor suggested.

Barker shrugged. "Maybe, but when we agreed not to, I took him at his word, particularly given the leak. Think about it. Millard has been close to this case right from the beginning. He knew where you lived with your family. He organised for you to go to the safe house at Ti Tree. And, as I understand it, he was an integral part of the illegal drug importation and distribution investigation team before he transferred to his current position. He had to know who all the players were. He probably knew, or at the very least suspected, who Ghandour used when he wanted someone hit."

"Williams and Boyd." Traynor nodded.

"Exactly. I think he might be the leak."

"I don't like to think about it. But what you say does make sense."

Suddenly, once again, the voice came loud from the veranda. "You pigs haven't gone to sleep in there have you?"

Barker stepped closer to the window. "No!" he called back. "We're not asleep!"

"I'm not going to ask again," Williams yelled. "Send Traynor out, or the old dude dies!"

"I'm not that old," Kirkwood muttered.

Williams rapped the caretaker on the head with the barrel of his weapon. "You shut the fuck up!" he hissed. "You're on borrowed time now, you fuckin' old prick. Any more smart-arse comments from you and you won't be getting any older."

"Your mother would be so proud," Kirkwood responded, rubbing vigorously at his head.

Williams hit him again, harder this time. "Are you deaf as well as stupid? Shut the fuck up!"

Kirkwood fell forward against the veranda railing; his glasses flew from his face and landed on the veranda deck at his feet. A thin trace of blood trickled down the side of his face.

"Hey!" Barker called from the shed. "Leave him alone! He's not involved in any of this!"

"He's involved if I say he's involved!" Williams called back. "Now, send Traynor out, or the old prick will get more than a smack on the head!"

"Are you Williams?" Barker asked.

Williams and Boyd exchanged surprised glances. "How the fuck do they know your name?" Boyd asked.

"That is your name, right?" Barker called. "Williams, or is it Boyd?"

"There's only one way they could know our names," Williams said to his partner.

"Traynor?" Boyd asked.

Williams nodded. "Traynor!" He turned towards the shed. "Come on out here, Jack!" he yelled. "We're gettin' tired of waiting! You wanna be responsible for old Billy Boy here gettin' one between the eyes?"

"There is a Task Force unit on the way!" Barker called. "How about we make a deal?"

"You gonna deal with these scumbags?" Jack asked incredulously.

"No, I'm trying to stall as long as I can."

"A deal?" Williams called back. "We don't deal with pigs!"

Sam looked at Foley. "That's twice he's used the *pig* word. I find that very offensive."

"You wanna go out there and tell him?" Foley asked.

Barker raised his hand to silence Sam and Foley and called back to the men on the veranda. "If you are still here when the Task Force gets here, there will be no way out for any of you. People are going to get killed! I have an offer for you that might just save your life."

"An offer?" Williams asked loudly. "Okay, arsehole, just for the fun of it let's hear your generous offer!"

"Send the caretaker in here to us. Then leave. We will not stop you."

"Not gonna happen, Porky!" Williams called back.

Barker looked at Sam. "*Porky*?" he said. "Now *I'm* offended."

"Poor breeding, boss," Sam offered. "That's what it is, poor breeding."

"It's a good offer!" Barker called back. "You would be wise to take it."

"Jam your offer!" Williams yelled. "Here's *our* offer! Send Traynor out here and you can have the caretaker! Take it or leave it!"

Traynor stepped up next to Barker. "Let me speak to him."

Barker shrugged. "Okay, but I don't think they're in any mood to negotiate."

"What's the caretaker's name?"

"Kirkwood. Bill Kirkwood."

Traynor moved closer to the window. "Hey, Williams!" he yelled. "It is Williams, isn't it?"

"Who wants to know?"

"Jackson Traynor!"

"Traynor, is that you?"

"Yeah, it's me."

"You kill the Mex?"

"He fell."

"Fell my arse!"

"You should listen to Superintendent Barker," Jack called. "This place is going to be swimming in police very soon. He's offering you an opportunity to get out while you still can."

"We'll leave, Traynor. Just as soon as you come outside and face us."

"Is Mister Kirkwood okay?"

"Not for much longer, arsehole!"

Jack dared a quick look out of the window. Long enough to notice the caretaker slumped against the veranda railing, a trace of blood on the side of the side of his face. "You okay, Bill?" he called loudly.

"Yeah!" Kirkwood called back. "Prick hits like a girl!"

Williams struck Kirkwood again with the barrel of his weapon. "What!" And then he hit him again, and again. "I hit like a girl! I hit like a girl! Does this feel like a hit from a fuckin' girl! Does it, you fuckin' crazy old bastard?"

Kirkwood raised his arms in a futile attempt to shield his face from the blows. He collapsed to his knees on the veranda floor, blood now running freely from an ugly gash on the side of his head. He teetered on his knees for a few moments and then fell sideways and collapsed on his back.

Williams leaned over Kirkwood's prone form. "How does it feel now, arsehole?" He spat on Kirkwood, drew his leg back, and kicked the caretaker in the ribs. "Get fuckin' smart with me, you fuckin' old geezer! Go ahead! There's plenty more where that came from!"

Boyd stepped forward and grabbed Williams by his arm. "Leave him, mate. Don't kill the old man yet. We still need him."

Williams turned from Kirkwood and stepped a few paces away. He leaned against the veranda railing, trying to calm his breathing and regain some degree of composure. "Fuckin' old coot!" he mumbled.

Boyd glanced down at the caretaker, satisfied himself he was still breathing, then joined Williams. "Mate," he said. "Maybe we should cut our losses and get the fuck out of here."

Williams glared at his partner. "What?"

"You heard them in the shed. This place is going to be swarming with cops very soon. Maybe we should get out now, while we still can."

"We've been paid a lot of money to do this job," Williams responded.

Boyd shrugged. "All we've done so far is trespass on the old dude's land and make a few threats. If Traynor gets to court with what he knows, Salim Ghandour, his drop-kick, drug-crazed son, and his entire outfit will spend the next fifty years in the slammer. How is he ever going to get his money back from us? Let's get, while the gettin's good."

"Have you forgotten about the deal we made

with each other all those years ago, when we first started in this business? If we ever found ourselves in a situation such as this, we would go out together, in a blaze of glory, and take as many pigs with us as we could."

"No, I haven't forgotten. But, if I recall, we made that deal after about a million beers and two bottles of bourbon. Have a look at where we are now, mate. We are independently wealthy, we know a thousand places we can disappear and never be found. Fuck Salim Ghandour, fuck Vaughn Millard, fuck Jack Traynor." He turned and indicated Rodolfo Herrera standing a few paces away. "And, fuck the chilli-eatin' Mexican."

"*Que?*" Herrera asked.

Boyd ignored Herrera. "What do you say?" he asked Williams. "Let's get out of here. This job has turned to shit. Forget about our deal years ago. If we stay here, we are almost certainly going to be killed. We've got money, plenty of it. We'll go north, towards Darwin. No one will ever find us."

Williams relaxed visibly. "Maybe you're right."

"You know I'm right, Don. Have a look around you. Look at this fuckin' place. It's in the middle of nowhere. It's like a fuckin' desert. Who wants to die out here?"

Williams looked around. The light was slowly fading as the sun sank towards the horizon in the west. If they were to stay and attempt to fulfil their contract with Salim Ghandour, the coming night would bring with it a different set of problems, not the least of which would be the arrival of police re-inforcements. His friend was right. They had to get away from Aningie Station and they had to do it soon. He turned back to face Boyd. "Okay. Let's get the fuck out of here."

Boyd stepped closer to the veranda railing. "Hey!" he called. "You in the shed! Can you hear me?"

"We can hear you!" Traynor called back.

"Your offer still on the table?"

Traynor looked at Barker who nodded his assent.

"The offer stands!" Traynor yelled to Boyd. "Is the caretaker alright?"

Boyd glanced back at the prone caretaker. "He'll live."

"Leave him and go," Traynor called.

Williams faced the shed. "We want free access to our bikes!"

Traynor looked questioningly again at Barker.

Barker shrugged. "Okay," he said quietly. "They won't get far."

Jack turned back to the window. "Okay! If you are going, go now!"

Herrera stepped forward, closer to Williams and Boyd. "You are leaving?" he asked.

"Yes, Pancho," Boyd answered. "We are leaving. You can stay if you want, but we are out of here."

"I weel leave also," Herrera announced.

Boyd shrugged indifference. "Suit yourself, mate." He turned to Williams. "You ready?"

"Yeah, I'm ready."

Both men moved to the steps leading down from the veranda. With their respective weapons aimed at the shed window, they made their way down the steps and across to where their Harleys were parked side by side.

35

Rodolfo Herrera watched the two gringos walk down the steps and climb onto their motorbikes. He watched as they placed matching black helmets on their heads, started their bikes and pulled away from the house. The loud, throaty burble from the twin Harley motorcycle engines reverberated loudly between the shed and the house.

Herrera was happy to see the belligerent gringos leave. He did not like them. He did not like the way they seemed to take control. This was his assignment, not theirs. He was never informed that the gringos would also be given the job of killing Jackson Traynor, something else he would have to take up with Miguel Alvarez when he got back home. However, now that they were gone, and now that Ignacio

Vargas was dead, he was alone. It was what he wanted all along, wasn't it? He always worked alone. Now that he was, why did it not feel the way it should?

What should he do now, he wondered? Police reinforcements were surely on the way and killing Traynor now seemed to be the only contract Rodolfo The Wolf Herrera was ever going to fail to complete. The whole thing had descended into a confusing chaotic shambles. The motorcycle riding gringos and their baseless threats to kill the care-taker were never anything more than bluff and bluster. They were never going to kill the old man, at least not while Traynor was still alive. They knew if they did, there would be nothing to stop the police from daring to attack and people would die, maybe even Traynor, maybe even himself. Herrera was not going to die here in the middle of nowhere in a foreign country. He needed to get back to Alice Springs and on board the first international flight out of Australia.

Alvarez would not be happy, but Alvarez could go fuck himself. This job had become way too complicated. Too many assassins, all trying to kill just one man. It should never have taken four professionals to do the job. The job should never have required Ignacio Vargas to accompany him to this awful country. Look how that ended! Vargas was dead. Laying on his back in the hallway inside the house, his neck all bent and twisted, like his legs.

Herrera doubted they would send Vargas's body back to Mexico. Not unless someone back home paid for it. Who was going to do that? Vargas had no family that Herrera knew of. Probably had no close friends either. He would probably be buried in some unspectacular cemetery somewhere in Australia, on the other side of the world from his homeland. No one would mourn for him. His name would pale into insignificance with the passage of time. Very little time, Herrera thought.

Such a fate, however, would not befall The Wolf. He would leave this place. Just like the gringo bike riders. It was not running, Herrera decided, it was a strategic withdrawal. Better to go back home and live to kill another day than to stay here and almost certainly die in this Godforsaken wilderness. He looked out over the wide expanse of barren country to the west of the homestead where the sun was rapidly sinking towards the distant horizon. Why would anyone live in this desolate, uninspiring land, let alone die in it, he wondered?

He looked down at the caretaker laying on the veranda clutching alternately at his bleeding head and his painful ribs. He stepped across to where Kirkwood lay and stood over him. "Today ees your lucky day, senor Kirkswood."

Kirkwood turned his head and looked up at the Mexican. "I told you, my name is Kirkwood," he mumbled.

Herrera shrugged. "Kirkswood, Kirkwood, ees no matter, senor."

"It matters to me."

"I weel leave this place," Herrera said, ignoring the caretaker's comment.

"You'll forgive me if I don't get up and see you off," Kirkwood said sarcastically.

"*Que?*"

"The whole fuckin' Northern Territory police force is on the way here, mate. If you're leaving, you better get your skates on."

"*Que?* What meens this 'skates on?'"

Kirkwood shook his head dismissively. The effort sent a wave of intense pain, like a thousand needles inserted behind his eyes, searing across his forehead. He closed his eyes and grimaced against the agony. "Thanks for coming," he muttered through clenched teeth. "Don't forget to write."

"*Que?*" Herrera asked again.

When the caretaker did not answer, Herrera stepped closer, drew his leg back, and kicked him hard in the ribs. The well-aimed blow struck in the same place as those administered by Williams. Kirkwood moaned once and slipped into blessed, pain-free unconsciousness.

"*Adios*, senor." Rodolfo Herrera smiled down at the unconscious caretaker and momentarily considered putting a bullet in his head. He decided against it; he never killed the innocent. He turned away, glanced briefly across at the shed thirty metres away, and then walked back into the house.

———

"What's happening?" Foley asked.

"The bikies have left," Traynor confirmed. "Herrera has gone back into the house."

"What about the caretaker?" Barker asked.

"He's not moving. Herrera gave him a kick in the guts as a parting gesture."

"Is he dead?"

"I don't know. I don't think so. Unconscious maybe...hopefully."

"Okay, let's get after the bikies." Barker turned to face Sam. "Sam, you want to stay here and check on the caretaker?"

Traynor grabbed Barker's arm. "I'll do it."

"Maybe you should come with Russell and me, Jack. We don't know where Herrera is. He came all this way to get you and that may still be his intention."

"You're wasting valuable time debating the issue with me. I'm staying. I'll check on the caretaker."

Barker frowned. "I don't think that's a good idea, Jack."

"I never said it was a good idea," Jack responded. "And your opinion is duly noted. I'm staying, nonetheless."

"We gotta go, boss," Foley said. "The bikies have a head start on us."

"Okay, okay," Barker conceded with an exaggerated shrug. "I'm only the senior officer here, who the fuck listens to me?" He turned to Traynor. "You get yourself killed here, Jack, that will really piss me off!"

"Getting killed is not my plan. I'm pretty good at staying alive in these sorts of situations, now go, get out of here!"

———

Herrera moved from the kitchen to the loungeroom, where he paused. He looked to his left, towards the hallway where Vargas's body lay on the floor. He crossed to the doorway and stared down at the body. "*Idiota!*" he hissed at the corpse. "*Nunca volveras a ver a Mexico*—you will never see Mexico again. *Adios, un hombre estupido!*" Herrera turned his back on the body and crossed quickly to the front door of the homestead.

Outside, the rental car he and Vargas came in

stood about twenty metres from the front veranda steps. Herrera descended from the veranda, hurried over to the vehicle and climbed behind the wheel. Slamming the door behind him, he reached down to the ignition. The keys were gone! Where were they, he wondered? He left them in the ignition when they arrived, he was positive. Frantically he began patting at his pockets. Nothing! Where were the damn keys? He leaned forward and scanned the floor at his feet. No keys! The keys had to be there. He never took them from the ignition...they should still be there.

"*Carajo! Carajo!*" he cursed loudly, the tiniest hint of panic tickling at the periphery of his senses. What did he do with the keys? He patted furiously again at his pockets. He lifted his feet and searched the floor again. He lifted his backside from the seat and felt around beneath him. No keys! He felt around the vacant passenger seat and searched the passenger side floor. Nothing! Exasperated, he leaned back in his seat, closed his eyes and thought hard about where the keys could be. In his mind, he retraced his movements from the time he and Vargas arrived at the homestead. He stopped the car...turned off the motor...he did not remove the keys from the ignition...he and Vargas climbed out of the car and entered the house. "*Carajo!*" he cursed again.

His eyes snapped open when he heard the sound of the police vehicle racing past the end of the house and away towards the long entrance road. He sat up and looked in the rear vision mirror. It was darker now, and the vehicle quickly faded from view in the rapidly increasing gloom. *"Jodidos cerdos gringos!"* he hissed at the image in the mirror.

He needed to find the keys. He opened the driver's side door and the interior light flickered on. Again, he searched frantically for the lost keys. Nothing. The keys were gone. *"Carajo!"* he yelled in frustration, banging his fists into the steering wheel.

———

Traynor hurried from the shed to the back veranda. In a few long strides, he was up the steps and kneeling next to the caretaker. Carefully, he examined Kirkwood and established he was alive, although badly hurt.

Kirkwood's eyes fluttered open. When he saw a kneeling man looming over him, he flinched and tried to move away. He moaned loudly as needles of excruciating pain seared through his head and ribs.

"It's okay," the man kneeling over him said. "It's okay. I'm a police officer."

Kirkwood looked up at the man. "You...you're a cop?" he muttered. He tried to lift his head and immediately slumped back as intense pain raged across his forehead. "Wh-where are they?" he groaned.

Traynor placed a restraining hand on Kirkwood's shoulder. "Lay still. You're going to be okay."

"Where are they?" Kirkwood asked again.

"They left. You're Bill Kirkwood, right?"

"Yeah. They're gone? Are...are you sure?"

"Yes, they're gone. I need you to stay here, Bill. I'm going inside to get you a blanket to make you more comfortable. Can you sit?"

"Sit? I hurt so fucking much I can't even blink! Arseholes b-b-broke my f-fuckin' ribs!"

"You're going to be okay," Traynor said again. "I'll be back in a minute, okay?"

"I ain't goin' anywhere," Kirkwood said, grimacing with pain.

Traynor gently patted the caretaker on the shoulder. "I'll be back, buddy." He stood up and entered the house.

In the kitchen, Jack unholstered his weapon and moved quickly but cautiously across the adjoining loungeroom. He picked up a blanket laying over an old, well used armchair and hurried back outside. He knelt next to the caretaker and draped the blanket over him. "This will keep you warm, Bill. Try not to move. I'll be back in a little while."

"Try not to move?" Kirkwood mumbled. "Try not to move! If that's your idea of humour, it sucks!"

"I apologise for my insensitivity." Traynor smiled at the caretaker.

"Where are you going?"

"I've got some unfinished business I need to take care of," Jack answered with a wink.

"Put one in the prick for me," Kirkwood said, knowingly.

Traynor patted Kirkwood gently on the shoulder and stood. He looked down at the injured caretaker and smiled again. "You're one tough old coot, Bill. Try to stay out of trouble while I'm gone."

This time, he walked back inside the house, through the kitchen, and across the loungeroom to the open front door, switching lights on as he went. He stepped out onto the front veranda and moved to the top of the steps leading down to a wide, clear, open space in front of the homestead. He stopped and focused through the rapidly darkening sky at the rental car approximately twenty metres away.

———

Something caught Herrera's eye. Movement. It came from the front. From the house. He looked up and squinted through the rapidly darkening light.

Standing on the front veranda, illuminated by

the light from the open front door behind him, a man stood at the top of the steps. In one hand, he held a hand-gun at his side. In the other hand, he held a set of car keys. He raised the keys and waved them at Herrera sitting in the car. "Looking for these?" He was smiling.

"*Santa Maria, madre de Dios,*" Rodolfo whispered softly. He reached for his weapon and then cautiously stepped from the car.

36

Senior Constable Jim Fowler parked the police four-wheel-drive Landcruiser sideways across the rough, dirt entrance road to Aningie Station so the front of the vehicle faced the rapidly darkening horizon to the west. Positioning the vehicle this way had less to do with obstructing the path of any approaching vehicle and more to do with offering himself and his partner some form of protection should they be fired upon. There were no fences at Aningie Station; where do you start to fence almost a million acres, let alone pay for it? This was open-range, beef cattle country on the fringes of the Tanami Desert and the stock had to roam freely in their search for feed. Annual rainfall was minimal at best and natural feed for stock was scarce. And, while the land around them was rough, corrugated, and covered in sharp, spiny, tufts of spinifex grass and gibber stones, an approaching vehicle could get around the police vehicle but it would not be a comfortable journey.

Fowler's junior partner Constable Mathew Rooney opened the glove compartment and removed a pair of small, powerful binoculars. Winding down the passenger side window, Rooney raised the glasses and focused through the gloom in the direction of the distant homestead.

"See anything?" Fowler asked.

"I can see the homestead in the distance, but it's too bloody dark to see much else."

"Okay, let's get out and position ourselves on this side of the vehicle." He opened his door and climbed out.

The Landcruiser was a two-door, tray-back model with a canvass covered cage mounted on the bed allowing for the secure transportation of offenders. From a specially fitted rack mounted above and behind the seats, Fowler removed a Remington .308 bolt-action rifle. "Pass the mag," he said to his partner.

Rooney reached back into the glove compartment, removed a four-shot magazine and handed it to Fowler. "You think we are going to need that?"

"I fuckin' hope not. But if someone comes out of the darkness shooting at us, I don't want to be scrambling around in the dark trying to get the gun out of the rack."

Rooney climbed out of the passenger side, closed his door and hurried around the vehicle to join Fowler. "This is a change from our every-day routine."

"You okay with this?"

"You mean with the prospect of being killed in a gunfight with a bunch of desperate hit-men?" Rooney asked with a sly smile.

"Yeah. Something like that."

"For what it's worth, I'd rather be home, cuddling on my couch with the bride."

"Yeah, me too. Oh...no...not *your* bride...I mean *my* bride," Fowler explained hurriedly.

"What's wrong with my bride," Rooney asked with a display of exaggerated offense.

"Nothing. Laura's lovely. But the three of us on your tiny couch...I don't think so. Besides, *my* bride wouldn't approve."

Rooney paused for a brief moment and stared into the darkness to the south, towards the distant homestead. Then, without breaking his focus, he said to Fowler, "Are we making light of a serious situation here?"

Fowler shrugged. "Nervous humour. It's a defence mechanism. It's how we cope with situations like this."

"Is that in the manual?" Rooney asked, jokingly.

"If it's not, it should be." Fowler looked across the bonnet of the Landcruiser. "There!" He pointed. "What's that?"

In the distance, two tiny pin-pricks of light appeared on the horizon. Rooney stared intently at where his partner pointed. "A vehicle?" he suggested.

"I think so. Grab the spotlight, mate."

Rooney opened the door, reached in and removed a powerful, hand-held spotlight from the seat. He plugged the lead into the vehicle cigarette lighter, wound down the driver's side window and passed the spotlight through. He closed the door to extinguish the interior light and then laid the light on the bonnet. "Do you think this is the baddies?"

"If it was our chaps," Fowler answered. "They would have the flashing lights on."

Rooney took a deep breath and exhaled loudly. "Okay, looks like show time." He unholstered his issue Glock pistol, clicked the magazine out, checked the load and then clicked it back home in the base of the butt.

A sound, too far off to identify, came to Fowler and Rooney through the surrounding desert silence. The noise seemed to accompany the distant lights and grew gradually in intensity as the lights became steadily closer.

Rooney raised the binoculars and focused on the approaching lights. "That's odd."

"What?"

"The lights. They're bouncing around all over the place."

"It's the road. We've been out to Aningie many times. The road's as rough as guts."

"Yeah, I know. This is different."

"Different how?"

"Look at them. The lights are not bouncing in sync," Rooney explained. "One light bounces up, the other bounces down. If it was a car, both lights would move up and down together. And, they are too far apart to be a car's headlights."

"What are you suggesting?"

Rooney paused, lowered the binoculars, and tilted his head to the south. "Listen," he said, finally. "That noise. It's not a car."

"What then?"

"Motorbikes! Two motorbikes!"

"Motorbikes? Are you sure?"

"Yeah, I'm positive. That's the sound of motor-bikes." Rooney lowered the binoculars. "Coming this way...fast!"

"They use motorbikes a lot these days for mus-tering cattle," Fowler said. "They're faster than horses, you don't have to feed them, and they don't tire out."

"Who musters cattle at night?"

"Point taken. Hit the lights!"

Rooney opened the door, reached in, and flicked on the vehicle roof lights. Suddenly, flashing blue and red lights lit up the vehicle and the immediate surrounding area. He closed the door and took up a defensive position next to his partner.

"They've stopped!" Fowler announced.

Up ahead, the distant lights had stopped bouncing and flickering. Now they had merged close together, almost as one, and did not appear to be coming any closer.

"They've seen the lights," Rooney said.

———

Don Williams and Luke Boyd slowed, manoeuvred their motorcycles close together so they could talk to each other without removing their helmets, and stopped. The twin Harley engines burbled softly as road dust settled around them.

"Fuckin' more cops!" Williams said, nodding towards the distant flashing blue and red lights.

"We knew they were coming," Boyd responded.

"Yeah, but I thought we might get away from this fuckin' place before they got here."

"What do you want to do?"

Williams turned his head and peered into the

darkness to the west and then the east. "How far away are they?"

Boyd shrugged. "Two, maybe three k's. But, they're not moving."

"What the fuck are they doing?"

"Waiting for us."

Williams nodded. "Yeah, that makes sense. What do you want to do?"

"The way I see it, we have two options. We can go wide, across country, and go around them, or we can revisit the original 'go out in a blaze of glory' plan."

Williams looked across at his friend. Through the face openings in their respective helmets, they locked eyes. Then Williams looked away and once again peered into blackness to the west and then the east. "Can't see a fuckin' thing out there. If we go around, it's gonna be a rough ride."

Boyd glanced down into his rear vision mirror. "Whatever we decide, we better do it quick. We've got them behind us as well."

Williams swivelled on his seat and looked behind them. Blue and red lights flashed in the distance, perhaps as far back as those were to their front. "Fuck!" he cursed loudly.

"Let's go wide," Boyd said. "No lights. If we go now, before those behind us get too close, they'll lose us in the dark." He patted the fuel tank between his legs. "These bad boys can outrun the fuckin' Jap shit-boxes they're driving."

"No lights?" Williams questioned.

"Yeah, if we go now...run dark...we can lose them."

"No, mate." Williams indicated the blackness around them with a sweep of his arm. "It's too dark out there. And the ground is too rough. If we can't see where we are going, and hit a stump, or a rabbit hole, or a wash-away, we are finished."

"Maybe," Boyd said, becoming anxious. "But if we stay here and get caught in a cross-fire, we are definitely finished."

"Maybe...maybe not. If we move up closer to the cops in front of us, the arseholes behind us will follow. We will be in the middle. Neither side is going to fire on us for fear of hitting their own men."

"So, we are going for the 'blaze of glory' option?"

Williams shrugged and smiled across at Boyd. "I've never killed a cop."

"Me either." Boyd reached across to Williams and the two killers touched fists.

No more words were spoken between them. Williams flicked his headlight off, followed immediately by Boyd. Suddenly, the surrounding darkness settled around them like a thick blanket. Only the flashing lights to their front and rear offered any indication they were not alone. Like a well-choreographed dance move, they kicked their respective machines into gear and began to move forward, slowly at first, allowing their eyes to adjust to the darkness and guided only by the flashing lights ahead of them.

37

Vaughn Millard shivered inexplicably from something he could not explain. It was late. Outside, night had fallen and brought with it an ever-present, accompanying chill of cold air drifting over the nation's capital from the not-so-distant Snowy Mountains. Although the Federal Police building was adequately heated against the night chill, it was not the cold that precipitated Millard's unease. Perhaps it was precognitive of events yet to unfold. Perhaps he was just plain tired. Or perhaps the long-anticipated finality of his situation had arrived.

It was time. He had made up his mind. If the situation unfolding at Aningie Station had not yet worked out as he had hoped, he very much doubted it ever would. He should have heard from Herrera and Vargas, or Williams and Boyd, by now. How hard can it be? Four professional assassins all gunning for the same man and still there was no word on whether Traynor was dead or alive. He had to assume the plan to kill Jackson Traynor had failed.

Millard knew there was a military helicopter en route to Aningie Station to pick up Traynor and take him to a military base in Darwin. The chopper might already be there by now for all he knew. If Traynor got on board the chopper, he would be impossible to get at. He would be held on a military base until the trial began.

Military bases in Australia were as secure, if not more secure, than they were in any other country. No one would get near Traynor if he made it to the base. Traynor was the conduit that would shut down Salim Ghandour's drug importation and distribution network. Ghandour, his son Hakim, and everyone involved in his outfit would go to prison for a very long time. It would be over.

Vaughn Millard's Federal Police career spanning almost thirty years would be gone. He would likely spend the rest of his life behind bars. The thought of spending the next thirty years locked away in a ten-by-four cell sharing his days with the worst of society's losers scared Millard even more than dying of old age in prison. Probably wouldn't even reach old age, he guessed. There were any number of

long-term gaol-birds who would just love to enhance their status amongst their fellow inmates by
killing a former cop. Crooked cops were even less
welcome in prison than paedophiles. He shivered
with the thought of it.

Now, he had to take matters into his own hands.
He could no longer sit and hope he would be contacted by Herrera, Vargas, Williams, or Boyd.
Aningie Station could well be swarming with police.
The four hired killers may be in custody, or even
dead. He could wait no longer. He was ready. His departure from the Federal Police Force was not going
to be the way he would have preferred, with a hand-
shake from the Commissioner and a healthy superannuation package to supplement his ill-gotten, off-
shore nest egg. That was unfortunate but he had
planned long ago for this possible eventuality. Superannuation notwithstanding, he had to go, and he
had to go quickly.

He pushed back from his desk, stood, cast his
eyes slowly around the room that had been his office for the last five years, and prepared to leave for
the last time. He had regrets; how could he not? If
he had his time over again he would never have put
himself in the precarious position he now found
himself. He was a good cop, or at least he used to be.
Back in the early days of his career he was considered by many to be a possible future Commissioner.

Sometimes, however, life turns to shit. When your life is at its lowest ebb, your marriage is in the toilet, your kids, swayed by their mother's bullshit, don't want to know you, it feels like you are drowning in the hopelessness of it all. Then along comes the money man. He offers you an insane amount of cash to look the other way, or provide a little information, or falsify a report; it's just a little thing, what real harm can it do? But, when you're swimming against the tide of alimony, child support, rent, and a mortgage on a house you no longer live in, it's not that difficult to succumb to the temptation. You only have to do it once, he reasoned way back then. But do it once and the hook is set and there is no turning back. Nevertheless, a couple of million dollars waiting for him in a secret off-shore account would go a long way to easing his conscience.

A light rap on his door snapped him out of his reverie. He looked up. Standing in his doorway was one of the two Federal Police assistant commissioners, Todd Jamieson. Jamieson stepped into the room and was followed immediately by a superintendent and two plain-clothes detectives. The superintendent, a man Millard went through the academy with almost thirty years ago, took up a position on the right of Jamieson. The two detectives stepped forward and positioned themselves on either side of the two senior officers.

Millard's heart skipped and his shoulders slumped visibly. This was not good. The stern looks on the faces of the assistant commissioner and his official entourage was evidence enough of that. One did not have to be a Rhodes Scholar to figure out the small contingent was not here to pass the time of day.

"Sir?" Millard addressed Jamieson.

Jamieson gave a slight nod. "Vaughn."

Millard looked from Jamieson to the superintendent and then to the two detectives. Finally, his eyes moved back to Jamieson. "What can I do for you?" he asked tentatively.

"You need to come with us, Vaughn."

"Oh? Where are we going?"

"We would like to talk to you about Jackson Traynor."

"Traynor, what about him?"

"It's over, Vaughn," Jamieson said. "We know about your involvement with the Ghandour family, and we know about the truckload of cash you have stashed overseas."

Fearing his legs would fail him and he would fall, Millard sat back down and slumped in his chair. He looked at the assistant commissioner, held his eyes for a few seconds, and then lowered his head and closed his eyes. Was it really over? Maybe Jamieson was bluffing. He lifted his head and looked again at Jamieson, desperately hoping to see something he instinctively knew was not there. No, Jamieson wasn't bluffing. It was there, in the assistant commissioner's eyes. His mention of the money was all the proof he needed. As he looked at Jamieson's stern, dead-pan face, he silently cursed himself. He had left his run too late. He should have left weeks ago, when the raids uncovered the biggest drug importation and distribution racket in Australian criminal history. Should have got out then. But, "should have, would have, could have" accounted for nothing now. They knew everything. He didn't know how they knew, and in the overall scheme of things it didn't really matter. In his mind, he could almost hear the cell door closing behind him. Prison! He would never make it. Some low-life, wannabe big-shot con would ram a shiv into his heart just for the honour of it.

"How?" he heard himself ask.

"We've had our suspicions for a long time, Vaughn," Jamieson began.

"Suspicions?"

"Yes. We interrogated a lot of people following the drug bust. Someone was always going to give up his sources in return for our recommendation to the court for a lighter sentence. We've been monitoring you for several months, building a case."

"Who rolled over?" Millard asked, in a voice barely audible.

"It doesn't matter who, Vaughn. But I will tell you this. About thirty minutes ago I had a telephone conversation with an old friend of mine from the Northern Territory. Does the name Cameron Barker mean anything to you?"

"You know it does."

"Barker told me that you assured him you told no one about Traynor being escorted to a cattle station north of Ti Tree."

"So?"

"So, how come all of a sudden four professional killers descended on Aningie Station looking for Traynor?"

"Maybe Barker told someone he shouldn't have told," Millard offered weakly.

"No, Vaughn. We all know that's not true. Maybe *you* told someone you shouldn't have told."

Millard shrugged and dropped his eyes. "I would like to call my lawyer."

"That might be a good idea. But first, let me caution you. You do know how that works don't you, Vaughn?"

"Yes," Millard muttered.

"You are not obliged to say anything further about this matter unless you wish to do so. However, anything you do say will be taken down and may be presented in evidence at any future court proceedings. Do you understand what I have just explained to you?"

"Of course I do."

"Is there anything else you would like to say in regards to this matter."

"No."

Jamieson noticed the mobile phone laying on Millard's desk. "I would like you to come with us now, Vaughn. Leave the phone."

Millard hesitated and the two detectives took a step closer to his desk. He raised his hands in a surrender gesture. "Okay, okay," he said. "I'm coming." He looked again at Jamieson. "Would you please extend me the courtesy of allowing me to walk out of here unrestrained, no handcuffs?"

"Of course."

Millard glanced down at his desk. "Can I have a moment."

"Okay, but just a moment."

Millard looked around the office. His attention lingered briefly on two Commissioner's Commendations, framed and hanging on one wall. He recalled the circumstances that earned him both and, for a moment, an immense feeling of regret threatened to overcome him.

"It's time, Vaughn," Jamieson said. "You need to come with us now."

Millard looked back at Jamieson and nodded. "Okay." He reached down and opened a drawer in his desk, placed his hand inside and came up with his police issue Glock 22 semi-automatic pistol.

Caught by surprise, the two detectives reached for their holstered weapons. They were a second too slow.

In one swift motion, Millard cocked the weapon and placed it in his mouth. With the muzzle touching the roof of his palate, he pulled the trigger. A 9mm round crashed through the top of his mouth and into his brain, killing him instantly. Now, for Vaughn Millard, it really was over.

38

Zaina Ghandour, her husband Salim, and their son, Hakim, were enjoying a family dinner in the sumptuous dining room of the home she shared with Salim on the expansive Ghandour estate. More accurately, Zaina and Salim were enjoying the meal, Hakim, not so much.

Hakim was restless, uncomfortable, and perspiring heavily, all tell-tale signs of substance withdrawal. He was an addict. He would never admit to being hooked on drugs and booze, addicts rarely do, and he was just as likely to fly into a rage if it was suggested to him that he may have a problem with illicit drugs and overindulgence in alcohol; a short fuse leading to anger management issues is often another sign indicating there may well be concerns directly related to his fondness for cocaine and strong liquor.

He mopped at his brow with his table napkin and immediately dropped his hand to his lap lest his mother, or his father, notice the developing tremor in his fingers. He had eaten little of his meal. With his lack of appetite and the shake in his hands, simply raising the fork to his mouth seemed to be an effort. However, he forced himself to eat, even made the occasional complimentary remark about how much he enjoyed his mother's cooking, knowing how it would upset her if he left food on his plate. Hakim knew Zaina loved to cook for her family, spending many hours in her vast, chef-style kitchen preparing these once-weekly family get-togethers. Disappointing her, and as a consequence raising the ire of his father, was not an option. If only he had a good bottle of red wine to help him get through the meal and still his trembling hand.

A strict observer of her Muslim heritage, Zaina Ghandour did not drink alcohol and forbade any alcoholic beverages at her dinner table. She was aware of her husband's fondness for an occasional whiskey or glass of outrageously expensive red wine, and she was acutely aware of her son's habitual, often excessive drug and alcohol abuse but, while she strongly, and silently, disapproved, if she didn't see it she could tolerate it. However, as a devout follower of Islam, indulgence in such disgusting substances at her table was never going to be tolerated.

When it came to matters of the home, Zaina was the boss. Despite how much it hurt her, what nature of poison Salim and Hakim subjected their bodies to when out of her presence was something she could not control and had long ago stopped trying. The consumption of alcohol and indulgence in illegal drugs was disrespectful, even insulting to the teachings of Islam, she considered. Such behaviour was a matter for her husband and her son to justify with Allah when the time for atonement arrived.

There was a fourth place-setting at the table, reserved for her late son Ahmed. Family dinners in Zaina's home were always planned for four. Zaina knew Ahmed was never going to sit at her table again, but she set a place anyway. In her heart, he would always be at the end of the table, opposite his father. He was the eldest son; it was only right that he occupied the seat at the end of the table opposite his father. Had he lived, he would be the head of the Ghandour family one day and, to her mind, the seating arrangements telegraphed the natural progression of the family dynasty.

Hakim raised the issue of the seating arrangements with her not long after Ahmed was killed. He believed, as the only surviving son, he should be entitled to sit in the place his brother once occupied. He was now the only surviving son, he reasoned, the next in line to become head of the Ghandour family. He learned very quickly that it was not wise to risk the ire of his mother, especially in matters related to her dead son, Ahmed. He never raised the subject again.

It was not that Zaina did not love Hakim. He was her son, her only son now. But Hakim was not Ahmed. He would never be Ahmed. Ahmed was a good boy. He was a respectful son. He never drank alcohol, did not use illegal drugs, and never missed a day where he would tell her he loved her. Even if he was away on family business, he would ring her and tell her he loved her and missed her. If only Hakim were more like Ahmed. And the whores! Don't get her started on the whores! He tried to bring one of his floozies to a family dinner once; he never did that again either.

———

Twenty-one heavily armed Federal police officers swarmed into the Ghandour estate at nine o'clock at night. Under the direct supervision of Assistant Commissioner Todd Jamieson, who had just a few hours earlier witnessed the suicide of Vaughn Mil-

324

lard, seven officers raided each house in the estate. Jamieson led the raid on Salim Ghandour's home.

They did not knock, unless crashing through the heavy, locked, ornate double front doors of Salim Ghandour's home with a battering ram could be considered knocking. They stormed into the dining room, surrounded the long, food laden table, all screaming at once, demanding Salim, Zaina, and Hakim spread-eagle themselves on the dining room floor.

There were seven of them, six dressed in black, tactical clothing, complete with helmets fitted with cameras and torches. They wore black, balaclava type face masks covering the lower half of their faces, leaving only their eyes exposed. The weaponry, an intimidating and threatening array of firepower ranging from semi-automatic handguns to fully automatic, high powered rifles, was aimed directly at the chests and backs of the three members of the Ghandour family. The seventh officer, Jamieson, wore a suit with a Kevlar vest visible underneath the jacket.

Zaina Ghandour screamed in fright. She immediately started crying, her chest heaving in great, gut-wrenching sobs. She flung her hands in the air, then grabbed at her chest, and finally clasped her hands to her head, the loud sobbing very quickly escalating into a loud, siren-like wailing. She seemed glued to her chair, unable to stand, let alone lay on the floor.

"Get on the floor!" one of the black-clad cops yelled. "Get on the floor!"

Salim Ghandour reached out and clasped his wife's hand. "Zaina, stop now," he said calmly. "Everything will be okay. Stop crying." He looked up at Todd Jamieson. "What are you doing here?" he asked, hatred burning in his eyes.

With a simple hand gesture to his men, the room fell silent, save for the deep sobbing of Zaina Ghandour.

"Get down on the floor, Salim," Jamieson said, calmly.

"Tell me why you are in my home?" Salim insisted.

Jamieson reached inside his jacket and produced a document. He dropped it on the table in front of Salim. "That is a warrant to search your home. Now, I won't ask again, get down on the floor!"

Salim's gaze did not waver. "Please show my wife some respect. My son and I will do as you ask. Do not force on my wife the indignity of laying on the floor."

Jamieson paused. "Okay," he agreed, finally. He looked at Zaina. "Mrs. Ghandour, please move across to the chair by the window and sit."

Zaina looked questioningly at her husband. "Salim, what is this? What do they want?"

Salim patted Zaina's hand. "It is okay. Please, go sit by the window. I will handle this."

Zaina hesitated. She fixed her husband with scared, pleading eyes. "Please, Salim," she sobbed. "Are they going to wreck my home again, and Ahmed's home?" She failed to mention Hakim's home, an omission which did not escape her son.

"Zaina, please," Salim said. "Go. Sit by the window. Allow me to handle this."

Slowly, hesitatingly, Zaina pushed her chair back and stood. Salim held her hand, fearing she may collapse with fear and shock at the sudden, un-expected intrusion into her home.

Zaina stood for a few moments, holding tight to Salim's hand. She stared down at her husband, her eyes filled with more tears. Then, from somewhere deep inside her, she found a courage she would never have believed she possessed. She pulled her hand from her husband's grasp and turned to face Todd Jamieson. "This is the second time you have stormed into my home with your army of soldiers," she said defiantly. "You disrupt our family, you dese-crate my dead son's home, and always you leave emptyhanded! We have nothing to hide! What do you want here?"

Jamieson took a step closer to Zaina. Salim

Ghandour immediately rose from his chair, intending to comfort his wife. Two officers moved forward and grabbed Salim by his arms, effectively restraining him.

"Ma'am," Jamieson said, "you need to sit by the window. Please do that now."

Zaina glanced quickly at her husband and then at Jamieson. "Please do not wreck my home." She turned away and moved across to the window and sat in one of two deep, plush lounge chairs on either side of a large bay-widow overlooking Sydney Harbour. Immediately, a dark-clad police officer moved across to the window and stood next to her, his weapon held loosely but nonetheless capably at his side.

Jamieson glared at Salim. "You and your son get on the floor," he ordered.

Salim hesitated. "What do you want here? We are on bail."

"Your bail has been revoked pending new charges. Now, get on the floor!"

Salim looked across at his son and nodded. "Do as they say."

Hakim began to rise from his chair. "Fuckin' pigs!" he cursed.

"Do not use such language in front of your mother!" Salim scolded. "Get down on the floor!"

Salim and Hakim dropped to their knees and then laid face down on the floor.

"Arms out, legs spread!" Jamieson ordered.

When Salim and Hakim had complied, Jamieson nodded to two of his men who dropped to their knees and patted father and son down, looking firstly for concealed weapons and, in particular, their mobile phones.

"No weapons," the officer searching Salim announced to Jamieson. He held up Salim's phone.

A few seconds later, the officer searching Hakim looked up at Jamieson. "Clean," he declared, holding aloft Hakim's phone.

"Cuff them!" Jamieson ordered his men.

Immediately, Salim and Hakim had their arms wrenched roughly behind their backs and handcuffs clamped tight around their wrists.

"You can get up now," Jamieson said.

Assisted by an officer on each side, Salim and Hakim were helped to their feet.

Todd Jamieson picked up the warrant document on the table and waved it at Salim. "This is a warrant for the arrest of you, Salim," he turned to face Hakim, "and you, Hakim."

"On what charges?" Salim asked.

"Conspiracy to murder."

"That's bullshit!" Hakim said loudly.

Salim looked at his son. "Be quiet!" he ordered.

Jamieson tossed the warrant casually aside on the dinner table. "As of now, you are both under arrest. You do not have to say anything further unless you wish to do so. Anything you do say will be taken down and may be given in evidence. Do you both understand what I have just explained to you?" He looked first at Salim and then at Hakim.

"Who, exactly, are we supposed to have conspired to murder?" Salim asked.

"Do you understand your rights as I have just explained to you?" Jamieson pressed.

"I understand," Salim growled. "Who are we supposed to have conspired to murder?" he asked again.

Jamieson looked at Hakim. "Hakim, do you understand your rights?"

"Yes!" Hakim spat, defiantly.

"Answer the question!" Salim insisted.

"That's not how it works," Jamieson answered. "*We* ask the questions...*you* answer them."

"It's a reasonable question," Salim pressed. "You are required to inform us of why we are being arrested."

"I told you...conspiracy to murder."

"Conspiracy to murder who?"

"Okay, you will find out soon enough anyway. Your intended victim was...*is*...Sergeant Jackson Traynor of the Australian Federal Police."

"You have nothing," Salim scoffed.

"Actually, Salim," Jamieson smiled wryly, "we have plenty."

"My lawyer will have us out before the ink on your warrant is dry," Salim insisted. "What is it exactly that you think you have on us?"

Jamieson shrugged. "Well, let's start with a conversation between yourself and Hakim we recorded in your study. A conversation in which you declared Traynor was not to reach Darwin alive. Then, if that doesn't work for you, there is the conversation between Superintendent Vaughn Millard of the Federal Police and one Don Williams, a professional hit-man, hired by you to kill Traynor." He looked at Hakim. "And finally, Hakim, there is the conversation you had with Millard. Is that *plenty* enough for you?"

"It's all bullshit!" Hakim insisted again.

"Shut up, Hakim!" Salim ordered. "You bugged my office?" he said to Jamieson.

"All quite legal." Jamieson smiled. "We had a warrant for that too." Then he turned to Zaina. "Ma'am, this warrant also authorises us to search the entire estate, including your late son's home."

Zaina lowered her head in her hands. "Nooo!" she sobbed. "You cannot do this again! There is nothing to find here! Nothing!"

"Zaina!" Salim called to his wife. "Zaina! Call

Akmal. Tell him what is happening here. Tell him to come quickly to the Federal Police office. Do not worry. Everything will be okay. Call Akmal, Zaina." He turned back to face Jamieson. "My lawyer will end this nonsense."

"Yeah, your lawyer Akmal," Jamieson said. "You must pay him well. I understand you are his only client. When he sees the mountain of evidence we have against you and your son, I expect he will be looking for a new client...in a new country. He's as crooked as you and your drug-addicted son." He addressed the officers standing behind Salim and Hakim. "Get these two out of my sight!"

39

D on Williams and Luke Boyd gradually closed the gap between themselves and the police waiting ahead of them. Occasionally, they glanced in their respective rear vision mirrors, assessing the progress of the following police vehicle. As they came closer to the road block ahead, they slowed their machines and eventually stopped about fifty metres short of the police vehicle parked sideways across the road.

"How do you want to do this?" Boyd asked.

For a moment, Williams did not answer. He sat astride his bike and stared at the vehicle ahead. Then he looked out into the darkness to his right and then to his left. "Do you still *want* to do this?" he asked, finally.

"Do what? Die in the fuckin' desert?"

Williams shrugged in the darkness. "We always knew it might come down to this."

"Do I sense some hesitation?"

"There may still be a way to get out of this in one piece."

"Okay, buddy. I'm listening."

"The pigs in front of us are what, fifty metres away?"

"Yeah, that's about right."

"And, they're parked across the road, right where it intersects with the road leading out to the highway."

"Okay," Boyd said. "What are you suggesting?"

"Well," Williams began. "You can see in the flashing lights, they're driving a utility vehicle with a cage on the back. That indicates to me there are only two of them. Probably the two local cops."

"I'll go along with that."

"We can still go around them. Get up to about twenty metres from them and then gun it. One of us left...around the front of the vehicle, the other right...around the back. The element of surprise. If we go hard, and fast, we can hit the main road in seconds. Go right and go hard all the way to the highway. It will take those two morons valuable time to get back in their vehicle, turn around, and follow. We can outrun that fuckin' piece of shit vehicle."

"What about the cops behind us?"

Williams glanced in his mirror. "They're still coming. But they're still a few minutes away. By the time they get here, we'll be gone."

"Sounds like a plan." Boyd smiled in the dark across at his partner.

"Okay, let's move closer. They will be taking cover on the other side of the vehicle. When I yell 'go!' you break left and go around the front. I'll go right. Fire a couple of rounds at the vehicle...that will put their heads down and give us a few valuable seconds. When we get past, we hit our lights...just for a few moments so we can see the main road. Turn right, go dark again, and head towards the highway."

"Do you think they will fall for it?"

"They'll fall for it. They're fuckin' small-town, dim-witted, Keystone cops. We start shooting, and they'll duck for cover. Get in each other's way tryin' to scramble underneath their car. If we're lucky, we might even hit one of them. By the time they crawl out from under the car and figure out what the fuck happened, we'll be several klicks down the road." Williams drew his 9mm Sig, actioned the slide to cock the weapon, and rested it on the fuel tank, between his legs.

Boyd did the same.

"Ready?" Williams asked.

"Ready," Boyd confirmed.

"Let's roll."

Simultaneously, each of them men kicked his bike into gear and began moving forward. Slowly at first, they drew closer to the police vehicle and the two officers taking cover on the driver's side.

———

"They're moving," Rooney said.

"Okay, be ready," Fowler responded. "Let them get close...real close, and then hit them with the spotlight."

Standing close together, side-by-side, Fowler and Rooney leaned over the side of their vehicle, steadied their forearms on the still warm bonnet, and watched the twin motorcycle lights approaching. Neither Fowler nor Rooney had ever fired his weapon in the course of his duty other than for target practice. Despite the distinct chill in the air, a common experience accompanying nightfall in the central Australian outback, both men found themselves perspiring. Occasionally, each wiped at beads of sweat stinging their eyes. This was a situation neither man had ever experienced to this point in their respective careers. This was serious. It was conceivable that one, or God forbid both of them, might die. It was dark, it was cold, and the tension in the air was almost palpable. Both Fowler and Rooney knew when they joined the police force they might one day be faced with a situation such as they faced now. However, the odds of actually being confronted with a life-or-death situation were considered about as long as winning the lottery. This was no lottery.

Twenty metres out, the motorcycles stopped. Beyond them, the lights of the pursuing police vehicle flashed blue and red in the distance.

"They've stopped again," Rooney said.

"Yeah."

"What are they doing?"

"I doubt they are considering the merits of surrendering. Hit 'em with the spotlight."

Rooney lifted the light from where it lay on the bonnet, aimed it at the stationary bikes, and flicked the switch. A bright, powerful beam from the Zeus spotlight knifed out across the space separating the vehicle and the bikes. In an instant the two riders were illuminated in the narrow, 900 lumens shaft of light like it was bright daylight.

———

"Fuck!" Williams cursed loudly. He threw his gun hand up to his face, protecting his eyes from the bright glare of the light.

Boyd averted his eyes and looked away to his

left, into the blackness outside the tunnel of light. "Fuckin' spotlight!"

"Go!" Williams yelled. "Go now!"

Simultaneously, both men gunned their machines. Dirt and small stones spat from their rear wheels in a thick cloud of dust as the Harleys responded to the sudden surge of power.

Boyd broke left and Williams broke right. In a split second, they were outside the beam of the spotlight and racing across rough, uneven ground, skirting wide around the front and rear of the police vehicle respectively.

Steering with one hand and holding a weapon in the other while trying to control a rapidly accelerating motorcycle bucking and skidding beneath you across rough, unforgiving terrain came with its own set of problems. Add to the mix the fact they were riding blind, without headlights, and the degree of difficulty increases exponentially. However, both Williams and Boyd were experienced bikers and, guided by the flashing lights from the police vehicle, coupled with the desire to get as far away from the waiting police and their road block as possible, they made good progress in their push to reach the main access road.

Boyd drew level with the police vehicle some fifty metres out to the front. At almost the same time, Williams drew level out from the rear. Both rode at the periphery of the glow cast by the vehicle's flashing roof lights. The powerful spotlight danced erratically across the night sky, chasing, searching for one and then the other, never seeming to find either of them.

———

"They're splitting up!" Rooney announced as the two riders separated and broke free of the spotlight beam. Suddenly, he didn't know who to focus on with the spotlight. "Fuck! Where are they?"

"They're riding dark."

Rooney swung the spotlight from his left to his right, and back again, searching the terrain across the front and the rear of the vehicle. In his haste, the beam danced haphazardly across the open ground, probing the darkness.

"Hold the light steady!" Fowler ordered. "I can't see them!"

"They're close!" Rooney announced as the deep, throaty roar of the twin Harley engines echoed out of the darkness.

Then just for a split second the spotlight illuminated one of the riders out to the front of the vehicle.

"There!" Fowler called, pointing to his front.

It was just a glimpse. The rider entered the light,

GARY S. GREGOR

perhaps sixty metres out, and then he was gone. Rooney waved the beam back and forth frantically, searching for the rider. "Where the fuck did he go? Can you see him?"

Then the gunshots started. They came from both the front and the rear. Bullets zinged and smacked against the body of the vehicle. Fowler and Rooney dropped to their knees, hugging the side of the vehicle.

"Jesus!" Rooney yelled. "They're shooting at us!"

"Kill the light!" Fowler screamed.

Rooney switched off the spotlight, instantly plunging them into semi-darkness. Now the flashing red and blue lights on the roof of the vehicle cast a carnival like hue across the vehicle and the two cops sheltering behind its bulk.

Bullets, fired out of the darkness, sprayed into the vehicle and the ground around where they knelt peppering them with dust and tiny, stinging pebbles.

"Return fire!" Fowler yelled to his partner.

Rooney opened fire, aiming blindly into the night to the front of the vehicle. Fowler did the same, firing to the rear. Neither man could see what he was firing at. It was more a case of blazing away into the darkness in the vain hope they might hit something.

Rooney heard a grunt from behind him. He

turned and saw his partner slump sideways and collapse onto the ground.

"Chook! Chook!" he called. "Are you okay?"

"I-I'm hit," Fowler hissed through clenched teeth.

Rooney reached down and grabbed Fowler's arm. "You're hit?"

"Ba-bastards got me."

"Where are you hit?"

"Missed...the vest," Fowler mumbled, grimacing with pain. "Got me high...in the shoulder."

"Hold on, buddy. Let me look." Rooney felt around Fowler's left shoulder and felt dampness and a tear in his uniform shirt.

Fowler groaned as his partner's probing fingers touched the wound. "Fuck that hurts! Is-is it bad?"

"There's a lot of blood. But I think it's missed all the vital stuff. Just a bad shoulder wound." He took Fowler's hand and lifted it to his shoulder. "Press down on here, as hard as you can bear it. Try to stem the blood. I'll get the first-aid kit from the vehicle."

"Wh-where are the baddies?"

It was only then that Rooney realised the shooting had stopped. He listened for a few moments and heard the sound of the motorcycles fading into the distance. "They're gone."

"Fuckin' arseholes!" Fowler cursed. "My wife is

gonna kick my arse," he added, almost as an afterthought.

"No, she won't. You are going to be fine."

"She'll kick my arse anyway," Fowler insisted.

Rooney smiled down at his partner. "Better a kick in the arse from the wife than a weeping widow at a police funeral," he suggested. He started to rise. "Keep the pressure on the wound. I'll get the first-aid kit."

Fowler cocked his head and listened. "What's that?" he asked.

"What?"

"Listen, that's a car."

Rooney quickly stood and looked over the bonnet of the vehicle at the rapidly approaching car. "It's Cameron Barker."

"Flag them down."

The oncoming car was close now. Rooney began waving frantically.

40

Following some distance behind the bike riders and closing fast, Cameron Barker saw the brake lights on the two motor cycles ahead suddenly glow brighter. He braked hard and the vehicle skidded, fish-tailing to a stop. "What are they doing?" he said, leaning forward over the steering wheel and peering out through the windscreen.

"They've stopped," Sam said from the rear seat.

"Yeah, but why?" Barker asked.

"They've obviously seen the lights at the road block up ahead," Sam suggested.

"That will be Fowler and Rooney," Foley said.

"Do I dare suggest we have the bastards?" Barker asked.

"Somehow, I don't think it will be that easy," Foley answered.

"I'll move up closer." Barker took his foot off the brake and the car began to roll slowly forward. He increased speed minimally, not wanting to get too close in case the bikers fired on them. "Be ready for anything," he said to Foley and Rose. "Who knows what these arseholes are going to do."

"I doubt they will lay down and surrender," Sam said.

"Like I said...be ready for anything."

Suddenly the bright glow of a spotlight illuminated the two bikers.

"Onya boys!" Sam said loudly. "Lit the bastards up like a Christmas tree!"

Then, suddenly, the twin red glow of the tail lights went out.

"What the...?" Foley exclaimed.

"They've killed their lights," Barker said.

"They'll go around," Sam said.

"What?" Barker asked.

"They'll go around. They'll split up and skirt the front and rear of the road block."

"In the dark?" Barker queried. "It's as rough as guts out there."

"They don't have a lot of options, boss," Sam said. "There's a road block in front of them and I'm sure they have seen us behind them. What are they gonna do? They have to go around. If they want to get away, it's their only option."

"With a bit of luck, they will both crash and burn," Barker said.

As he spoke, the two motorcycles separated and disappeared from view into the darkness beyond the glow of the spotlight.

Barker increased speed even more, the vehicle headlights probing the darkness ahead. "Do you see them?" he asked Sam and Foley.

"No," Sam and Foley said in unison.

"Like I figured," Sam said. "They have separated."

"There, look!" Foley cried, pointing to the police vehicle parked across the access road. "It's one of the local lads!"

"He's waving us down," Barker said.

"If we stop, the perps are gonna get away," Sam said.

"He's waving us down," Barker said again. "We've got to stop. Something might be wrong."

Barker skidded to a stop at the rear of the cage-vehicle. Immediately they noticed Chook Fowler sitting, propped against the driver's side of the vehicle.

"That's Chook," Barker said.

"He looks hurt," Foley said.

Foley, Sam, and Barker climbed quickly from their car as Rooney dropped back to his knees alongside his injured partner.

"Chook's been hit!" he called to the three new arrivals. "He's been shot!"

"Fuck!" Barker hurried across to Rooney and Fowler and squatted next to Fowler. "Where are you hit?"

"Shoulder," Fowler mumbled. "Bastards got me." He grimaced with pain, pressing harder against his wound. Blood seeped through his fingers and ran freely down the front of his uniform shirt and underneath the Kevlar vest.

Rooney rose to his feet, opened the door of the station vehicle, and rummaged behind the driver's seat. "Here, sir," he said finally. "There's a dressing in our first-aid kit." He knelt back down next to Barker and Fowler and opened the kit.

Barker rested his hand on Fowler's good shoulder. "You are going to be fine, Chook. Let's get the vest off you and have a look at the damage." He carefully removed Fowler's Kevla vest and unbuttoned his uniform shirt, exposing the injured shoulder.

"How bad is it?" Fowler asked, grimacing with pain.

"You are going to be fine. It looks to be right at the top of your arm, in the fleshy part. I'm no doctor but it might be a through-and-through wound. Hopefully it missed the bone. We'll get something on it to stop the bleeding and get you out of here as soon as we can."

"You're gonna have to send me to some remote corner of the world where my wife won't find me. Because if she does, she's gonna finish what those two pricks started."

Barker smiled. "I met your wife earlier today. She will be fine."

Barker stood and looked up at Foley and Rose. "Russell, you and Sam get after the bikies. I'll stay here with Mickey and take care of Chook. Don't let those bastards get away."

"Okay, boss," Foley said. "You sure you are okay here?"

"We'll be fine. Get going!"

"Let's go, Sam," Foley said, hurrying to the driver's side of the vehicle.

"Behave yourself, Chook," Sam said, looking down at Fowler.

"Yeah, right," Fowler chuffed. "Don't let those bastards get away."

Sam climbed in the passenger seat and, as he slammed his door closed, Foley accelerated quickly. The rear wheels spun uselessly in the loose gravel for a second or two and then found purchase. Suddenly, the car lurched forward and sped away leaving a cloud of dust in its wake.

Sam struggled to fasten his seat belt against the

sudden lurching. When it clicked home, he grasped the hand-hold above his door and braced his feet against the floor. "What the fuck!" he said. "Are you a rally driver now?"

Wrestling with the steering wheel as the vehicle bucked and skidded across the rough ground, Foley answered, "Defensive driving, Sam."

"More like kami...fuckin'...kaze driving if you ask me."

Suddenly, out of the darkness, the main access road loomed in front of them. Foley braked hard and simultaneously spun the wheel to his right. The rear end of the vehicle skidded left, heading straight for the left-hand verge of the dirt road. Half way through the slide, Foley wrenched the steering wheel back, turning the vehicle's front wheels into the skid. At the same time, he hit the gas and accelerated out of the dangerous slide. The vehicle straightened, the wheels gained purchase on the road, and the car accelerated away in a shower of loose dirt and gravel towards the distant Bruce Highway.

Rubbing vigorously at the side of his head where it had hit the window, not once but twice, Sam looked across at Foley. "Jesus! That was fuckin' close!"

Foley did not turn his head to look at Sam. He leaned forward over the steering wheel and peered intently through the windscreen, concentrating on the road in front.

Even in the dull light inside the vehicle Sam saw a hint of a smile on Foley's face. "What are you smiling at?"

"Smiling? I'm not smiling, I'm concentrating."

"You nearly killed us both," Sam said, rubbing harder at his head.

"I'm a good driver, Sam. I had complete control of the car. We were never in danger."

"You're full of shit, Russ."

"Why don't you stop whining? You're still alive, aren't you?"

"Yeah, by the grace of God. Not by your driving skills."

Foley's smile widened marginally but he chose not to dignify Sam's comments with a response. Instead, he said, "Keep your eyes peeled for the two bikie dudes."

Sam changed the subject. "What do you think Traynor is doing?"

"I'm guessing he wants a little one-on-one time with the remaining Mexican."

"I'm surprised Yap Yap let him stay back at the homestead. He has to know that what Jack has in mind is almost certainly not legal."

Foley shrugged. "Self-defence is legal. And, after

GARY S. GREGOR

what happened to his family, whatever Jack has in mind is okay with me."

"Me too."

Suddenly, up ahead, two red tail lights appeared out of the darkness.

"There they are!" Sam announced.

"So much for Yap Yap's 'crash and burn' theory," Foley said. He pushed down harder on the accelerator.

41

"Ah, Senor Traynor?" Rodolfo Herrera said to the man standing on the veranda. At his side he held his .45 hand gun, cocked and ready to fire. He lowered his eyes and saw Traynor also had a weapon at his side. "You are Senor Jackson Traynor, right?" he asked. The man on the veranda did not respond. He stood unmoving, staring back at him in silence.

"Finally, we meet," Herrera said. The man still offered no response.

Twenty metres separated the two men but Herrera sensed there was something about the way the man on the veranda stood silently staring down at him, something about his demeanour that conveyed more than words ever could. It was like he could see, even feel the hatred in Traynor's eyes burning

GARY S. GREGOR

into his own despite the darkening night and the distance between them.

Rodolfo Herrera was not afraid. He could not remember a time when he was afraid of anything, or anyone. Perhaps when he was a young boy there might have been a time or two when he was afraid of the wrath of his father following an indiscretion, but that was a long time ago. If there ever was an occasion way back then when he did feel afraid, he could no longer recall what might have precipitated his fear. If you could not recall ever being afraid, any such incidence did not count, he reasoned.

There was always going to be a confrontation between himself and Jackson Traynor. It was inevitable. That's why he came half-way around the world. His job was to kill the silent man on the veranda. He never expected the inevitable confrontation would be here in this remote, hot, dusty, God-forsaken place, but here he was. Life was full of unexpected experiences. This was just one more.

The Wolf always chose to kill from behind. A bullet to the back of the head. It was quick and it was humane. If the target never saw it coming, he would not take his last breath with his heart filled with fear. It was the decent thing to do. Most people, even those of strong character, when faced with imminent death did not handle the situation well. They displayed in their eyes, and in their demeanour, a terrifying fear. Often, they wept uncontrollably and pleaded for their life. The Wolf reasoned that if someone had to die by his hand, there was no need for them to suffer needlessly before they did so.

This time was different. It was a first for him. Herrera was going to kill Traynor, there was not the slightest doubt in his mind about that, but this time he would kill while looking into the victim's eyes. What would that be like, he wondered? Would he see fear in Traynor's eyes? Perhaps not. It was too dark and Traynor was too far away to clearly see his eyes. But perhaps he would sense the *rata's* fear. It would be a new experience. Maybe he would enjoy it enough to employ it again with his next target. Strangely, as alien as the concept was to him, he found himself looking forward to it.

He took a sideways step, away from the car. He could not see Traynor's eyes, but he felt them follow him. This man would be good, he thought. But, The Wolf was better. Either way, this would be a challenge.

"Do you know who I am, senor?" he asked Traynor.

"I know," Traynor confirmed from the veranda. His voice was direct and unfaltering.

"Do you know why I am here?"

"To see the many attractions of my country?" Traynor suggested with undisguised sarcasm.

"I do not like your country, senor."

"Tell someone who gives a shit."

"Eh? Your words are...how you say? ...confusing, senor."

"You murdered my family," Traynor said.

"No. You are wrong, senor. I did not kill your family. I do not kill the innocent. Eet ees not my way."

"You were there. Maybe even stood there and watched."

"Senor Vargas murdered your family. I was not even in your house when he did those things to *tu esposa* and *tu hija*."

"My daughter was twelve years old. She was raped and butchered. My wife also. You were there, you sick fuck! And you did nothing to stop it! You knew Vargas. You knew what sort of animal he was. You left him in my house with my wife and daughter. You knew what he was doing to them and you did nothing to stop him."

Herrera shrugged. "I am sorry for your loss, senor," he said, unconvincingly. He took a further step sideways away from the vehicle and the dull glow of the interior light. Best not make too much of a target for him, he reasoned.

"I did not come here to listen to your hollow apology," Traynor said.

"You came to this place to hide," Herrera said. "Like the *rata* in his *agujero en la suelo*."

"I don't speak Spanish."

Herrera shrugged again. "Eet ees no matter," he said indifferently. "I theenk also you did not come here to have the conversation with me, no?"

"No, I did not come here to talk to you."

"You came here to kill me, senor?"

"No, *you* came here to kill *me*."

"Ah!" Herrera smiled. "So now we get to the... how you say...the neety, greety."

"Close enough."

"Ees true, senor. I came to thees place to kill you, and so I must do thees now."

"Good luck with that."

"*Que*? You wish me luck, senor?"

"You're going to need it."

"I am very good at what I do, senor," Herrera announced, as if it might have some influence on what Traynor did next.

"So I've heard," Jack said. "But I'm better."

Herrera slipped his finger inside the trigger guard of his weapon. "*Que*? Better? I do not theenk so, senor. I have killed many men," he boasted.

"Yes, you have. You killed them all behind their back, like the coward you are."

"You theenk I am the coward? How many men have you killed, senor?"

"Too many."

"There ees the difference, senor. You do not like to kill. Eet is my work. I love my work. I am very experienced at the business of killing."

Like Herrera, Traynor could not see the other man's eyes. It was too dark, and the distance was too great to clearly see his face. However, the look in his eyes was irrelevant. He was not looking at the Mexican's face. He was looking at his gun hand. Herrera held a big gun; at least it looked big in the small hand of the Mexican. Probably a .45, Jack thought.

Then, across the distance separating him from Herrera, he saw the slightest movement of his hand. His finger had moved inside the trigger guard. Jack guessed he was poised to raise the weapon and fire. It would come at any moment.

Jack had two weapons, the Sig Sauer 9mm and a Colt .45 calibre semi-automatic. Right now, he was glad he chose to carry the Sig Sauer 9mm as opposed to the Colt. The Sig was slightly lighter, had less recoil than the .45, and although the Colt would kill or incapacitate more quickly, he was not about killing the Mexican quickly. He wanted Herrera to die slowly. He wanted him to know that he was dying. Just like his wife, April, and his daughter, Jessica, must have known they were dying when he and Vargas crept into his home and slaughtered the two people he loved more than life itself.

Traynor was familiar with the feeling men experience when about to go into combat. All such men were afraid. Those who claimed they were not were lying, perhaps as a false display of bravado masking their fear from their comrades. Some demonstrated real, tangible fear, a fear you could see in their eyes and almost smell seeping from the pores of their skin. Others wept silently, their lips moving in a whispered prayer to God asking Him to keep them safe. Then there were those who did not sweat, did not tremble, did not weep or pray. These were the men who were totally lost in the 'thousand-yard-stare.'

The thousand-yard-starers were the hardest to reach. It was like they were oblivious to everyone and everything around them. There was nothing wrong with their sight or their hearing but they behaved as if they could neither see nor hear. They were in another place. A far-away place. They were unreachable. These were the unlucky souls who were the most likely to die in the ensuing battle. Many of them simply zombie-walked into the chaos of combat and were almost always among the first to fall.

Jackson Traynor was afraid. He was afraid at the battle of Shah Wali Kot near Tizark back in 2010. He had experienced fear many times during his deployment in Afghanistan. It was healthy to be afraid before going into combat, he believed. The hard part was mastering the fear. If you could control the fear rather than let it control you, it kept you alert. Kept you focused on the training that ultimately led you to the situation you now found yourself in. All you had to do was harness the fear. Own it. Embrace it. Traynor learned how to do that on the battlefield in Afghanistan and he was doing it now. Breathing slowly, deeply, through the nose. Slowing his heartbeat. Steadying his hand. Focusing on the Mexican's gun hand rather than trying to read his eyes. It was dark, and getting darker. Herrera would have to make his move soon; if he didn't, it would be too dark to see any hand movement.

Jack was not wearing a Kevlar vest. If Herrera got the first shot away, and if it was a good shot and the .45 calibre round hit him in the chest at around 850 feet per second, it would kill him. The Mexican had to react. What was he waiting for? Was he smarter than Jack gave him credit for? Was he waiting for the light to fade completely?

Then, there it was. The slightest movement of Herrera's hand. The barrel of the .45 began to rise.

Jack was faster. He whipped the Sig up and fired. The two movements, the raising of the weapon and the trigger pull were almost simultaneous.

Herrera fired a fraction of a second later. The .45 calibre round ploughed into the ground at the foot of the steps leading to the veranda where Traynor stood.

The 9mm round from the Sig hit Herrera low in the abdomen, perhaps a little lower than Jack would have preferred, but it was a hit nonetheless. For a moment, the Mexican showed no reaction. Then he lowered his head and looked down at his waist. Blood was already seeping through his shirt and spreading like spilled red wine on a tablecloth.

The Wolf lifted his eyes and looked at the man he came to kill. Traynor stood at the top of the stairs, his weapon pointed directly at him. "You... you shot me, senor," he said, his tone almost disbelieving. He lowered his eyes again and looked at the spreading red across the front of his shirt. "You shot me." There was no pain, just bewilderment. His grip on the .45 relaxed and the barrel dropped, almost like the weapon had suddenly become too heavy to hold. His eyes shifted from his waist to the gun. He stared at it, struggling to comprehend what was happening to him. Then, his hand opened involuntarily and the gun fell from his fingers and landed with a thud in the dirt at his feet. He looked down at the fallen gun, then at his open hand, his confusion mounting rapidly. He looked up again, towards the veranda.

Traynor had moved. Now he was standing on the ground at the foot of the steps, his weapon still aimed directly at Herrera.

"Wh-what?" Herrera muttered. "You are leaving, senor?"

"No, I'm not leaving. Not yet."

"Ees good, senor. Ees good you stay." Herrera felt his legs beginning to fold beneath him and looked down at them. "Wh-what is 'appening?" he mumbled softly.

"You're dying," a voice very close said.

"*Que?*" He raised his head and Traynor was right there in front of him, just a metre away. Then, all feeling in his legs was gone. Slowly, he sank to his knees. His head dropped, he stared uncomprehending at the ground for a moment before lifting his head again and looking up at Traynor looming over him. "I am dying?" he mumbled.

"Yes, you are dying. Very slowly."

"I would like to go home."

"Not going to happen."

"I do not like this place."

Then, the pain hit, like a white-hot knife being slowly pushed into his gut and twisted. He moaned and closed his hands over the wound in his belly. Blood seeped through his fingers and ran freely over his hands. He looked down, staring absently at the blood running uncontrollably. "Ooh...Holy Mary...

Mother of God!" he moaned. He leaned forward, his head almost touching the ground. "Ooh...*hacer que el dolor desaparece*—make the pain go away!" He rocked slowly, back and forth, clasping his hands tight over his wound. Then he stopped, lifted his head, and looked up at Traynor. "You must...finish it, senor," he pleaded.

Jack extended his arm until the Sig was just a hand's length from Herrera's face. "Say hello to your friend, Ignacio Vargas," he said.

"He ees...not...my friend," Herrera said defiantly. "Instead, I will say *hola* to your pretty daughter."

Jack fired at point blank range. The 9mm round ploughed into the centre of Rodolfo Herrera's forehead.

42

Slowly, the distance between Foley and Rose and the two motorcycles began to widen. Foley pushed the police vehicle hard over the rough, dirt road corrugations. The speed was dangerous but worth the risk, he thought. He leaned forward, gripped the steering wheel tightly, and focused on the twin tail lights ahead as they appeared and then disappeared in a cloud of thick dust billowing behind the Harley Davidsons.

Sam gripped the hand hold above the passenger window so tightly, his fingers began to cramp. His free hand pushed against the dashboard in front of him, bracing himself against the incessant spine-jarring jolting as the car raced after the bikers. "How...far...to the highway?" he asked, his voice stuttering in concert with the noisy, staccato bumping of the vehicle.

"Almost there," Foley answered.

"If they get to the highway before we...catch them, they will outrun us on the bitumen."

"I can't push this heap of shit any harder," Foley responded. "I-I've got the pedal flat t-to the floor now."

Then, up ahead in front of the two motorcycles, two headlights appeared, blinking on-and-off in a random pattern through the dust cloud.

Foley eased off the gas pedal and the vehicle slowed dramatically. "What's that?"

"It's a vehicle coming the other way, Russ."

"What's another car doing way out here?"

"Might be some of the local indigenous lads heading back to their outstation."

"Or it might be the Task Force vehicle," Foley suggested, hopefully. He pulled to the side of the road and stopped. He reached for the radio controls and switched to a frequency used for vehicle-to-vehicle communications. "Major Crime One to Task Force One, do you copy?" he spoke into the handpiece. A few moments passed with no response and then the voice of Sergeant Wayne Donaldson, a twenty-five-year veteran of the force and senior member of the Task Force, crackled from the speaker.

"Task Force One copy. Donaldson here. That you, Superintendent Barker?"

"Negative. Russell Foley and Sam Rose here. What's your location, Wayne?"

"We are at the intersection with the Stuart Highway. Adjacent the car park and viewing area of Central Mount Stuart."

"Hold there," Foley ordered. "We are in pursuit of two suspects heading your way."

"Roger that." Donaldson indicated to the driver to stop the BearCat. "We see headlights ahead," he said into the radio handpiece.

"Two motorcycles, heading your way fast. Request you stop and apprehend."

"Roger that."

"Suspects are armed," Foley cautioned.

"Copy that."

Suddenly, a bright light ahead of the bikers lit up the night sky and the road ahead. Through the glare of the light, the familiar red and blue rooflights of a police vehicle flashed.

"Yes!" Foley said, fist-pumping the air.

"Well," Sam said. "I take back everything bad I've ever said about those pussies."

Foley looked across at his partner. "Everything?"

Sam shrugged. "Almost everything. They *are* late, as usual."

"Right on time, I would suggest." Foley shifted

the transmission into reverse and began backing away.

"What are you doing?"

"Moving out of danger. If the scene up in front of us turns into a shooting match, I don't want to be in the line of fire."

"Good thinking, Russ. That's why they pay you the big bucks."

———

Don Williams and Luke Boyd skidded to a halt a hundred metres short of the blinding spotlight ahead.

"Fuck!" Williams cursed.

"Where the fuck did they come from?" Boyd asked.

"Doesn't matter where the fuck they came from. They're here."

"Can we get around them?" Boyd asked, scanning both sides of the road.

"Maybe. They're close to the intersection with the highway. Near to the car parking area at that place we passed coming in. We can go left past them, across the car park and out onto the highway."

Boyd looked down into his rear vision mirror. "Can't go back," he said. "We've got the bastards behind us as well."

"There's nothing but more desert behind us anyway," Williams said. "What do you think?"

"Whatever we do, we need to do it fast."

"Well, I think we should go for it."

"How you wanna do this?"

"How much ammo you got?" Williams queried.

"Half a mag."

"Me too. Do we make a run for the highway?"

"Sounds like a plan."

———

In the front cabin of the Lenco BearCat armoured response vehicle, the driver sat behind the wheel with the transmission in neutral, and the powerful Caterpillar 300 horsepower turbo diesel engine idling softly. His role as driver was to remain in the cabin, poised to react instantly if required. On the command of the man sitting next to him in the passenger seat, Sergeant Wayne Donaldson, ten members of the Territory Special Reaction Team spilled out of the vehicle and took up defensive positions surrounding their truck.

Dressed from head-to-toe in black tactical clothing, complete with helmets and balaclavas covering their faces, the team was a well-trained, disciplined unit, heavily armed with Glock sidearms and semi-automatic rifles.

Satisfied all was in readiness, Davidson leaned forward and focused his attention on the approaching headlights. Brilliant light from a set of powerful spotlights mounted on a rack across the roof of the vehicle penetrated the darkness for several hundred metres ahead, illuminating the road, the patchy scrub on either side, and two motorcycle riders.

Like rabbits caught in the sudden glare, the motorcycle riders skidded to a stop a hundred metres ahead of the BearCat. Donaldson flicked another switch and two large public-address speakers, also mounted on the roof, buzzed loudly. He reached for a handpiece and addressed the bikers. "Northern Territory Police! Switch off your engines and climb off your motorcycles! Place your hands on your head and step away from the bikes!"

He received no response. He called again. "This is the Northern Territory Police! Climb off your motorcycles and step away with your hands on your head!"

When still he got no reaction, he spoke to his team through individual communication devices each man wore inside his helmet. "Stay alert," he ordered. "Open fire only on my command." He called again to the bikers. "This is your last chance! Step away from your motorcycles with your hands on your head!" He turned to his driver. "Move up, Thommo. Slowly."

The driver, Senior Constable Max Thomms, slipped the transmission into drive and the BearCat began to move slowly forward. The team members, walking five-abreast on either side of the armoured vehicle, raised their weapons to the 'ready' position.

Donaldson again addressed the bikers. "Move away from your bikes with your hands on your head!"

———

"They're coming," Boyd said as the BearCat began to move slowly towards them.

"Ready?" Williams asked.

"Yep. It's been a hell of a ride, mate."

The two men touched fists, kicked their respective bikes into gear and accelerated rapidly towards the approaching BearCat. Controlling a speeding motorcycle with one hand while firing indiscriminately into the blinding light with the other was always going to be problematic. With the Task Force team moving towards them and more police at their rear, Williams and Boyd did not have the benefit of time to consider an alternative course of action. It was what it was. Might just as well face it head-on and hope for the best.

———

"Shots fired! Shots fired!" one of Donaldson's team members yelled from his position outside the vehicle.

"Stop!" Donaldson commanded the driver. "Return fire!" Donaldson ordered his team.

A cacophony of noise erupted from each side of the BearCat as ten high-powered, semi-automatic rifles spat a withering barrage of gunfire at the approaching riders.

———

Intending to pass on the driver's side of the BearCat and race across the viewing area carpark, Williams and Boyd veered towards the left-hand side of the road, both firing blindly into the glare of the spotlights.

Boyd was the first to go down, followed almost immediately by Williams. Under a deadly hail of bullets, both men were hit multiple times. Each speeding bike, now uncontrolled, simply fell over, dislodged its rider, and skidded across the hard, dirt and gravel road in a cloud of dust.

Luke Boyd died instantly, at least three rounds hitting him in the head through his open-face helmet and many others peppering his upper body. His body lay in a rapidly expanding pool of blood a few metres from his bent and twisted Harley.

Don Williams, despite his horrific wounds, took a little longer to die. Somehow, his helmet had come off and he lay on his back on the verge of the road, his legs folded awkwardly beneath him. He tried to turn his head to look for Boyd but could not move. He tried to move his arms. Nothing. There was no pain and for a moment he wondered if perhaps he had escaped unscathed. If he was unharmed, why could he not move? He stared up at the sky. Through a fine film of dust slowly settling around him, he noticed the stars, high above the glare of the light. Millions of them. He remembered some-where, a long time ago, reading something about the beauty of the night sky in the Australian out-back. It occurred to him as he lay on the remote, gravel road a long way from civilisation, staring up at the night sky, that these were incongruous thoughts, but he could not get them from his mind. Then suddenly, strangely, he was overcome with an immense tiredness. *I'll just take a short nap*, he thought. *Then I'll find Luke and we'll get out of here.* He closed his eyes and the stars disappeared.

43

Having reversed for several hundred metres to a position that would put them in an area of relative safety, out of range should a firefight erupt at the scene ahead, Foley again pulled over to the side of the road and stopped. Just as he shifted into park and applied the handbrake, the firing started. Even at this distance, and with the car windows closed, he and Rose could hear the gunshots. Like distant fire crackers, a cacophony of shots echoed against the stillness of the night.

"Jesus! Those boys are really going at it! Are you sure we are far enough away?" Sam asked, sliding lower in his seat.

"Yeah," Foley answered. "We're safe here."

"The bikers will never know what hit them."

"Yeah. The Task Force chaps love their work,

and they are bloody good at it even if a tad too enthusiastic at times."

"It's what they do. I heard some of them have the words 'Be certain—kill them twice' tattooed on their butt."

The next few moments were surreal. The scene that unfolded in front of Sam and Foley was like a violent movie played on a large, outdoor screen at a drive-in theatre. As they watched, the two motorcycle riders, illuminated by the powerful spotlights, came together and attempted to race down the driver's side of the BearCat, only to ride directly into a hailstorm of gunfire.

The loud crackle of gunfire, incongruent against the surrounding quiet, carried to them over the distance separating them from the action ahead.

It lasted less than thirty seconds. As quickly as it started, the firing stopped and an eerie silence descended around them, reclaiming the night.

Foley and Sam sat and stared in awe as several Task Force members, weapons at the ready, moved cautiously forward and examined the fallen bikers.

Finally, Sam asked, "What the fuck was that?"

"That, Sam," Foley muttered, "was the Territory's finest at work."

"Jesus! Remind me never to piss those blokes off."

"What happened to your earlier 'pussies' remark?"

"I recant the remark," Sam said earnestly. "They're not pussies. They are the kings of the jungle."

"Perhaps you might like to tell them that. I'm sure they will be very happy to hear how you feel about them."

"Now, now, Russ. I don't think we need to go that far. We don't want them to get all big-headed and overcome with their own self-importance."

Foley looked across at Sam in silence.

"What?" Sam asked.

"You're an idiot," Foley said dismissively.

"Task Force one to Major Crime one, do you copy?" Donaldson's voice crackled through the radio.

"Copy, Wayne," Foley answered. "What's your situation?"

"Two suspects down...deceased. A minor hand wound to one of my chaps. Situation under control. Is Superintendent Barker with you?"

"Negative," Foley repeated. "We have a man down on the road into Aningie Station. OIC at Ti Tree, Chook Fowler. Yap Yap is with him and his partner."

"Serious?"

"Shoulder wound. He'll be okay."

"Need any help?"

"That's a negative. We are returning there now. You have a satellite phone in your vehicle, right?"

"Affirmative."

"Good. John Singh is at Ti Tree with a Forensic team. Request you contact him and get a couple of his chaps out here to process the scene."

"Roger that."

"And, secure the area until they get here," Foley added.

"We'll lock it up tighter than a nun's knickers," Donaldson answered.

"Thanks, Wayne."

"No problem. Task Force One, out."

Foley replaced the radio handpiece, completed a U-turn, and accelerated away, back towards Aningie Station.

Sam looked across at Foley. "'Tighter than a nun's knickers!' What's that about?"

"That's Donaldson," Foley said, as if it was all the explanation needed.

"Not exactly correct radio procedure."

"Should I assume from your tone that your 'kings of the jungle' comment no longer applies?"

"I am just pointing out that there is a protocol in place for correct radio procedure."

Foley glanced across at Sam. "This from a man who has, at one time or another, broken just about every protocol in the book," he said, with no attempt to disguise the sarcasm.

"Point taken," Sam acknowledged with a shrug of indifference.

———

"You lose them?" Barker asked when Foley and Sam arrived back at the Ti Tree vehicle.

"No, not exactly," Foley said.

"What do you mean 'not exactly?'"

"Fortunately, Wayne Donaldson and his Task Force chaps arrived."

"And?"

"The bikies made a run for the highway. They didn't make it."

"We have them in custody?"

"No. They're dead."

"Dead?"

"As a door-nail," Sam added with a nod.

"The bikies tried to get past the BearCat, firing as they went," Foley continued. "Task Force returned fire with everything they have and both bikies were killed."

"Any Task Force injuries?" Barker asked.

"One," Foley said. "Minor hand wound."

"Broke a nail," Sam said.

"What?" Barker asked with a scowl.

"Sorry, boss. Couldn't help myself."

Foley continued. "I asked Donaldson to contact John Singh and request he come out and process the scene."

"Good," Barker said. "Well done."

Sam looked down at Fowler, sitting on the ground leaning back against his vehicle. "How you holding up, Chook?"

"I'll live. Bloody glad to hear those two arse-wipes are dead. I would love to have been there."

"It was quite a scene," Sam said with a smile.

Foley turned to Barker. "Sam and I are heading back to the homestead, boss. We need to see if Jack is okay. Do you want to come with us?"

Barker spoke to Rooney. "Mickey, will you and Chook be alright here until we get back?"

"I would like to get Chook back to the medical centre at Ti Tree," Rooney said.

"Okay." Barker looked down at Fowler. "Do you think you can travel back to Ti Tree?"

"Yeah, I'm okay."

"Is the vehicle okay, Mickey?" Barker asked Rooney.

"One headlight out, and a couple of holes in the panel-work, but the engine's good to go."

"Good, let's get Chook into the vehicle and then I'll go back to Aningie with Sam and Russell."

Sam and Foley leaned down to help Fowler to

his feet. Rooney hurried around to the passenger side and opened the door.

"Are you sure you are okay?" Barker asked Fowler as Sam and Foley lifted him.

"I'm fine, sir. It's not the shoulder wound I'm worried about. It's the damage my wife's going to do when she finds out I got myself shot."

Barker laughed. "She'll be fine, Chook. I've learned that police wives are more resilient than we give them credit for."

Jim Chook Fowler smiled. "With respect, sir, you're not married to my wife."

44

Jackson Traynor went back into the house, paused momentarily at the doorway to the long passage, and looked at the body of Ignacio Vargas. Then he continued through the kitchen and out onto the back veranda.

The caretaker, Bill Kirkwood, lifted his head and looked up at Traynor. "I heard gunshots."

"Yeah. There were a couple."

"You get the bastard?" Kirkwood asked, hopefully.

"Yeah. I got the bastard."

"What about the biker pricks?"

"I don't know. My colleagues went after them. They haven't come back." Jack squatted down, close to Kirkwood. "You okay, Bill?"

"I've been better. But it would take more than a

smack in the head and a kick in the ribs to finish me."

Traynor smiled at the caretaker. "I've already figured that out about you, Bill. I told you before, you are one tough old coot."

Kirkwood tried to stand. "You wanna help me up? This floor is hard on my bony arse."

Jack reached out, helped the caretaker to his feet and gently leaned him back against the veranda railing. "Take it easy, mate. Rest here for a moment and then I'll get you inside."

"Feels like I got a knife in my fuckin' ribs, and my head's spinnin' like a top!" Kirkwood groaned.

"I'm not surprised. He worked you over pretty good."

"You got a name?"

"Jack Traynor."

"You the dude they came looking for?"

"That would be me," Jack answered with a smile.

"Someone must want you pretty bad for four of the bastards to come for you," Kirkwood suggested.

Jack shrugged. "It doesn't matter now, Bill. Let's get you inside where it's more comfortable." He put an arm around the caretaker's shoulder and slowly helped him inside the house. In the loungeroom, he sat Kirkwood down in a well-worn but comfortable looking armchair in the middle of the room, directly opposite the open passage doorway.

Kirkwood turned his head and looked into the hall at the body of Ignacio Vargas sprawled ungainly on the floor. "I would like to have a word with your boss about bringing all this here to my home," he said.

"I'm sorry about that, Bill," Traynor said earnestly.

"Don't suppose it's your fault." Kirkwood nodded towards the hallway. "What's the deal with that prick and his mate?"

"Professional hit-men. Sent out here by the head of an international, illegal drug syndicate based in Mexico."

"All the way from Mexico? That's some pretty heavy shit."

"Yeah, it is. Can I get you anything? Glass of water? Something stronger?"

"No, thanks. I'm good. Might just sit here for a while and rest."

"Good." Jack smiled. "I'm going outside to get some air. I'll check back on you in a little while."

"Then what?"

"Then we'll take the Mexicans' car and get you to Ti Tree where we can get you some help for your injuries. Might even buy you a beer."

"Quit drinking years ago, thanks anyway. Though all this shootin' and killin' crap could easily make me want to start up again."

"If you quit, it's probably not a good idea to start again."

"I won't. Just a momentary thought flashed through my mind. Must have been the crack on the noggin'. Got me thinkin' all sorts of dumb shit."

Traynor smiled. "Okay. I'll be just out front. Call if you need anything." He turned to leave the room and paused when Kirkwood spoke.

"Thanks, Jack."

Traynor turned and smiled widely at Kirkwood. "You're welcome."

———

Outside, Traynor sat down on the top step of the wide, front veranda of the homestead. Light from the open front door and loungeroom window behind him cast a dim glow over the veranda and a small portion of the front yard. He looked beyond the extent of the light, towards the silhouette of the Mexicans' rental car twenty metres away. A faint, narrow shaft of light from the interior of the vehicle seeped out through the open driver's side door, illuminating the body of Rodolfo The Wolf Herrera.

As Jack stared at the corpse, a heavy blanket of sadness descended slowly over him. He wiped absently at an errant tear that somehow escaped from his eye and rolled slowly down his cheek. Involuntarily, his mind began to wander.

It was sad, he thought, that the one thing he seemed to be proficient at above all else was killing. Oh. He was a good cop; at least he believed he was. And he had been a good soldier before he ever became a cop. He was also a good husband and father. His work kept him away from his family way more than he would have preferred, but he loved his wife and daughter and, when he was home, he never failed to let them know just how much they meant to him. Unfortunately, despite his prowess at soldering, policing, fathering, and being a husband, he was better at killing.

Traynor hated killing. Intentionally taking the life of another was not, and never had been, part of his psyche. It was as alien a concept to him as anything he could think of. So why was he so good at it, he wondered? The military was where he learned to kill, and on the battlefield in Afghanistan was where he perfected it. In war, killing was, for the most part, an unavoidable consequence of military conflict. You had to kill the enemy or they would kill you, or your mates. When faced with the situation of kill or be killed it made sense to be better at it than the enemy, Jack reasoned. Over there, in the heat of battle, the killing was justifiable. You kill or you die—logical in its simplicity really. But, justifiable and logical notwithstanding, Jack never found anything pleasurable in the killing of another human being. Someone's husband, someone's lover, father, or brother, died by his hand, and he found that immensely sad.

It was understandable, he thought, why many former soldiers, even some cops, suffered late in their lives with Post Traumatic Stress Disorder. Watching people die, regardless of who they were or what terrible things they might have done, or indeed being the instrument of their death, surely has to have an adverse effect on the emotional well-being of both the watcher and the perpetrator. *Perhaps that's where I'll find myself in a few years*, Jack thought. *FITH—Fucked In The Head,* as the acronym goes. He blinked back another tear.

The two men who participated in the brutal rape and murder of his wife and daughter were dead. But, now that they were, he felt no sense of gratification. Herrera and Vargas were evil men. They were men who took great pleasure in killing. It was their profession. What sort of person does it take to make a living out of killing others and derive great pleasure from it, Jack wondered? Any reasonable man would suggest the world was a better place for their leaving it and that Jack should feel proud that he was responsible for their departure. Perhaps he should, but he didn't. There was some

sense of vengeance for the loss of his family perhaps, but there was no pride. His wife, April, and his
beautiful daughter, Jessica, were still dead. He felt
only sadness, a suffocating, all-consuming sadness.

———

Jack turned at the sound of shuffling behind him.
Kirkwood, holding his ribs and breathing heavily,
leaned against the front door jamb. Jack started to
rise.

"No! Don't get up. Stay there," Kirkwood said.

"What are you doing, Bill?" Traynor asked. "You
should stay in the house where you will be more
comfortable."

Kirkwood shuffled slowly over to the top of the
steps, leaned against the railing and paused for a
moment. "All I'm doing in there is staring at the
dead guy in the hallway," he said, finally. "Thought
I'd come out here and sit a while with you, if that's
okay."

"Of course it's okay." Jack nodded towards the
body of Herrera lying in the dirt twenty metres
away. "You'll be staring at another one out here.
Here, let me help you." He reached up and took
Kirkwood's arm, guiding him down to sit next to
him on the top step.

Kirkwood sat down with a quiet groan of pain.

He leaned forward, holding his ribs tightly. Then he looked up and squinted into the darkness ahead. "That the other Mexican prick?"

"Yeah." Jack placed a hand on the caretaker's shoulder. "You okay?"

"I won't be ridin' horses or rounding up cattle for a while," Kirkwood answered with a grimace. "But I'm alive and I suppose I should be grateful for that."

Both men sat in silence for a few minutes, each of them lost in their own thoughts, staring into the darkness beyond the reach of the faint glow from the house and the Mexicans' vehicle.

Eventually Kirkwood turned his head and looked at Traynor. "I heard the two Mexicans murdered your family."

Jack continued to stare ahead. "Yeah, they did."

"I'm sorry about that," Kirkwood said, softly.

Jack's focus did not shift. "Thank you."

"I also heard you used to be a soldier."

Jack nodded. "Yeah, I did."

"Saw action?"

"Yeah. Afghanistan."

A few more moments of silence followed and then the caretaker spoke again.

"Hurts, don't it?"

"What?" Jack asked, turning his head slightly to look at Kirkwood.

Kirkwood looked directly into Jack's eyes. "Killing people."

Jack turned away and focused on the darkness again. "Yeah, it hurts," he said, almost in a whisper. He swiped hastily at yet another tear.

45

Traynor heard a vehicle approaching. He looked up and saw headlights in the distance. He unholstered his weapon and laid it on the step next to him, his hand resting lightly over it.

"More visitors in the last twelve hours than I've seen in all the years I've been here," Kirkwood said. "Who do you suppose that is?"

"Don't know. I hope it's the three Territory chaps coming back."

"And if it's not?"

Traynor pulled the Glock a little closer to his side. "I'll worry about that when they get here."

They watched in silence as the car approached. When it arrived, it stopped behind, and to one side of the Mexicans' rental car. The headlights illuminated the body of Herrera sprawled awkwardly on the ground.

Cameron Barker climbed quickly out of the rear seat, followed by Sam and Foley from the front of the car. The three men cautiously approached the body, stopped several paces from it, and stared down at the crumpled form.

Finally, Barker looked up at Traynor and Kirkwood sitting on the top step of the veranda twenty metres away. "You okay, Jack?" he asked.

"Yeah."

"You, Mr. Kirkwood? Are you okay?"

"Hurts like a bitch," Kirkwood answered, haltingly. "But, yeah, I'm okay."

Barker swung his eyes back to Traynor. "You do this, Jack?" he asked, indicating the body at his feet.

"I did," Jack answered.

Barker moved forward and crouched next to Herrera's body.

"He dead?" he heard Sam ask from behind him.

"Very," Barker answered, getting to his feet. He stepped around the body and moved forward, closer to the house, followed by Foley and Rose. All three stopped at the foot of the steps.

"I can tell from the bullet holes in him he didn't stumble, fall, and break his neck, like his mate."

"No, he didn't break his neck," Jack confirmed.

"You put two in him?" Barker asked.

Jack shrugged. "It was dark. My first shot went low," he said, somewhat casually.

"Your second shot, in the middle of his forehead, was a great shot...given it was so dark."

Jack shrugged again. "Got lucky, I guess," he offered by way of explanation.

Barker nodded. "He has a gun laying in the dirt next to him. Can I assume that you acted in self-defence?"

Kirkwood uttered a quiet, indistinguishable noise. Barker looked at the caretaker and immediately saw the remains of a smile fading from his lips. He looked back at Traynor. "Tell me this was self-defence, Jack."

"You look hard enough, you'll find a bullet hole somewhere in the house behind me," Jack responded. "You find the bullet, you'll see it matches the Mexican's gun."

Barker paused for just a moment, as if he might be analysing Traynor's version of events. "Okay. Self-defence. That's good enough for me."

"What about the arsehole who knocked me around?" Kirkwood asked.

"Dead," Barker answered.

"And his mate?"

"Also dead."

"Couldn't happen to a couple of nicer blokes," Kirkwood said sarcastically.

"Self-defence?" Traynor asked with a wry smile.

Russell Foley answered. "It wasn't us, Jack. They ran into our Task Force chaps and figured they could get past them."

"You blokes want a coffee?" Kirkwood asked.

"Coffee sounds good, Bill," Sam said.

"Well, you're gonna have to make it yourself. It's gonna take me twenty minutes to get back on my feet."

"That's okay, mate. You stay there. Russell will make the coffee."

Foley turned to Sam. "What?"

"You make good coffee, Russ," Sam explained.

"I'm always making the coffee," Foley complained. "Anyone can make coffee, Sam, even you." He paused for a moment. "On second thoughts, I've tasted your coffee. I'll make it."

Sam smiled. "Milk, one sugar for me."

Foley looked at Barker, Traynor, and Kirkwood. Like watching a tennis match, their eyes darted from Sam to Foley and back again. "What?" he asked of all three.

Kirkwood answered. "You are right. No one makes bad coffee. Why do you think he does that?"

Foley considered the question momentarily. "So I'll make the coffee?" he suggested, questioningly.

"There it is!" The caretaker laughed.

Russell Foley climbed the steps, passed Traynor and Kirkwood, and moved to the front door.

"Kettle's in the kitchen cupboard," Kirkwood said to his back.

"What now?" Jack asked Barker.

"Now we wait. There is a military chopper on the way. It will pick you up and return to Darwin. You will be housed on an army base there until the court date and then you will be escorted to Sydney to testify against the Ghandour family."

"What will you do when this is all over?" Sam asked Jack.

Traynor looked pensive for a few moments. "I don't know," he said, finally. "I haven't thought that far ahead."

"Do you think you will go back to work with the Feds?"

"Well, that far ahead I have thought. No, I won't go back. My job with the Federal Police cost me my family. If I went back, that would follow me every day of my career. I don't want to forget, but I don't want to be constantly reminded of it either."

"You know," Barker said, "we could always use someone with your experience up here in the Territory."

Traynor looked questioningly at Barker.

"Just a thought," Barker added. "We have some good men and women in the job up here, and cops of your calibre would be more than welcome. I'm sure we could circumvent some of the prerequisites."

Traynor looked up at the star-filled sky. "It's nice here." He placed an arm around Bill Kirkwood's shoulder. "I appreciate the kind words. The first thing I might do when this is all over is come back here and visit my new friend Bill, if he'll have me for a week or so."

Kirkwood looked at Jack. "Anytime, mate. And you can stay as long as you like." He glanced at Barker and Sam. "That goes for all of you," he added.

Just then, Russell Foley came out of the front door. "If you ever decide to consider the boss's suggestion, Jack," he said. "I could use a new partner."

"What?" Sam said.

"Nothing," Foley said, smiling widely. "Coffee's coming," he called as he turned away and re-entered the house.

THE END

Dear reader,

We hope you enjoyed reading *Safe House*. Please take a moment to leave a review, even if it's a short one. Your opinion is important to us.

Discover more books by Gary Gregor at

https://www.nextchapter.pub/authors/gary-gregor

Want to know when one of our books is free or discounted? Join the newsletter at

http://eepurl.com/bqqB3H

Best regards,

Gary Gregor and the Next Chapter Team

You might also like:
Steel and Shadows by Stuart Field

To read the first chapter for free, please head to:
https://www.nextchapter.pub/books/steel-and-shadows

Safe House
ISBN: 978-4-86745-173-1

Published by
Next Chapter
1-60-20 Minami-Otsuka
170-0005 Toshima-Ku, Tokyo
+818035793528

10th April 2021

CPSIA information can be obtained
at www.ICGtesting.com
Printed in the USA
LVHW091218080621
689681LV00001B/70